Anita Desai (née Mazun
Mussoorie, India, and grew
Hindi and Urdu. Desai ma
Cry, the Peacock and was immediately praised as the finest of her generation of writers. This was followed by an equally well-crafted *Voices in the City*.

Her novels and short stories evoke characters, events and moods with recourse to a rich use of visual imagery and details, which has led to comparisons with the modernist sensibilities of T. S. Eliot, William Faulkner and Virginia Woolf. Throughout her writings Desai focuses on personal struggles and problems of contemporary life that her characters must cope with.

She has received numerous awards, including most recently in 2005 the Grinzane Cavour International Prize — *Una Vita per la Letteratura* (a Life for Literature) — one of Europe's most prestigious literary awards and often said to anticipate the Nobel Prize.

'She is a novelist of the human psyche, and approaches her subjects quietly and delicately. She is one of world's most distinguished novelists in English.'
   Alan Lightman, Prof., Writings & Humanistic Studies,
MIT, USA.

By the same author
in **Orient Paperbacks**

Cry, the Peacock
Where Shall We Go This Summer
Voices in the City

Bye-Bye Blackbird

anita desai

Orient
Paperbacks
DELHI | MUMBAI | HYDERABAD

www.orientpaperbacks.com

ISBN 13: 978-81-222-0029-4
ISBN 10: 81-222-0029-X

1st Published 1985
This edition 2007

Bye-Bye Blackbird

© Anita Desai

Cover design by Sandip Sinha for Vision Studio

Published by
Orient Paperbacks
(A division of Vision Books Pvt. Ltd.)
5A/8 Ansari Road, New Delhi-110 002

Printed in India at
Ravindra Printing Press, Delhi-110 006

Part I

The Visitor

1

The morning light slid down the lane-lengths of telephone wires, perched a while on the peaks of television aerials and then rolled down the drain pipes into the new-leafed hedges and through the silver caps of the milk bottles on the steps, rang the brass door knockers and set the birds and bottles clinking and clanking in informal good-morning voices that rose up to Dev's window and politely woke him. But when he pulled out his watch from under his pillow he was disgusted to find it was barely five o'clock. He wondered if it had died in the night of an inability to acclimatise itself, but its steady ticking asserted itself through the bright beadcurtain of bird-and-bottle sounds and he shoved it away with a groan, then put his head beside it under the pillow. But he had mistakenly left the window open at night and now the milky fingers of morning reached through and scrabbled through his winter coverings like a giggling tease and eventually he had to emerge, half smothered, from the dark pillow and face the window now swimming with liquid light in which the red roofs and blackened brick walls of Clapham stood steady as the keels and hulls of sound old boats that had weathered the wash and swell of another day's tidal wave.

He propped himself up on one elbow, trying to conjure some of yesterday's excitement and buoyancy out of the tiredness of a night's sleep begun too late and ended too early. Groping about for the support of a tranquillising smoke, he found he had left his cigarettes on top of the brass-knobbed dresser at the far end of the room.

There was nothing for it but to roll out of his dishevelled bed, leap up into the air as his feet touched the freezing floorboards, race across to the dresser, snatch up cigarettes and matches and take a flying leap back into his blue quilt. Trying nervously to nurse it back to warmth and keep the ashes from falling on the blue satin, he thought with momentary bitterness of the cup of tea that would have been brought to him if he were at home in India now, by a mother fresh from her morning prayers, or a servant boy scorched and sooty from a newly made fire. By no stretch of imagination were his host Adit Sen or his wife Sarah likely to do this for him: there was an eiderdown-smothered silence from their end of the flat. Once the cigarette had dwindled to a stub and he had to leap up in order to fling it out of the window into the hedge, he felt he might as well wrap his earthen brown shawl about him and go out to find the kitchen and make himself a cup of tea. It was the first lesson his first day in London taught him: he who wants tea must get up and make it.

In the kitchen he was confronted by last night's dishes piled up to the level of the tap in the sink, encrusted with the frozen gravy of the chicken curry with which the Sens had celebrated his arrival in England and their home. He lurched towards the window and broke it open, knocking down a starving potted plant as he did so. Cold air, bits of pottery and handsful of earth flung themselves at him so that he staggered. Looking down at the grisly sink — the decapitated head of last night's party, now caked in yellow blood and the smell of decay — he reflected that earth might be useful in scrubbing these plates clean: he had seen that now sorely missed servant boy use a handful of mud and ashes on the dishes at home with impeccable results. He picked the plant out of the sink by its lank hair and dropped it into the plastic pail that seemed to collect all the rubbish. The stench was quickly being diluted by the morning air and he felt refreshed enough to grope about the cupboard for a kettle. All he could find amongst the mops and brooms was a saucepan which he set on a small electric heater, not feeling capable of tackling the big black gas stove that took up most of the place in the kitchen. Later he remembered to fill it with water. While he waited for it to boil he decided to layout teacups for everyone and was amused to find each of a different colour and design. Then he found an enormous Kashmir teacosy on a chair. He stood patting the pattern of irises and kingfishers in blue crewel embroidery, wondering at its history — it was so ample, so substantial it was sure to have some history. Had Adit's mother sent it out from India to her ash-blonde and unknown daughter-in-law? Had Adit bought it at one of those Indian stores that dealt in tinned mangoes, spices and brassware and brought it home to his Clapham flat in a little seizure of nostalgia? And what did it mean to Sarah? Then he felt it quiver beneath his hand and, lifting it up, found a great orange tomcat curled up beneath it like some tame deity of the hearth. The creature leapt up, alarm blazing from its green eyes, and shot out of the window with a sound of claws screeching on tiles that made Dev shiver.

'*Paji*[1],' he hissed after it. Teacosy in hand, he recalled all the stories he had heard of the Englishman and his pets. He looked at the matting of cat's hairs on the inside of the tea cosy with distaste inflating his nostrils. The saucepan boiled over.

He drank three cups of Typhoo tea and when he had poured out the dregs of the teapot, Adit stumbled in, wearing his wife's pink, fur-lined slippers and a dressing gown of cornflower blue that looked particularly resplendent with the collar and trousers of a pillar-box red nylon sleeping suit emerging from it. His sleep-crumpled face looked incongruous with this brilliant outfit and was rather like a paperbag mask stuck on top of a gorgeously dressed and opulently stuffed scarecrow.

In a sleep-snarled voice he growled, 'Tea — give me a cup — why must you wake up the whole house at six o'clock on a Sunday morning? Tea, quick, hot. Even on a working day I don't get up before eight-thirty,' he grumbled. He sat at the table and ferociously rubbed his eyes and hair.

'No *puja*[2] to the rising sun on the banks of the Thames? That's bad, Sen. Must write and tell your mother you've become an — what do you call them — destroyers of idols — iconoclasts?'

---

[1] Scoundrel.
[2] Worship.

'Don't know. Not at six in the morning.'

'It's seven, and it's your language now, Sen,' Dev told him severely, looking austere in the folds of his great shawl and a growth of beard on his jaws.

'Only adoptive,' Adit maintained.

'Make an effort.'

'Make me tea.'

'There's no kettle.'

'O God,' Adit moaned and rose from his chair to switch on the bright electric kettle on the white table. 'What did you take this for?'

Dev stared at it, certain it had not been there before. 'An electric kettle. Do you want me to be electrocuted and find my dead body when you come in for your breakfast?'

Adit began to come to life with a chortle as of a slow-starting car. 'I thought you came to study electricity or engineering here. You won't go far with that attitude.'

'Engineering!' Dev spoke with scorn. 'Do you think I want to join the Sikh fitters of Bradford, and live in their ghettoes and do the dirty work for the British engineers? Not me. I'm going to study at the London School of Economics.'

'It's not so easy to get in there, I'm told.'

'I know. That's why I came well in advance to make all the right approaches.'

'Approaches! Do you think you can get into an English college by sending the Principal a basket of mangoes? All you can do is fill in the forms and pay the entrance fees. There's no such thing as bribery here, you know.'

'There's no poverty either. But it's typical of you to immediately think I mean bribery and corruption. All I had in mind was approaching the professors and impressing them with the subtle complexities and the deep wisdom of the Oriental mind.'

The kettle let out a shriek and raised its lid on a spume of smoke. Tea was made, cups were clattered, Adit sang a song from an old Indian film, *Toofan Mail*, and in a while Sarah came in, holding about her a dressing gown of beige wool. In contrast to her colourful husband, she was all in tones of colourlessness that went with the long, straight fall of her pale hair. She went straight to the tea cosy and raised it tenderly.

'Where's Bruce?' she cried. 'Did you let him out, Adit? You shouldn't have, you know how he is these days.'

'I let him out,' Dev confessed unwillingly. 'But how is he these days ?'

'On heat,' she said.

'Oh, I didn't know. I picked up the tea cosy and he reared out like a cobra.'

Sarah smiled at his simile and sat the tea cosy on the teapot.

'But it's full of cats' hairs,' Dev protested.

'They make very good insulators,' Sarah told him, lighting herself a cigarette to go with her cup of tea.

'What a house! You keep pets for insulation?'

Adit, setting his cup down with a flourish, suddenly lifted his hand, let it quiver in the air like a flag and burst out in a choked voice; *'Questa o quella per me pari sono.'*

Then he slapped Dev hard on his back. 'Opera, my dear chap, one of the delights of the Western world with which you've never met. Oh! Verdi, oh God...' and he lifted his hand, making it flutter again, and roared: *'A quant alter d'intorno d'intorno mi vedo.'*

Sarah winced and rose from the table to go to the sink and start washing the dishes with an equanimity of expression Dev could not have believed anyone could summon on being faced with dishes made so loathsome with the leavings of last night. But she smoked her cigarette, the tap steamed, the dishes conversed lightly with each other, and in a little while she and Adit were frying eggs from which

Dev fled, turning only to call, 'When do we go to a pub? My first pub, it's time you took me to my first pub, you know.'

Sarah laughed. 'They don't open so early.'

Dev was disgusted. 'Too early for a drink? But this is a *jungly*[3] city, this London of yours.'

Adit sang joyfully: *'La donna e mobile muta d' accento e di pensier,'* and, in turning over a fried egg, tossed it high in the air. It fell on the floor and the yolk exploded.

'Oh-ho-ho. La-la-la,' Adit trailed off abashed.

'But is it old ?' Dev enquired with some anxiety as they pushed through the door into the rich, plummy, semi-darkness of the local pub, lit by the gleams of glass, brass pale ale and Sunday leisure.

'Not very,' Sarah smiled at him they settled down on a wooden bench by the wall. 'I shouldn't think more than a hundred years or so.'

'Then it is old,' Dev said, unable to keep the reverence from his tone, and now he raised his head, now turned, now swivelled as he took in, recognised and named the 'mullioned windows,' the 'horse brasses' shining against the stained woodwork, the 'casks' and mugs and portly British faces. He had known them all, he had met them before in the pages of Dickens and Lamb, Addison and Boswell, Dryden and Jerome K Jerome; not in colour and in three dimensions as he now encountered them, but in black and white and made of paper — and yet how exact the reproductions had been, how accurate he realised as he recognised the originals around him, within reach at last. He passed the palm of his hand slowly over the scarred tabletop and bowed his head, just a little, acknowledging the past introduction which had imprinted itself so finely, so imperially on his mind that it was simple enough to pick up acquaintanceship after all these years, in the sound assumption of future familiarity. Nothing in his past twenty-two years had resembled remotely this world he had entered by stepping through the door of

---
[3] Wild.

the King's Arms, this world of beer-soft, plum-thick semi-darkness and its soft, thick characters. Yet it was known, familiar, easy to touch, enjoy and accept because he was so well-prepared to enter it — so well-prepared by fifteen years of reading the books that had been his meat and drink, the English books that had formed at least one half of his conscious existence. It had been an education begun under compulsion by the black-frocked Jesuits of St. Xavier's School in Calcutta, at the chalk-scrawled, ink-grooved desks of the brawling classrooms. But soon it had become compulsive, a thing of habit and instinct, conducted half-unconsciously under the slowly ticking electric fan of the summer holidays and by the moth-battered lamp on the veranda at night. In those hours this world had been constructed for him, a paper replica perhaps, but in a sense larger than life, so that what he now saw and touched and breathed was recognisably the original, but an original cut down to size, under control, concrete, so that it no longer flew out of his mind and hovered above him like some incorporeal, winged creature.

Staring, staring — yet unsurprised by all, he was able to recognise the bald old wheezing man at the bar — caretaker, newspaper seller, wheel-barrow pusher or tramp — who had brought in his blind and dusty dog with him; the pale, intense faces of a youthful foursome at a table, dressed in suede jackets and nicotine stains, who all spoke together in low, glum voices; and the creaking, orange-tinted harridan, her paint all cracking and peeling, who downed her bitters in the outcast's corner before she unsteadily arose and faltered out into the Sunday nowhere. Flaxen triangles of cheese on salt-crusted biscuits, and the rich foam of ale frothing over the tumbler tops. New moons and half moons of tumbler stains on the worn tabletops. The strange and hieroglyphic variety of horse brasses dangling from the wainscot. The tumblers hanging upside down on their hooks. The pop and gurgle and swizzle and gush. The growl and hum and chuckle and swish.

Sarah opened her bag and let spill all the coins inside in a fine, ringing fall of plenitude. 'Pennies here —' she sorted them out in a row for Dev to study and memorise. 'Ha'pennies here and threepennies there.' He felt them between his fingers, committing to memory their size, their thickness, the feel of their thinly sculptured surfaces, their scored rinds, their disced pettiness.

> 'Half a pound of tuppenny rice,
> Half a pound of treacle,
> Mix it up and make it nice...'

he whistled, with an ease and an abandon that somewhat shook him who, in India, had found it necessary always to be on the defensive in public, to assume an arrogance, a superiority to the rest, however unpleasant and disagreeable. But here, surrounded by the easy, informal Sunday people, smiling to themselves at the thought of their Sunday roast and amiably talking of horses and dogs and the Labour Government, he found it easy to lose this self-consicousness, to think only of what lay outside and around him, and concentrate comfortably on the six-pences and shillings, the half-crowns and farthings that Sarah laid out and counted for him.

> 'Up and down the City road,
> In and out the Eagle,
> That's the way the money goes...'

Fingering them in a heap under his palm, he felt himself Director of the East India Company. This was what the cardamoms and cloves of India had been bought with, the cottons and the Kohinoors, the sandalwood and the rhinoceros horns, the people and their lands. Now he owned them, now he clasped them, now he clinked one against the other, now he built a silver tower of them, higher and a little higher still. Now it toppled and scattered, now he shoved the bits carelessly back into Sarah's bag.

> 'Every night when I go out,
> The monkey's on the table,
> Take a stick and knock it off,
> Pop goes the weasel.'

His mood of carelessness, so easy and so fluid, of familiarity and ease, changed quickly out on the High street where he was a stranger again and all was strange to him. Yet not — he paused and faltered, bumping into a passerby or two — so strange after all. Somehow recognisable too, faintly surrealistically for, strolling lopsidedly down the High Street, it seemed to him he was strolling down the Mall of a Himalayan hill station, the Mall of Simla or Mussoorie or Darjeeling or anyone of the little towns that heat-maddened, homesick British colonists had created in the incongruous Himalayas, created in the shape and memory of little English country towns and little English suburbias left oceans behind. The Himalayan ranges, aloof and mystical in their splendour, were no more familiar to them than to the Indian plainsmen but at least the climate was familiar, cold and refreshing and often wet, and the flowers of their home were to be found blooming in the Himalayan forests, fanned by the wings of tropical butterflies. Dev knew them from the summer holidays of his childhood, knew the strange combination of wild mountains with unoriental small towns of stone churches, chimneytops smoking on red roofs, silent marmoreal cemetries, bow windows and geranium boxes, and the ubiquitous Mall twisting and turning between book stalls, confectionaries and curio shops. Now, recognising in the High Street those echoes of the Indian hill station Malls he realised that the holiday retreats of his childhood had not been the originals he had taken them to be, but copies. The original existed over here, in the High Streets of London's suburbs and England's villages. Here were the bow windows and the red rooftops, the coffee shops and the dipping side lanes, the strolling crowds and dogs on leashes, the cakes and flowers and magazines on display.

Too dazed to retain any haughty poise, he exclaimed, 'But this is the Mall!'

'What Mall?'

'The Mall in Simla. Or Darjeeling. All the Malls.'

'Rot. Absolutely different.'

Absolutely different too — he agreed — in the gleaming prosperity and sparkling contemporaneity that had certainly never been reflected in those Himalayan copies but here flowered and spread and twinkled in a manner wholly new to Dev for it was something beyond his Indian imagination and experience: supermarkets with their pyramids of frozen food packets, delicatessens with their Continental fruits and wines and cheeses, the clothes shops with their waxy, surprise-eyed models in windows starred with gloves and lace handkerchiefs, the pubs and fish-and-chips shops, the welter of high, aristocratic perambulators and hairless pudding-faced, lollipop-stoppered babies, the well-groomed dogs on leashes, the trim nylons on the womens' stout legs, the red umbrellas and blue mackintoshes, the drizzle and the sunshine, the high prices and the easy trade.

While waiting at the door of a delicatessen Sarah had found to be conveniently open, he tried to pull together his self-assurance but could only muster a show of it. Then, while waiting for the bus in a cluster, 'Wog!' said a damson-cheeked boy in a brass-but-toned blazer to him. Only under his breath but, just before he leapt aboard the bus, 'Wog!' he said again, quite loudly. Dev, disconcerted, swung around to catch Adit's reaction, to catch a cue for his own, but Adit turned carelessly aside and pointed out something in a show window to Sarah, his shoulders in an elaborately nonchalant slope.

'*Paji!*' swore Dev and did not invoke the names of Johnson and Boswell again, or of Dryden or Pope, but chewed an unlit cigarette and sucked its black, bitter shreds.

Staggering under the bilious weight of an Anglo-Indian lunch — Sarah's rice was very sticky, her lamb curry very hot, and they had fried and eaten innumerable *papadums* — they stumbled across the Common which was slowly emerging from its noontime somnolence into an afternoon brightness and liveliness. On the sunburst pond a boy in a blue blazer sailed a small red boat. A dog — terrier about its ears and labrador about its tail — streaked over the grass after a blue ball. A big man in a blue pullover (London loved blue, London loved red, the Union Jack blew everywhere) strode through the high grass, bearing a great kite over his head and his children stormed around him, agog to see the kite launched. A man and a woman lay together, arduously crushing small daisies in the grass, shutting the world out of their love by using the ostrich's simple expedient and covering their heads and shoulders with his jacket. Beyond a clump of trees — chestnuts opulently green and hawthorns dressed in crinolines of dark pink blossom — a game of cricket proclaimed itself by flicker of white on green, by click of bat on ball. Dev and Adit were not in a shape to become involved in the game, not even as spectators; they dropped under the trees and lay, stupid with food and sunshine, their conversation pitched at an unusually low note.

'You don't starve do you?' Dev murmured. 'Your mother worried.'

'I don't. I taught Sarah to cook straightaway. No British broths and stews for me.'

'Taught her well,' Dev murmured, mellowed by the sun and the buoyant green and the distant sounds of the cricket game.

'Mmm,' Adit agreed from under his spread scarf. '*Charchari*, she can even make that.'

'No!'

'Oh yes. Poppyseed. I get poppyseed in that shop off Tottenham Court Road and we grind it and put that in. It makes authentic *Charchari*. And last Christmas I told her, you can have your plum pudding but my idea of a proper party pudding is good, rich carrot *halwa*. I made five pounds of it.' Overcome by the memory of those five pounds of rich red sweet and the sugar and the almonds and the cream that went into it he groaned.

'Pig.'

'Pigs — there were six of us. We had Samar and his wife Bella — he's a doctor, she's sweet — and Jasbir, an anaesthetist, and his wife Mala — a good solid Punjabi female. We were six pigs together.'

'You think too much of your food here,' Dev complained, sufficiently over his luncheon greed to give food an objective and disapproving look. 'At home you would just take carrot *halwa* for granted but here you go ga-ga over it. You get your proportions all wrong, you emigrants.'

'Immigrants, I think we are, and it's values you mean.'

'Don't get me tangled up in your language. It's a mad language. It has no logic.'

'You speak it all the time.'

'Only out of politeness.'

'You — polite !'

A breeze moved, leaves fell — the pale, curled ones, too delicate and new to stick. It was not altogether comfortable in the shade of the chestnuts, but a glimpse of the periwinkle sky and the sounds of cricket and the odour of grass created an illusion of summer warmth sufficient to keep them horizontal on the lush grass. The stupor of a holiday afternoon flattened them so successfully, they seemed asleep and, having nearly stepped on them, old Mrs. Simpson in her brown tweed skirt, taking her spaniel for a run, muttered aloud, 'Littered with Asians! Must get Richard to move out of Clapham, it is impossible now.' The odd dog, half-terrier and half-labrador, no longer interested in the blue ball, sniffed at their boot toes but was given no indication of adventure by them and raced off, with its peculiar rocking-horse motion, after a bee it had seen buzzing about the lower branches of the hawthorns.

Suddenly Dev exploded.

'That boy at the bus stop — he called us wogs. You heard him.'

'I did not.'

'Adit, I saw you turn, I saw your face. You can take that — from a schoolboy?'

'It is best to ignore those who don't deserve one's notice,' Adit said but not grandly — he said it quite softly, in the care-paced voice of one who has learnt it as a lesson.

Dev made a spitting sound and sat up, hugging his knees, now unquestionably chilled by the green, unripe shade of the chestnuts and by the encroaching evening. 'I wouldn't live in a country where I was insulted and unwanted,' he said grandly.

'No? Why have you come then?' Still Adit's voice showed no hostility, only laziness.

'To study. You know that. I will go back to India an "England-returned" teacher. I will teach. It's a pity I have to come all the way here for a proper education but there it is — I must.'

'Oh! noble, noble man. When you go back — to enlighten the dark races with Keynes's theory of economics — they will award you the Padma Bhushan, Class II, on Republic Day. How fine you will look with it shining on the front of your dirty purple pullover.'

Dev threw grass at him, covered him with earth and leaves, 'Laugh. Go on. That's all you people do, you lazy immigrants. God. You should go mad — mad, when even schoolboys can call you names on the streets, when you find that the London docks have three kinds of lavatories — Ladies, Gents and Asiatics. But what did you do? You laughed.'

'And what did you do? You queued up at the Asiatics. "At the Wogs".'

'Of course. I wouldn't step into a dirty white man's lav if you paid me to. I wanted to show them I preferred the Asiatics.'

'Generous of you.' Then Adit sat up, showering earth and grass. He yawned hugely and patted Dev on the knee. 'Stop it, *yar*[4]. You've come abroad to study and see a new country. Stop making — what does Sarah call 'em — storms inside teapots.'

'Teapot! Never heard a more apt name for this fat little island. Adit, aren't you coming back at all? Do you mean to stay on?'

'Yes,' Adit said, 'I do. I love it here. I'm so happy here, I hardly notice the few drawbacks. I'll tell you — I did go back, three years ago, when I got engaged to Sarah and my parents wanted me to

---
[4] Friend.

come with her. I stayed there looking for a job for four months. All I could find was a ruddy clerking job in some Government of India tourist bureau. They were going to pay me two hundred and fifty rupees and after thirty years I could expect to have five hundred rupees. That is what depressed me — the thirty years I would have to spend in panting after that extra two hundred and fifty rupees. I took a look at some other people who had to live on that much and I said, no thank you, I'm not made for this, and I came back and told Sarah we'd stay. I'm happy here. I like going into the local for a pint on my way home to Sarah. I like wearing good tweed on a foggy November day. I like the Covent Garden opera house — it has a chandelier like a hive of fireflies; when I stand under it, I feel like a millionaire. I like the girls here — I like their nylon stockings and the way their noses tilt upwards, and I used to like dancing with them. I like steamed pudding with treacle. I like — I like thatched cottages and British history and reading the letters in *The Times*.'

'Like being called a wog. Like choosing between three kinds of lavatories...'

'I like the pubs. I like the freedom a man has here: Economic freedom! Social freedom! I like reading the posters in the tube — oh, I must take you to see my favourites, two of them hanging side by side —. "Beware of VD" and "I got it at the Co-op." Do you get that kind of fun on your way to office in Calcutta? And I like the Thames — I'll take you to see it from Raleigh's Walk up in the Tower and you can imagine yourself back in any period of British history you like — I like the ravens there — mad, black witches, croaking and raving. I like the feeling I can nip across the Channel for a holiday in Paris when I win the football pool, and no damned P-Form *wallah* or Reserve Bank today to stop me...'

'Like being at the bottom of the ladder in your office. Like knowing you can never get to the top because there'll always be an Englishman there...'

'Why should I care, *yar*? I like old Ma Jenkins who cleans my room. When I say, "Good morning, Mrs. Jenkins, and how are you this morning?" she says — hands upon her hips, here — she says,

"Like half a dog, Mr. Sen — still on me two legs." Ha ha! Oh I like these fat old London women with faces like buns full of currants. And I — I like strawberries in summer. I like a weekend at the seaside. I even like the BBC !' he ended with a shout of triumph.

'Boot-licking toady. Spineless imperialist-lover,' Dev said. 'You would sell your soul and your passport too, for a glimpse at two shillings, of some draughty old stately home. You'd probably vote for the Tory Government if you could, and for the Immigration laws and Mr. Oswald Mosley and the Nottinghill louts and —'

'You're daft, *yar*,' Adit roared, shaking his head like a horse bothered by flies. 'You're daft. You just don't want to admit this is the land of opportunity and you've come adventuring in it. Admit it, you know it.'

'Opportunist yourself!'

'You haven't changed, Dev. You're the same kill-joy you always were in college. If anyone suggested going to the coffee house, it was you who pointed out that no one had money. If anyone thought of going for a moonlight drive, you pointed out that there was no moon and none of us had a car. You think black by habit.'

'And you?'

'Oh, I think gold, Dev, gold. I see gold — everywhere — gold like Sarah's golden hair. It's my favourite colour,' and he got up, dusting off grass and ladybirds and looking refreshed. They strolled off towards High Street. Adit singing softly and sentimentally.

> 'Pack up all my cares and woe,
>   Here I go, singing low,
> Bye-bye, Blackbird.
> Where somebody cares for me,
>   Sugar is sweet and so is she,
> Bye-bye Blackbird.'

The bouncing dog suddenly gave up the fleeing bee, veered around and, homeless adventurer that he had seemed, now made for some positive destination. He had a bowl of bones and beef broth waiting for him after all, in the shining kitchen of some Sunday villa.

Some crouched, some lay before the convex screen, pale and fierce as the sun in eclipse, its restless shifting of black and white reflecting on the faces it held captive, now darkening, now illuminating them with its mercurial whims. It seemed even to dictate their attitudes — by highlighting the stiff angles of raised knees and crossed legs, by setting a pair of black eyes momentarily ablaze, it made them representatives of dark defiance; by casting them into a well of soft shadows that rounded their backs and gave their heads and hands a sleeping limpness, it made them creatures of laze, of lazy acceptance. No one displayed any active response to the twitching figures that scribbled across the screen or to the drum, the trombone and the electric guitar that assaulted them with their persistent monotone of beat — thrum, thrum, thrum, without a change, without a break: the language of a mental defective who is unable to escape from its restrictions. Only towards the end did the tone rise, just a bit, but — defeated by its own effort — failed and faded away and, with it the jerking, palsied figures of the musicians.

White fluorescent letters flickered upon a blank white screen. The audience shifted, seemed to strain. The letters stood clear in white heat. Then shifted. Shifted again. Unrolled themselves. STRANGER IN BRADFORD followed by a curious tumble of British and Muslim names. The figures on the silent carpet stirred, lifted. Bottles and glasses were passed from hand to hand but the liquid sounds of drinks being replenished were drowned by the wistful music of an Indian flute as an unknown, but familiar, face appeared on the screen and turned around, looking at the landscape of chimneytops and television aerials, washing lines and factory gates, dustbins and babies' prams.

'He looks cold,' someone said. Adit sang:

> 'The north wind doth blow
>> And we shall have snow,
>> And what will poor Robin do then?'

'Shush!'

'Poor thing,' he sang, but stared as intently as the others at the Pakistani fitter who now stood in a queue for a job, descended to the blackened heart of a smoking factory and stood there amidst the embers, gazing about him expressionlessly before going to his tools and lifting them, one by one, with tentative and oddly delicate movements, like those of a pilgrim fingering his saint's holy relics.

'Stupid peasant!' growled Dev.

'Shush!'

They watched motionlessly while the young man, huddling his arms about him, a Kashmiri fez upon his head, wandered down long streets in search of a room. In one bleared window was a handwritten sign, *Room To Let*. He rang the bell. The door opened. A hatchet-faced woman in a plastic apron appeared. Her thin lips parted, chopped a bit, then snapped shut, soundlessly. The boy pointed to the sign, his lips moved dryly. The woman jerked her chin and her mouth opened wide. A man with three chins appeared at her side. His hand moved in peremptory jerks, as though he held an invisible stick. The Pakistani shrugged, walked off.

> 'He'll sit in a barn
>> And keep himself warm
>> And hide his head under his wing,'

sang Adit softly.

'Poor thing,' sang some of the others. Dev, placing his arms on his knees, grunted, and Sarah exhaled smoke.

The next scene showed the barn — a large uncurtained room with an immense television set for furniture, and three young men in their vests and striped pyjamas busy around a stove, kneading dough, rolling out and frying thick *rotis*. They sat down at an uncovered table and ate, their fingers breaking the newly made bread quickly and cleanly.

'Ahh, *roti* and *dal*,' said someone on the carpet.

'Slurp, slurp.'

'Open the window — what a disgusting smell!' piped someone else in a mock-BBC voice, and they all laughed.

Saturday night was ushered in with that manic beat of drum, trombone and electric guitar. In a steaming dance-hall, the Pakistani stood with his back to the wall, pressed in by his countrymen, mugs of beer in their hands. He watched with soulful, romantic eyes the blonde girls in their short, tight skirts stomp and twist and scribble about the crowded floor, and he said, 'My religion forbids me to drink or smoke or touch a woman. But here, in this country, what am I to do? I also do the things I see other men doing,' and there he was, on the floor, frightenedly clasping a girl by her waist, and moving his feet hesitantly and self-consciously, out of step with the quick, brisk music.

The audience on the carpet whistled and made ribald comments on Pakistani fitters and landladies' daughters. Sarah was seen to close her eyes slowly. She did not hear their laughter or understand their language. She seemed to hear nervousness and shame and sadness, if such things can be said to have speech. Shame. The shame of it all.

When she opened her eyes again the young man was lying on his bed and playing his flute, the melancholy flute that had ushered in the landscape of iron railings and smoking chimneytops that was his landscape by adoption. The young men in vests and striped pyjamas began to sing and clap their hands and the song, following upon the inane jigging of the dance hall music that had preceded it, seemed genuine and emotional to Sarah, the voices spiralling and enlarging and breaking with an intensely felt passion. Then they were off their beds and broken chairs, and dancing around their bare, uncurtained room, flinging out their arms, bending their knees and leaping high in an inspired *Bhangra*. One of them pulled out a handkerchief and waved it over his head. There was no breeze to ripple it but their ardour made it ripple, and the harvest was brought in on marigold-hung bullock carts, the rainclouds appeared, the rivers swelled, the mango ripened and it was the night of the peacock, the lion and the full moon — till the loud thumping of an indignant broom on the ceiling broke up their joy and their intoxication and there was a silence in which a voice was heard demanding, 'Wrap it up, you blighters, where d'you think you are, eh?'

The limp figures on the carpet that had seemed to go limper, almost to melt and disintegrate during the singing, as though an unsuspected sea had risen from the floor in great, warm waves to lap at them, sweep about them and drag them to and fro with its lurching rhythm, now sat up, stiff and straight, rubbing their eyes, coming out of a dream.

'What, the peasants of Punjab take that lying down?' Dev asked. *'Hai, hai,* the disgrace. What happens to them when they come to England? What would their fathers think of them, the milksons? There ought to be a riot, vengeance, murder.'

'Shush!'

The scene changed, the music changed, new characters appeared. They looked into a school room, swarming with the dark, oiled heads of Pakistani and Indian children, and at a teacher at the blackboard painstakingly drawing a picture of a man with an upraised arm. When it was done, she shouted, 'Police!' The children were awed and solemn and, with solemnity, they mimicked, 'Pulleece!'

Now the commentator himself came on, his square shoulders and bald head taking up all the space. His dehumanised and precisely phonetic voice made its cool little summary, its chilling predictions and was quickly blotted out by a blank, shivering glare of white before the next programme began — and was switched off.

The mock BBC voice spoke up from the darkness.

'Two civilisations at loggerheads. Period of transition. Awful responsibility. The future. The point is — does the Commonwealth really exist? If so, why doesn't everyone use the same lav?'

The lights went on amidst laughter. Glasses were refilled, uncomfortable cushions beaten, and the room brimmed with talk. Someone waved a copy of the *New Statesman* over their heads, folded to the *This England* column, and read aloud an interview with a Soho stripteaser who confessed she had only 'gone with white men' till one day she met a black man and now said she would 'never look at white again — unless it was for marriage.'

There was a welter of laughing sounds from which Dev's voice emerged in disgust. 'Now what do you make of people like that! How the hell is one to unravel the twists and turns of such perversity?'

'Oh, *perverse*,' someone scoffed. 'It's just too funny to be called such serious names.'

'The trouble with you immigrants,' said Dev, 'is that you go soft. If anyone in India told you to turn off your radio, you wouldn't dream of doing it. You might even pull out a knife and blood would spill. Over here all you do is shut up and look sat upon.'

'No, no!' shouted Jasbir. 'It's only these Pakistani Punjabis who go soft. The Lahore *wallahs* were never known for their strength. You wouldn't find an Amritsar man or a Ludhiana man looking like such a spaniel.'

'Huh, you Punjabis are all talk and swagger. Only the Bengalis can show real defiance,' claimed Samar, the doctor, who looked like nothing so much as one who needed his chest X-rayed. 'You only get worked up when the mood moves you, and it never lasts. We follow our reason and carry things out to their logical conclusions. A man gets in the way of your living the way you want to, so the man is shot.'

'Huh!' retorted Jasbir. 'You Bengalis have so much trouble tying up your *dhotis*[5], you'd never get into the fight till it was too late.'

---

[5] A kind of clothing, often worn by males in India to cover the lower part of the body. It consists of a long cloth knotted round the waist, passed between the legs and tucked in at the back.

'Jasbir,' his wife warned, 'you have three hostile Bengalis glaring at you from every corner.'

'I can take on six of them,' he roared. 'And that one —' He jerked his thumb at Samar, 'he's not even a Calcutta Bengali. The Delhi variety is like a hen when it comes to fighting — he just scratches in the dust and leaves it to the cocks.'

This provincial bantering grew more and more heated, the jeers louder, the taunts more obscene, all four men participating with violence and ribaldry. Mala, the Punjabi wife, laughed too, able to follow the nuances of communal and provincial prejudice and myth, language and custom. But Sarah and Bella sat in stiff silence, their Anglo-Saxon faces impassive. They had learnt exactly how much of this foreign world was theirs to tread and had given up their early attempts, made out of curiosity and a desire to join, to interpret jokes which seemed to depend entirely on such matters as a Bengali's accent or a Punjabi's eating habits or a Bihari's intellectual limitations, of which they naturally had no experience or comprehension. Bella, thrusting out her little chin, sometimes burst into a giggle. She herself had been brought up on jokes about stingy Scotsmen, wily Welshmen, drunken Irishmen and Cockney backchat, and could faintly comprehend a similarity of humour planted on soil so different, grown in a climate so extreme that it had undergone a radical change, retaining just a faint accent of resemblance. Sarah, who was only vaguely aware of the existence of such jokes, had her lips pressed together in a thin smile of boredom. Occasionally she shot a look at the statuesque Mala, at the way her black hair gleamed in the light and her white teeth sprang out in a big laugh at a remark Sarah had considered smug or unkind but was evidently not so, and there was a thin envy on her face — or so Dev thought as he regarded her, every now and then, from over the top of his beer mug.

Finally he said, 'What do *you* think Sarah?' using her first name for the first time.

She jumped a bit and her sleepy eyes widened. 'I?' she croaked. 'I — I think we should all have some hot chocolate — I'll make it,' and she went to the kitchen with a rush of relief.

'Is that a hint, Sarah?' Jasbir roared after her. 'Is it already time to throw us out?'

'I'll go help,' said Bella and got up, pulled down her tight little skirt and went off. Mala made no such effort, merely lolled against a cushion, only too grateful for a respite from housework, and told a story about her small son whom she once watched being chased up the stairs by a gang of English children, screaming at them in despair, "I'm *not* black! I'm *not* black — I'm *grey!*" Mala laughed with a gay, clanging sound at her son's wit.

'It's all very well,' said Jasbir, 'to draw a line between a Pakistani fitter and a Bengali professor, but what is the difference to the salesgirl at Woolworths or the bus conductor — what *is* the difference?'

'None,' laughed Mala, 'none.'

'Do you know what happened to me yesterday when I was going to hospital ?' asked Samar, curled tightly around his glass of brandy like a surprised loris. 'I was waiting in the queue when it started drizzling, so I opened out my umbrella. It's my old Calcutta umbrella — big and black, Hunter brand. Then a fat red man behind me hissed, "It's not raining".' Samar made a grotesque attempt at imitating a hearty huntin' and fishin' man's accent. 'So I said. "But it is, you know, it's just started," and he snapped at me, "No, its *not*." So then I just turned my back on him and I heard him say, under his breath, "Bloody Pakistani." Dammit, I heard him, I did.'

Jasbir and Adit roared. They slapped their thighs and threw themselves back into the sofa cushions and then jumped up to dance around the room, patting each other on the back and coughing.

Dev said, 'You're hysterical, the two of you.'

'So speaks the great new leader of the abused and the downtrodden!' shouted Adit, raising one arm above his head in salute.

'You clowns, why don't you stop it? Why didn't you hit him with your umbrella, Samar? You said it was a Hunter brand umbrella.'

'It is. That's why I didn't dare hit him — it would have broken in two and I would have got wet.'

The others laughed but Dev said, 'Why didn't you use your shoes then? Your fists? Anything. Why do you let them get away with it?' He was getting heated but Sarah and Bella came in just then with a tray full of blue-and-white striped mugs in which the hot chocolate steamed, spreading a sweet aroma through a room overripe with smoke, liquor fumes and fraud. With unexpected diplomacy Dev quietened down and sipped his cocoa.

'This is Sarah's way of saying it's midnight and we mustn't disturb her landlady any longer,' said Jasbir. 'Come, Mala, I suppose we must go.'

Sarah smiled with serenity, her hands folded about her cup.

'There's always the sofa,' said Adit, reluctant to see his friends leave, although he helped them with their coats and scarves. 'Dev has the spare bed now.'

'It's a nice sofa but not good enough, I think, for a memsahib,' said Samar and took Bella's arm.

'Wait, wait!' Adit shouted, unable to end the evening so soon. 'I'll come to the bus stop with you. Come on, Dev, be gallant. Let's guide them down the street. They might be assaulted by teddy boys. Arm yourselves with your walking stick, your umbrella, your *kukri*[6].'

'It's not teddy boys any longer, daddy,' Bella smiled a smile as bright as the big bell of marigold hair about her face. 'It's rockers now, and mods.'

'Ah, my dear, we belong to different generations. Alas, alas. Wash up, Sarah dear, and go to bed and don't mind me when I fall over the cat,' and Adit and Dev went out with their friends, unable to part with the warmth of shared experience and shared humour, leaving Sarah to pick up empty cups and glasses and full ashtrays and yawn her way to bed.

---

[6] Dagger favoured by Nepalis.

They had not come to the end of their cigarettes when they got back to the house and they stood by the gate awhile, unwilling to let the rich colours and the ringing sounds of their Indian friendships dissipate in the damp chill of the spring night and the white billows of invading sleep.

'The people downstairs are still up,' Dev said, trying to peer through the ragged lace curtains.

'They're never down,' Adit said with some bitterness. 'When there's nothing on the telly, they'll manage to find something on the radio,' and it was true, the lighted windowpanes were vibrating with an insomniac's frenzied ryhthms.

'Who *are* they?' Dev asked suddenly. He thought he glimpsed a blue costume like a sari behind those white tatters.

'Didn't we tell you? Sikhs — from Ludhiana, *yar,* the authentic stuff. About four generations of them in those two rooms, I should think. First the young men came, then they sent for their mothers, and the mothers sent for wives for the sons, and they all had children together.'

'What do they do here? Do they work?'

'Oh, the young men work in factories, the old ones in garages and warehouses, and the women cook and the children watch the telly. They drive us mad with their noise and their quarrels and singing and comings and goings.'

'Poor old Sen,' Dev laughed freely and delightedly for the first time that evening, as they went up the tiny gravel walk between the privet hedges on which the Sikhs had left some pieces of washing, yellow in the darkness. 'You've tried so hard to show Sarah what a sahib a *babu* can be, and then you're let down by the brown rabble downstairs. Hard luck.'

'Don't try to be funny,' Adit growled as they unlocked the door. 'And for God's sake, don't shout or half a dozen of them will pop out for a little bit of friendly *gup-shup*[7] that wakes up the whole of Laurel Lane.'

---

[7] Gossip.

'Really, Sen,' Dev pounded up the stairs, 'how can you stand for it? Really must write a letter to *The Times* about these hordes of black invaders who are spoiling your emerald isle.'

Adit made a threatening noise inside his throat but tiptoed carefully all the way up to their own door, then suddenly boomed out, 'Don't be so funny or I'll break your neck one day, *yar.*'

'Shhh,' hissed Dev, suddenly delicate on his toes, 'You'll wake Sarah.'

'So what?' Adit roared. 'She's used to being woken up. These English wives are quite manageable really, you know. Not as fierce as they look — very quiet and hardworking as long as you treat them right and roar at them regularly once or twice a week.'

'Not so different from the meek Indian gazelles then.'

'Shut up. This, you know, is what is called Abuse of Hospitality.' said Adit as he flung open his bedroom door in a lordly fashion. *'Namak haram*[8] — ungrateful for the very salt you eat.'

'Waker up of English wives,' Dev hissed back but the door shut in his face and there was nothing for it but to go to his own room and bed.

---

[8] Ingrate.

2

Shutting the green door quietly behind her, Sarah walked on cat's feet down the stairs, down the gravel walk to the gate, and was out on the morning road with swiftness that suggested feline magic. Yet, in that short passage, her personality and appearance made a rapid change, an automatic and switch-swift adjustment to the world outside. Amongst her blue-rimmed cocoa mugs, her potted plants, she was laconic and reserved, but self-possessed and casual. Striding down Laurel Lane, her satchel swinging from one shoulder and her long hair caught in a tortoise-shell band on the nape of her neck, she had the hurried rush and tough briskness of one suspicious, one on the defensive. She clutched at the collar of her green mackintosh as though she were hiding something inside, or protecting a weak chest. She darted along the pavements as if on sliding skates, widely skirting the parked milk van, hurrying her step at the sound of approaching footfalls as though she were fleeing, holding this thing, this weakness inside her coat, hidden from them, from their curiosity, their questions, their touch.

Old Mr. Crummidge who was always out, patting his cabbages and sniffing through his warts at his two rose-trees, at an hour when others groaned at being woken by the alarm clock, watched her fleeing down the lane every morning and every morning, grumbled, 'What's up with 'er now? Got the police after 'er or what?' and, every morning, his wife, watching from the window where she stood holding a hairbrush matted with her pepper-coloured hair, growled,

'There 'e is — at it again — always got 'is old eyes on the dames, 'e has.'

But Sarah did not hear them, Sarah did not see them. Sarah had crossed the road and was out on the Common which she liked to cross on foot rather than take the bus around it, at least in fine weather. Here she could slow her pace and relax her hold on her coat collar, but she kept a sharp lookout for those who walked their dogs at this hour, keeping to the loneliest path, walking under the trees and drawing across her face a mask of secrecy. Those who glanced at her made aware of her by the violence with which she turned away from them — felt apprehensive, but, since she was a stranger, gave it no thought.

What was Sarah's secret? Once even Adit had wondered when, by chance, she got onto the bus that he had travelled across the river on and he had had, by force, to observe her from a distance as a great press of people going home from work kept him from pushing his way to her side. Across the overcoats and newspapers and damp hats, her anguish had struck him in a salt wave, silencing the clamour he was about to make to attract her attention. 'Mrs Sen, Mrs Sen,' he had wanted to call, raising his umbrella over the heads of parcel-laden matrons and paper-wrapped clerks, but seeing the look on her face, turned as it was to a window curtained with raindrops, he had sat back, sat silent, shocked by that anguish. An anguish, it seemed to him, of loneliness — and then it became absurd to call her by his own name, to call her by any name: she had become nameless, she had shed her name as she had shed her ancestry and identity, and she sat there, staring, as though she watched them disappear. Or could only someone who knew her, knew of her background and her marriage, imagine this? Would a stranger have seen in her a lost maiden in search of her name that she seemed, with a sudden silver falling of the light of glamour, to an unusually subdued and thoughtful Adit? Or would she have seemed merely an anaemic working girl on her way home from work with nothing to look forward to that evening that could bring any warmth to her white forehead or her grey eyes? 'I must take her out tonight,' Adit thought with some agitation. 'to visit one of her friends, not mine,' and, immediately on getting off the bus and taking her arm, he had made his bid to recover her vividness, the sure, quick quality of her humour that he had known when he fell in love with her. Curtly she had refused. But why, he protested, did she never see her old friends anymore? She did not care to, she replied, and said nothing more till they were inside their flat with the green door shut behind them, and then she sighed, shook the rain from her hair and allowed him to put his arms around her there in the rain-drummed kitchen.

Sometimes she had a great stretch of the Common to herself when she could see no intruder, not even a shivering errand boy or a strolling dog. Then she thrust out her chin, lifting her face to see the green dragonflies droning through the mesh of morning light and note how the leaves on the chestnuts had achieved full span on their twigs and quivered with a summer pride, and hoped she had remembered to put some chocolate in her bag for that freckled child who brought the registers in to her.

She came to the edge of the Common just as a bus rolled to a halt and out tumbled a load of children in their summer freckles, their crosses of sticking plaster, the remains of their breakfast egg and toast, and aggressive, freshly combed and washed morning cockiness. As she darted through their throng, they pretended not to notice her at all but, once she was across the road, she heard them scream, 'Hurry, hurry, Mrs. Scurry!' and 'Where's the fire, pussy cat?'

The concrete courts of the school were already awash with the ink of blue blazers and tunics. Earlier busloads of children were playing tribal games with marbles on chalk-drawn squares and circles, while some still fierce knots gathered in corners to whisper and plan the battles to be fought that day, the treacheries to be undertaken, the triumphs to be won. None had attention to spare for Sarah and she slipped into the school, still strangely dark, to her little back-room under the stairs. She shut the door behind her, briefly pressed her hands together as if in a little prayer of gratitude, and, sitting down at the desk, she heaped about her registers and copy books, like a fortress.

From within this paper fortress she conducted her day with a misleading show of self-confidence, even of command. The Head sent her a time-table to check. Letters were opened, signed, pinned, put in this tray and that. Bills paid, cheques written out. Lunch duty and games duty and recess duty allotted fairly, justly and irrevocably to this teacher and that. Keys jangled in cold steel bunches of authority, cupboards were unlocked and their contents counted and marked — so many boxes of chalk, so many bottles of ink, arithmetic books and readers, pencils and erasers. Counting, tidying, taking out and putting in — some mechanism had taken her over, wound her up with a key and set her moving and working in a comfortably assured and uncomplicated way, performing the daily tasks evenly and smoothly, with the conviction of a priestess that if all the rites were performed, all the rules observed, life would be, after all, simple. The wrinkles came out of her forehead, her hands stopped fumbling and seemed to know just what to do, she might have seemed quite happy to anyone who looked in — and then someone did.

It was Philippa Goodge, the child with a picture book face of a jack-o'-lantern, yellow teeth carved between the gaps, a handful of straw for hair, always adorned with a fancy-dress, polka-dotted ribbon, carrying a register half as big as herself in her pink sausage arms.

'Hullo,' Sarah smiled and bent down for her bag to look for the chocolate she had decided to give Philippa, when Philippa spoke.

'Please,' she said, 'have you any of those Indian stamps to give me, ma'am?'

Her bag opened, Sarah stopped and felt that secret, that nut fall out of the cracked shell of her being. Out it tumbled, rattling, terrible — a nut, a crab, a grain of sand. There it lay — her secret.

'Indian stamps?' she faltered.

Indian stamps — that tiny triangle of mauve on a purple background that was stamped even on her white forearm; that Indian teaplanter in a cowl, picking her way through green tea bushes, who was her secret companion; those many inscrutable faces of statesmen, philosophers and unknown Indian sages who were her oracles — these figures of the Indian stamps were hers, hers to ponder over, mull over, to acquaint and align herself with, in an effort to know India, become Indian — these were her secrets. To have anyone pry upon them, break in upon the shadowed intimacy of her relationship with them, was violent, shaking, terrible.

'Indian stamps?' she faltered, staring at Philippa, hardly able to believe this picture book clown to be an aggressor, a spy. (Had the children on the road that morning called her, perhaps, 'Hurry, hurry, Mrs. *Curry?*') Quickly she withdrew her hand from the bag and shut it. 'No, no.' she muttered, 'not today,' and, taking the register from the child's arms turned away and the bar of chocolate stayed in her bag.

But unreality had swamped the paper walls of her fort, turning them soggy, making the pages float away on dim waves. In the centre she sat, feeling the waves rock her, and then the fear and the questioning began. Who was she — Mrs. Sen who had been married in a red and gold Benares brocade sari one burning, bronzed day in September, or Mrs. Sen, the Head's secretary, who sent out the bills and took in the cheques, kept order in the school and was known for her efficiency? Both these creatures were frauds, each had a large, shadowed element of charade about it. When she briskly dealt with letters and bills in her room under the stairs, she felt an impostor, but, equally, she was playing a part when she tapped her fingers to the sitar music on Adit's records or ground spices for a curry she did not care to eat. She had so little command over these two charades she played each day, one in the morning at school and one in the evening at home, that she could not even tell with how much sincerity she played one role or the other. They were roles — and when she was not playing them, she was nobody. Her face was only a mask, her body only a costume. Where was Sarah? Staring out of the window at the chimneytops and the clouds, she wondered if Sarah had any existence at all, and then she wondered, with great sadness, if she would ever be allowed to step off the stage, leave the theatre and enter the real world whether English or Indian. She did not care, she wanted only its sincerity, its truth.

She did not hear the bell ringing till Miss Pimm flew in like a wintry draught, crying 'Haven't you put the kettle on? Ooh Sarah, I won't have time for a cup of tea, ooh dear.'

With so urgent and necessary a task to be done, Sarah was quickly the brisk, the active secretary again. She apologised over and again for having overlooked the time, and now hurried about the business of lighting the gas ring, getting out the chipped cups and the lump sugar and rushing to the dining room for a bottle of milk while poor Miss Pimm sucked her aspirins and wailed about the agony of teaching the multiplication table to her three West Indian pupils. 'They just don't concentrate, they just don't care. You never saw the like of them, Sarah. And my migraine is just killing me, I really oughtn't to have come, I ought to have told the Head to fill in for me today, that's what my mother said this morning and I wouldn't listen to her, I wouldn't.'

'Have your tea. I made it extra strong.'

'That's a dear, you are. Ooh, isn't it nice and strong? Another lump of sugar, dear, I think you've forgotten I take three.'

'Ah yes, it's Julia who takes two. I'm sorry.'

In a while Julia Baines came in for her tea, more like a languid afternoon breeze than a draught. She half-lay across Sarah's desk, smoking a cigarette and laughing off Miss Pimm's agitation. 'Give them lines to do,' was her advice. 'I just wait for one desk to slam, one giggle in the back row, and I give the whole lot lines to do. Then the Head tippytoes up, peeps in and squeaks, "Oh my, aren't we a model class?" Ha ha,' she laughed, crushing her cigarette in the dregs of her tea, which made both Sarah and Miss Pimm shudder with distaste. 'Just don't get so worked up,' Julia continued, 'you won't be here forever, will you?'

'Why not?' squealed Miss Pimm. 'I don't see myself taking off for Monte Carlo on my savings, 1 don't,' and she suddenly laughed a big, braying laugh that shook the bony shoulders under her grey cardigan.

'Well, I don't see myself slaving away in this crummy school forever and forever. Let the Head find out about my teaching when the examinations come around and the kids tell her I never made them open their arithmetic book once in all the year, and I'll be happy to be sent on my way. Adventure, adventure! Isn't that right, Sarah? Course you're the adventurous one, really. Still waters run deep, eh? You'll desert all one horrid, foggy day and make off for sunny India, I know.'

Sarah put down the tea pot and said, as quietly as she could, 'I don't know. Why do you say that?'

'Why? Well, your husband isn't going to stay here forever, is he?' Julia shouted aggressively, and Sarah stood still trying to make out what she meant by that, when two more teachers came bouncing in for their tea, complaining so loudly of the children who had held them up that Sarah could quietly withdraw to the gas ring without Julia noticing or following. Julia was giving them advice, but they hooted at it loudly.

Sarah made no effort to join them. She was still breathing hard at having so narrowly escaped having to answer personal questions. It would have wrecked her for the whole day to have to discuss Adit with Julia, with Miss Pimm, in this sane, chalk-dusted, workaday office. She was willing to listen for hours to Miss Pimm's diagnosis of her aches and pains. She was willing to listen, though somewhat less readily, to Julia's description of last night's dance in Streatham and the boy who took her home. She was able to smile at the extravagant exaggerations of Mrs. Goodall as she repeated the naughty words that Tommy Banks had scribbled across the blackboard. But to display her letters from India, to discuss her Indian husband, would have forced her to parade like an impostor, to make claims to a life, an identity that she did not herself feel to be her own, although they would have been more than ready to believe her. When she had started working at the school, she had been less practised at withdrawing, at sidestepping, at not only going off on a tangent herself but leading others on one as well. There had been some dreadful tea breaks when they had compelled her to explain the various ways of cooking curry, when they had questioned her about her parents-in-law and their whereabouts, when they had even come close, dangerously close, to asking her 'her plans,' her husband's 'plans.' She had stammered out her replies, too unhappy even to accuse them of tactlessness or inquisitiveness and, for her pains, had heard Julia sniff, as she left the room, 'If she's that ashamed of having an Indian husband, why did she go and marry him?' So she had had to learn, through the years, to keep others talking of themselves rather than allow them to refer to her, and the tea break was for her an exhausting, demanding and hair-raising exercise in such tactics.

When the bell had rung a second time and they had disappeared, leaving her to deal with the dirty cups and the disorder, she had only an hour and a half before lunch in which to calm her nerves, straighten out their knots and rest herself by immersing her mind in the school accounts. If only, she cried out once before the tangle of figures succeeded in drawing her thoughts wholly to them if only she were allowed to keep her one role apart from the other, one play from the other, she would not feel so cut and slashed into living, bleeding pieces. Apart, apart. That enviable, cool, clear, quiet state of apartness. Then she spotted an error in addition, and another, and grew absorbed in correcting them.

Lunch time was not the ordeal that the small and intimate tea break was to her. The length of the plastic-topped table with fifteen children seated at each side of it separated her from Miss Pimm and they were so busy shouting, 'Don't eat with your mouths open' and 'I want to see every bit of that cabbage eaten up,' that there was not the vaguest chance of any personal remark being made, though Sarah felt, uneasily, that Philippa Goodge, the jack-o'-lantern child, was eyeing her in a curiously cold, speculative way. (*Had* it been 'Hurry, hurry, Mrs. *Curry?*') Once the discoloured, spotted bananas had been handed out and the discarded skins collected, and the children sent out to play, Sarah watched the teachers depart with them into the pale drizzle on the courts where they nevertheless threw themselves into their tribal sports with undampened abandon. Sarah was to be left to herself and to her work for the rest of the afternoon. Only once did she come close to disaster. While she was collecting her belongings and waiting for the last bell of the school day to sound, Julia Baines, who always managed to slip away before anyone else, put her head in at the door — looking rather fuzzier than it had at the start of the day — and cried, 'Come and have a cup of tea with me at the corner, Sarah. Come on, do now — we haven't had a chat in a long time.'

Sarah dropped an armful of registers on the desk and turned a mottled pink. 'Oh no,' she cried in dismay. 'Oh no,' and then, collecting herself and her books, she added, 'It's my ironing day, you see. I'm so sorry but I've been putting it off for days, you know how it is.' Julia went off without another word, leaving Sarah to feel not only wretched but in the wrong.

It was still drizzling thinly as she came out of the school, some time after the roaring, rushing mob of children had left, leaving a litter of paper on which the ink ran in the rain. The bus was so long in coming that she went into the supermarket to wander amongst the stacked shelves in an absentmindedly happy way for she loved the supermarket, only just remembering to snatch up a bottle of mango chutney and a Lyons blackberry pie in order not to arouse the accountant's suspicion. The supermarket was a soothing place to her. Here she could buy her Patna rice and her pickles without acquiring the distinct personality these purchases would have marked her with, had she shopped for them in one of those pleasant little shops at the end of Laurel Lane where, in no time, the berry-faced broom-wielding proprietor would have come to recognise her and to ask. 'Now how about a nice salmon head for your husband, Mrs. Sen ? I know how these Bengali gentlemen love their salmon heads and I've got a nice big one for you.' But inside the sparkling halls of the supermarket where walls of soap and cornflakes hid her from strangers' eyes, she could be as eccentric. as individual as she pleased without being noticed by even a mouse. She walked out into the soft, muzzling rain with her packages, reassured to find herself an unidentifiable, unnoticed and therefore free person again. The bus came and she found herself a seat next to the door so that she did not need to push past or touch anyone and she turned her face to the blurred window, observing the melting greys and greens of the Common with that fixed expression of stark loneliness that had so stirred her husband on another rainy afternoon.

On the table a steaming mug, blue-rimmed, and an orange cat, sleeping, its paws folded symctrically under its chin. A pair of hands, white, blue-veined, folded about a letter, stamped with the purple triangle of India in a mauve wash of the Indian Ocean. Sarah sat holding it, gazing at it, bemused, rousing herself only to reach out for the cup and drink a sip of tea or touch the cat's ears and start in its throat a low, grudging purr. Rain streamed down the windowpanes she had deliberately left uncurtained for she loved the sight of it closing about her, shrouding her, separating her from the world with its lustrous curtain.

She did not start at the rap on the door for she recognised the hesitant, faltering, three or four little raps and shuffle of feet on the door mat. It was only Emma Moffit who rapped at the door in that manner and Sarah rose composed to open the door and admit Emma, for Emma would not disturb by even a ripple this afternoon hour of meditation. Emma, the landlady who lived like some aged mouse in the attic of the house, was the one person who, with Sarah, could sit sipping tea and gazing upon letters from India with precisely the same expresion of wonder, awe and study as though awaiting a sudden exploding revelation, a flash of light that would illuminate all. To have Emma with her was merely like having a mirror in the room — so Sarah had once confessed to Adit and appalled and horrified him for he could see no resemblance whatsoever between his tall, fair wife with her long countryside stride and her laconic good nature and this nervous, spidery old lady, always a composition — untidy and distorted — in grey and mauve and green, with her rundown flannel slippers, her great brooches, her scattered hairpins and her grey, mauve and lunatic face. 'But if you hadn't married me, or if you were to leave me, I would grow to be just like Miss Moffit,' Sarah explained to him in a rare fit of introspection, and Adit was furious. 'You have no heart,' he cried. 'How can you imagine such things? How can you say such things? An icicle — I have married an icicle !'

'You have a letter,' Emma noticed at once as she pulled up a chair to the table. She reached out her purple hands, chilblained even in summer, as though to touch the letter, or the cat — but she touched neither.

Sarah poured out her tea and sliced a lemon. 'It is always in Bengali,' she said, wistfully.

'Such beautiful script,' Emma breathed, staring at the sheets Sarah drew out of the envelope to spread beneath the cat's drooping head. 'When I think of Tagore writing out his poems in that script' — Emma drew a loud breath that made her nose tremble as if in ecstasy.

'Tagore? Oh. Oh yes — but I thought he painted.' 'That too, Sarah. Everything. Sometimes he would write a poem and then convert the script into a painting. I have seen prints. Such weird, wild things, Sarah, you never saw.'

'No,' said Sarah, 'I haven't. I must ask Adit's father to send — your tea, Emma, drink while it's hot.'

'Yes, yes.' She gulped down her tea so hastily that some of it crept over her underlip and trickled down her chin. ('Dirty old bag,' Adit called her. 'Does she bathe? I don't think so. That's why she doesn't mind those Sikhs living on the ground floor and mucking it all up. Really, Sarah, how can you stand her?') Suddenly Emma ducked her head between her shoulders like some tortoise, her eyes lit up as though her spectacles had suddenly liquified and she gushed forth. 'I came to tell you something, Sarah. *Two* things. Do you know that sweet young Mrs Singh — the young one who came out just last year — is going to have a baby? Yes! She came up and told me herself and brought me the most delicious sweets, "to celebrate," she said. *Burfee* sweets she called them, with silver paper on them, *real* silver, you know, not tinfoil !' Her eyes rolled in amazement, with pleasure at the memory of the sweetness of these sweets. 'And she is to have a baby this winter. Won't that be lovely, Sarah? A darling little Sikh baby in my own house, oh my. She told me she will be coming to give you some of that *burfee* too.'

'Oh no,' cried Sarah in dismay. She dreaded Indian sweets. She dreaded meeting young Mrs. Singh who dressed in pink or parrot green satin *salwar-kameez* and who always, even in the coldest weather, had two half-moons of perspiration showing under her shining satin armpits. The thought of her breaking into this cat-quiet kitchen, with a jingle of glass bangles, bearing a plate of rich, silvery sweets, made Sarah shrink with dread.

'Yes, she did. Isn't that *sweet?*' cried Emma so that Sarah could already feel the incredible, the impossible sweetness of the silver *burfee* in her mouth. 'And that's only *one* of the nice things that happened today. The other is — more *important,*' she breathed slowly. Her eyes expanded, protruded and bulged out of her powdery face and she spilt some more tea down her chin. 'Do you remember,' she went on in a suddenly hushed and conspirational voice, 'I told you I was going to form a little club? A little *Indian* club to which my Indian friends could come on Wednesday afternoons — I chose Wednesday because it always rains and strangers would be happy to have somewhere to go and have something to do. They could meet some really interested, intelligent English people and tell them, teach them about India.' Her way of pronouncing 'India' was to savour the first syllable with her lips and tongue all pursed together into a little grape, and then to let her lips part and to breathe out the large second syllable gustily, romantically.

Sarah nodded, misgivings closing in upon her like a dampness, taking all the warmth out of her teacup, her sleeping cat and the rich, purple-stamped mystery of the unread letter. 'Yes,' she sighed, 'you've spoken of it often.'

'*Well,*' cried Emma Moffit, bringing down one hand flat on the tabletop with a slap that startled the cat and made its furred brow wrinkle up in a frown of disapproval. 'I think — think it is going to start functioning at last. My own little India Club! I've had so many replies to the letters I sent out — you should have seen the mountain the postman left for me today, that *dear* man — and the *most* important one was a letter from Swami Binodanand who lives in Hampstead, a very wellknown Swami — in his circles. He wrote to say he would keep his Wednesday afternoons free for my little club, to give lessons in yoga.' Miss Moffit spaced the last three words with care and emphasis, breathing slowly and deeply to let their importance make their effect. Then she leapt up, her long chain of onyxes clattering suddenly and wildly against her bony chest. 'Don't you think it is *wonderful,* Sarah? *Don't* you?'

Sarah's heart sank and she folded her hands in her lap and nodded dumbly.

'Every Wednesday then, we shall have a yoga class. And all free, you understand — there will be no money transactions at all in *my* club. Then, when famous Indians visit London — philosophers or painters or musicians — we shall invite them to come and address the Little India club! *There!* Aren't I getting ambitious?' She laughed and laughed and her skeletal figure seemed to grow quite disjointed in her pleasure and her exertion — her knees flung apart, her onyx rattling about her neck, her hairpins showering out of her white, windy hair. 'But do you know why, Sarah? I said to myself this morning, as I opened my letters, said to myself — here I am, in contact with such wise, wonderful people like the Swami Binodanand of Hampstead. and it is a challenge to me to make, to create a meeting place where these great, wise people can come and lecture to us lesser beings, us *little* ones, and help us to expand, to set our sights on farther, on *Eastern* horizons. I said, I said to myself. "Come out of your shell, Emma Moffit. You've lived in your shell for thirty years." ' Here her voice thinned out and dwindled... 'Thirty years it is now, Sarah, that I've lived inside my lonely shell. But now, now at last something has come to draw me out of it. What a challenge, it is — *frightening!'* She shook open her mane, all pins scattered from it, and twined her hand about her necklace tightly. 'But so wonderful — it will be wonderful,' she whispered.

(Emma Moffit's obsession with India, the romantic affair she had with India, had a reason for it so obvious that it risked an appearance of banality: she had once been engaged to a young British soldier who had served in India and died there of dysentery. He was buried in Ambala. She had kept his letters and gifts to her wrapped in a cashmere shawl for thirty years now.)

Sarah nodded, and nodded wretchedly. The more Miss Moffit came to life, animatedly jerking her skeleton about and clicking her teeth, the more still and reserved grew Sarah. She had hoped to spend a pleasant half hour with a woman who, like her, knew India, knew it well but at one remove and they sat together on many afternoons, often in silence, their curiosity and imagination in curious harmony, talking desultorily of a book one of them had been reading about Himalayan flowers or bandits in Rajasthan, of Adit's family in Calcutta, of a new Indian recipe Sarah had tried out the night before. To Emma, as to Adit, Sarah could voice her curiosity about the whiterobed widows who, she had heard, lined the banks of the Ganges in Benares, about the composition of *henna* that women used, she had heard, to draw patterns on the palms of their hands and tbe soles of tbeir feet. Together they would contemplate a land composed, for them, of rich, drowning perfumes — Emma had had sent to her once a leather case with tiny, thick bottles of rose and violet *attars*[1] — of the droughts, monsoons, famines and floods of which they read in the papers, of the ivory elephants and subtly flavoured tea and tingling pickles they bought in London's Indian shops, of the weird, tantalisingly unresolved music they heard on Adit's records of Bismillah Khan's *shehnai* and Ravi Shankar's *sitar,* of the descriptions of weddings and feasts and festivals in letters from Adit's family, and of the great landscapes of river and desert, the incomparable dawns and sunsets and night skies of which they dreamt nightly. Mostly Sarah constructed the India of her imagination in silence and solitude and she therefore enjoyed, once in a while, speaking aloud to Emma who shared and understood. But now she had an awful suspicion that Emma was moving, moving fast, dangerously and inescapably towards the underlit and suspect world of fake Swamis, of hoarse, sweaty seances in damp darkness, of the naked and oily contortions of yogic postures, of thick lumpy sweets and phoney sages...the things that made her shudder, discreetly, as she sat quietly, only half listening. while Emma clicked her big teeth, rattled her necklace, breathed gustily and talked, talked on.

All of a sudden much sooner than she had dared hope, Emma flew up, crying, 'All that work to be done, to be written. and here I am gossiping away with you. My dear. I must fly!'

---

[1] Perfumes / fragrant essential oils.

Sarah was so relieved she felt ashamed and at the door she said, 'About the rent, Miss Moffit, I'm ever so sorry but you'll have it by the end...'

'My *dear*, don't mention it,' cried Emma surprisingly, for she was in the habit of slipping very curt, stern little reminders into Sarah's letter box by the end of the first week of the month, in complete contrast to her gushing goodwill and disorganised but selfless generosity. 'I wouldn't have — If it hadn't been my Oxfam subscription that simply has to be sent in this month. You know it is only for that that I let out my rooms and collect the rent. Otherwise, how I would love to have all you lovely, lovely people as my guests.' She gave Sarah a swift peck on the cheek and streaked up the stairs like a gust of grey wind.

'Hmm — hmm — hmm — father's knee is bad again... hmm — hmm — Nikhil's exams are over, he thinks he's done well... hmm — hmm — mother is going on a pilgrimage to Amarnath,' read Adit, now and then consenting to translate, inadequately for the intently listening Sarah. He came to the end of the letter, tossed it down on the rug and raised his arms over his head in a great yawn. 'Mother going to Amarnath!' he blinked 'I can just see her setting off over the mountains with trunks full of saris, bunches of keys, stores of pickles — she can't go across the street without taking at least half her belongings with her.'

'But,' said Sarah, holding aloft a darning needle in one hand and a crimson sock in the other. 'I thought one went on foot, over glaciers.'

'Yes, but safely, with a retinue of coolies and mules,' Dev told her. 'The spiritual East rarely manages to be spiritual except on a solid bulk of materialism like the strong backs of coolies and mules.'

'You make fun of everything.'

'Not at all. Haven't you heard of the tourists' India, that land of contrasts, of the mythical and the modern? Haven't you heard about our bullock carts and naked fakirs jostling with the buses and trams on the streets, etcetera, etcetera?'

'I must go,' said Sarah with decision and urgency born of that long day of torments and silences. 'Adit, we must go.'

Adit had gone to fetch himself another drink. Returning with it, he looked fierce. 'Have we the money?' he growled. 'Or the time? Do you know how long a boat takes? Do you know how much an air ticket costs? It's all very well for my mother to be a pilgrim and set off on a mule over the Himalayas, but here we are, attached with ropes — ropes of steel to the aeroplane age, the jet age, the age of hurry, the age of the weekend. Now if I were a student, I could have jumped on a cargo boat, or hitch-hiked — I did that once. But you can't do that if you have a wife — let me warn you in advance, Dev.'

Sarah looked penitent and Dev asked resignedly, 'All right, tell us about the time you hitch-hiked.'

'Right across the continent to Aden,' said Adit with pride, holding aloft his glass of Guinness.

'A beautiful Swiss redhead drove him from Germany to Aden in her shining white Volkswagen. She hoped to be taken along to India from there,' said Sarah, bending over her workbox to extract another sock.

'I don't believe it — not with that ugly mug of his,' Dev protested, and Adit sat beaming as if in remembrance of a plateful of cream.

'Well, she wasn't exactly beautiful,' he said modestly, 'she was a hundred pounds overweight for that. But she did want me to take her to India, that's quite true.'

'She paid all the bills on the way,' Sarah explained.

'So that I would have enough for two tickets. But all I had was enough for a third-class ticket on the Haj boat. A third-class ticket means being a deck passenger. When I got onto that boat with my neat little bag, I thought I'd find myself a nice quiet corner, put up a hammock and go to sleep for five days. Hell, there wasn't place for me to sit on my bag leave alone lie down anywhere. Everyone else had got onto that boat at Mecca. Those pilgrims had brought along their women, their trunks, their bedding rolls, even goats and chickens and stoves. They would slaughter the beasts and roast them and there would be blood and feathers and coal all over the decks. A dirty great slaughter-house, that's what the boat was. At night they'd eat and sing and then great fights would burst out all over the ship like bonfires. You'd hear women screaming and see men beating each other till blood ran and the captain came to tear them apart. Then, five time a day, they would roll out their prayer mats and say their prayers. And there was I, miserable Hindu, with not enough room to squat in, and babies vomiting into one pocket and defecating into the other...'

Sarah held up a sock before her pinched face. She had heard the description many times but Adit never ran out of new, highly coloured embroidery thread with which to adorn it.

'What did you do ?' Dev asked, fascinated.

'For two days I just sat on my heels. Then I climbed up the wall into a porthole. There was a sailor lying on his bunk there. I fell on my knees, folded my hands and begged him, pleaded with him to let me use his toilet. Dammit, 1 had real tears pouring down my cheeks like the Ganga and the Jumna together. Finally he gave me permission to climb up once a day, at four o'clock in the morning, and use his toilet. Then, I'd crawl down again and sit on my heels and recite all the Sanskrit prayers I could remember — silently, of course.'

'But what did all the others do? About the lavatories, I mean?'

'Don't press me, *yar*,' Adit said, glancing at Sarah 'My wife has such a delicate stomach, don't you know? But I can tell you, I didn't eat once in those five days. The men would sometimes look across at me and offer me a piece of roast sheep, but I would clutch my belly and stick out my tongue and they would leave me alone. I think they imagined I was in the early stages of cholera and hell, so did I. When I was pushed off the boat in Bombay, I couldn't find my bag. But I didn't give a damn. Only my brothers and sisters were disappointed I hadn't brought any presents.'

'That,' said Sarah, daring to breathe again, 'is the saga of how he lost the Swiss redhead.'

'Yes, didn't she go with you after all?'

Adit sat smirking. 'She wanted to, all right. So I took her along to the booking office in Aden — you see, I hoped she would pay for my fare as well, that's all I was thinking of, Sarah — and the man at the counter took one look at her and then he said to me, "You want to take her on the Haj boat?" Then he took me aside and said, "Look, here, it's your business, not mine, but there is no guarantee, absolutely no guarantee, that she won't be raped within five minutes of her getting on board that ship." '

'And of course you didn't see yourself as the knight in shining armour, did you?' Dev laughed. 'Good to think of you being forced to be realistic for once.'

'Naturally, *yar,*' Adit scratched his ear. 'After I'd taken one look at those vast bearded Muslim stalwarts and knives with which they were slitting their goats' throats, I had no illusions about the latent strength of the Bengali *babu*[2] at all.'

'Does anyone feel like dinner tonight?' Sarah asked in a discouraged tone.

Dev admitted, 'All that talk of slaughtered sheep and chickens has given me an appetite,' and Sarah left cat under one arm, to put the rice on.

'So this time,' said Dev, 'you'll go by Air-India cared for by the little Maharaja and his sari-clad *houris,* carrying a neat blue airbag full of French perfumes for the family?'

'This time I'll go by air, with a bag full of luxury goods from Woolworths,' Adit agreed. 'When I have a whole month of leave saved up, I'll go. My mother will cook *hilsa*[3] fish wrapped in banana leaves for me. My sisters will dress Sarah in saris and gold ornaments. I'll lie in bed till ten every morning and sit up half the night listening to the *shehnai* and sitar.'

---

[2] Gentleman.
[3] Fish of the roe family.

'What I can't understand about you is — if you long that much for *hilsa* fish and the sitar, why don't you get the hell out of here and go home where these things fall into your lap for the asking? If that is the life you crave — what keeps you from having it?'

'Ah, but when I'm there — and I was, you know, for four months, looking for a job before I married Sarah — I take these things for granted again and I only notice the laziness of the clerks and the unpunctuality of the buses and trains, and the beggars and the flies and the stench — and the boredom, Dev *yar*, the *boredom* of it. Then I'm mad to get back to England and the nice warm pubs and pick up a glass of Guinness and eye the girls and be happy again.'

'In other words, *yar*, a dilemma.'

'A dilemma? Nothing of the sort!' Adit snorted. 'It's only complicated, worrying, thinking people like you who get caught in dilemmas. I live for the moment. I don't think. I don't worry.' He lifted a finger in the air and sang,

> For every evil under the sun.
> > There is a remedy or there is none.
> If there is one, seek till you find it,
> > If there is none, never you mind it.

'Ha!' snorted Dev and Adit withdrew yodelling to the kitchen where Sarah chopped and stirred and sprinkled in whorls of aromatic steam. Then he stopped singing and exploded in anger.

'If my mother were to see this Sarah, she'd — she'd have a heart attack. How can you be so filthy? I'm not going to eat that damn rice, I'm not, after your filthy cat has been sticking his nose into it.'

'He is not filthy. He is as clean as clean can be.'

'Don't give me any of that. Cats eat rats, don't they? He noses in the rubbish bin outside, doesn't he? Throw it all away, at once. Cook some clean rice.'

Dev, who had heard it all now got up to shut the door quietly. Although he himself loathed the thought of the cat sniffing the food he was to eat, he felt quite sorry for Sarah to whom he had grown quickly attached — even to that part of her which he found, at times admirably cold and reserved. At that moment he could understand why a loud Oriental voice, uninhibited by any consideration, could grate on the selfconcious and silent Englishman's ears. At that moment Adit's voice grated even on his ears, accustomed as they were to noise of all kinds, at every hour. But soon he heard it drop to a growl, then a grumble and, much before it would have taken to cook a fresh helping of rice, he was called in to dinner. But then his own appetite dwindled to think of eating the unclean rice and he pushed it about his plate with a fork.

Sarah gave him a sharp look and said, exasperatedly, 'You don't go in for pets much in India, do you? I don't think I could live in a house without pets somehow.'

'They're dirty,' Adit growled.

'But you have your sacred cows, Adit, right in your streets?'

'That's quite different,' Adit said sternly, 'quite different.'

Dev began to laugh and Sarah looked up in surprise but did not say another word throughout that meal. After clearing the table, she went straight to bed with Kipling's *Plain Tales From the Hills* and fell half-asleep listening to the rumble of talk and laughter in the next room, followed by the profuse strumming of sitars and pounding of drums on the spinning records. The music sounded all dissonance to her ears as did the voices, and she fell asleep from the fatigue of trying to place them, string them, compose them, into a pattern, a harmony. To her closed eyes the darkness moved in a tumult of black shapes that would not settle. Her dreams too were in pieces, tormented, like the night slit and torn by long blades of rain.

Part II

Discovery and Recognition

3

Riding on the top of the 139, right up in front with only a sheet of glass to separate them from the blue-grey waves of London, they rode, they swam, like porpoises, through the city between banks of clayed brick walls. Adit, assuming familiarity with it all, assuming the disinterest of a native of the city, lowered his head into the Country Properties column of the *Times,* but Dev, his head aggressively uptilted, stared ahead, turned this way and that and confronted the Battersea power station with the eyes of a conquering soldier marching into Egypt. He had determined to be *blasé*, even contemptuous, for he had found early on cynicism to be the easiest and safest of postures, but there were things in London — and the Battersea power station was the first of them that threw him off his guard, shook him out of his normal attitude of cynical coolness and now, like an idolator catching sight of a renowned shrine, he raised his arms in an unconscious frenzy of excitement at the vision of the four great pillars, one at each corner of the massive grey temple of power, pouring vast billows of dark smoke into an empty, breathless sky.

Battersea, Battersea, Battersea power station! Words of worship roared inside his throat and when he opened his mouth a strangled sound came out to make Adit look up in amazement.

'What's the matter with you, *yar?*' he whispered, fiercely annoyed at such unsophisticated, such outrageous behaviour which so brazenly marked them as strangers, visitors, bumpkins even.

'What's the matter with *me?* Look there, *yar,* look at that — that building.'

'That's the Battersea power station,' Adit hissed.

'Ah, it must be the most magnificent sight in London! God, I'm sure the pyramids have nothing on it. Look at its bulk, look at the way it squats, square and weighty and unremovable on the ground. Look at those vast blank walls — like those of a secret vault of mighty emperors. Look at those towering chimney-stacks sending out the smoke of sacrificial fires. Can't you see the *puja* being conducted in its locked chambers, by priests in saffron robes and vestal maidens in white? Can't you see the great bonfire they've built inside and the herbs, the spices and magic potions they hurl into it? Can't you hear the clanging of great gongs and the blowing of long horns and singing of sweet hymns? I believe the electricity of London is generated by that sacrificial bonfire, right in the innermost heart of that temple. We ought to stand up and bow, Adit. We ought to kneel down and pray. We ought to sing out a hymn — the Vedic hymn to Fire —' and, to Adit's agony, Dev began to intone shrilly in Sanskrit:

> 'Produce thy streams of flames like a broad onslaught,
>   Go forth impetuous like a king with his elephant.
>   Thou art an archer.
> Shoot thy sorcerers with thy hottest arrows,
>   O Agni, send forth thy heat, thy winged flames...'

'Chelsea Bridge!' sang out the conductor. 'Chelsea Bridge !'

* * *

Rain on Sunday. Damp raincoats swinging from the gallows in the corner, wet umbrellas bleeding into a bucket. Electric heaters glaring red like inflamed eyes. Sunday papers littering the floor. Sarah expressionlessly following the thundering vacuum cleaner about, Adit sitting immobile in front of the television screen. Smell of rain, fish, mildew and mud.

'You must be masochists to live in this climate,' declares Dev, for his eyes are burning, his head exploding after an endless morning of reading close print on thin paper and seeing the shadows flicker across the shivering screen. 'Masochists. What a climate, what a stinking climate.'

Adit suddenly jerked into life, joyfully suggests, 'Make a bonfire to the great god Agni. Go on, go to Battersea power station and offer up your flannel underwear, your knitted socks. Ask Agni to send us heat.'

Laurel Lane. To begin with this is Dev's London — the small side lane banked with its brick-walled houses, partly obscured by privet hedges, by lines of washing and, now and then, a creeper of crimson roses or a bush of azaleas as delicate, as fine and airy as a host of pink and white butterflies hovering over a garden gate. In the small pebbly gardens and on narrow pavements, an occasional abandoned toy wagon or garden rake, but rarely an owner of these objects, rarely any human attachment. Lives lived in Laurel Lane are indoor lives. Occasionally a door opens, a stout and chinless matron in a flowered dress and an old cardigan appears with a tub of washing under one arm and clothes pegs stuck in her mouth like outsize teeth, or a younger woman comes out to wheel a sleeping child in its pram. There is a certain hour every afternoon — so Dev has noticed on his indoor days — when Mr. Yogi's icecream van drives up, playing a gay little tune to summon the children of Laurel Lane. Then, even in wet and freezing weather, an astonishing number of junior citizens explode into the lane, clutching their pennies, to buy ices of great variety in colour. Rough children they look, with patched clothes and dirty boots, but with what fresh faces, what achingly red cheeks and bright, alive eyes, — National Health Service children, brought up on free orange juice and good milk and with money to spare for Mr. Yogi's ices.

But Dev is rarely there to watch the appearance and disappearance of this Pied Piper of ices and Laurel Lane remains, to him, a place of shut doors and curtained windows. Spidery aerials perched on rooftops like ritual totem poles are evidence of television sets by the dozen, but never a sound does he hear from them. He does not hear his neighbours — their radios, their quarrels, their children are all kept behind closed doors.

'Now if this were India,' he explodes one dull day, standing at the window, 'I would by now have known all my neighbours — even if I had never spoken to them. I'd know their taste in music by the sound of their radios. I'd know the age of their child by the sound of its howling. I'd know if the older children were studying for exams by the sound of lessons being recited. I'd know what food they ate by the smells of their cooking. I'd know which men quarrelled with their wives, which mothers-in-law beat their daughters-in-law — everything. If I lived on a road like this in Calcutta, I would be aware — as aware as can be — of everyone around me. But not here. Here everyone is a stranger and lives in hiding. They live silently and invisibly. It would happen nowhere in India.'

'That must be nice,' says Sarah wistfully, strangely, for she had never struck Adit or Dev as being a neighbourly or even curious person. But somehow the picture Dev has coloured for her — bright, verbal crayons sweeping across the black-and-white of the wellknown page — appeals to her.

'It isn't,' growls Adit. 'It's bloody noisy and dirty and smelly.'

'But alive,' Sarah protests.

'And this isn't. Or it wouldn't be if it weren't for the pets. There are always the pets,' Dev muses at the window.

The canary in the brightest window, its brass cage sparkling with the freshest polish. Even the most nondescript dog has the brisk air of confidence which is born of the certainty of a good dinner at home, and almost always there is a concerned and affectionate human being at the other end of the leash, sometimes even making human noises at it. But the ones that really captivate Dev — although he will not admit it are the cats, larger than any he has seen before, fluffed out in billows of fine hair, stalking sedately, royally down the garden paths to settle in a patch of sun of the walls, and serenely — with only the faintest expression of curiosity, subtly dissembled — watch the world go by. They are Bustopher Jones, Deuteronomy and Jennyanydots in person. They do not dart away at his approach, as he is used to having cats do, nor do they glare discouragingly down their noses at his overtures, but look up inquisitively, almost inviting a pat and a bit of conversation about the fine weather, unalarmed and comfortable in their eiderdown furriness. Nothing lean or scarred mars this golden landscape and so captivated is Dev that he cannot bear to speak of it — at least no more than to admit grudgingly, 'Of course they do keep pets. I know which houses keep what pets.'

Dev ventures into the city. He descends, deeper and deeper, into the white-tiled bowels of Clapham tube station. Down into the stark caverns artificially lit, by way of long, ringing staircases where draughts sweep icily up and down and yet leave the Underground airless, suffocating. The menacing slither of escalators strikes panic into a speechless Dev as he is swept down with an awful sensation of being taken where he does not want to go. Down, down and farther down — like Alice falling, falling down the rabbit hole, like a Kafka stranger wandering through the dark labyrinth of a prison. On the platform, with blank lights glaring at the cold white tiles all around he stands fearfully with his fellow travellers and darts horrified glances at the strange look these people, who had seemed natural enough in the sunlight of High Street, have acquired in these subterranean depths. Here in the underground their faces have become withdrawn, preoccupied, and are tinged with an unearthly, Martian green, their movements are grown furtive and their voices — on the few occasions when they do speak out — chill him with their hollow, clinging harshness. In a panic he throws himself into the tube that has come slipping in like a long worm, and is carried off by it, hurtling through black tunnels in which the air is choked with soot and cinders and the very air is black as in a tomb. Dev is swamped inkily, with a great dread of being caught, stuck in the underground by some accident, some collapse, and being slowly suffocated to a worm's death, never to emerge into freshness and light.

He does emerge, to his amazement into the most natural freshness and light of Leicester Square — its little park ringed with tulips and green benches on which old men sit, under early summer foliage, reading their papers and scattering crumbs to fat, overfed pigeons. Exhilarated as a man snatched back from the tomb, he walks off, staring at the posters over the theatre doors, advertising plays he has so far only read of but now can actually walk in and see — a miracle that quite unsettles him.

But twice that day he is to relive the experience of delving into the tunnels of London's grim earth and of emerging into the radiance of natural light. In the galleries of the Tate he stumbles upon his own horror of the underground in Sutherland's crazed, dark, blood-stained visions. In considerable agitation, he tries to keep his voice down as he falters, 'Look. Look, Sen, that is what I mean, that is what I was talking about.'

Adit, fearing another pagan outburst as he had suffered on the bus, tells him sternly, 'Those were drawn in wartime, don't you know, when the tubes were used as bomb shelters.'

Stammering with the effort of maintaining his dignity, Dev insists, 'They are no different now,' and he is able to breathe only when Adit leads him into a gallery illuminated with the rosy, noontime visions of the Impressionists.

Similarly, at the National Gallery after walking, awed and subdued past the sombre and gigantic Tintorettos, El Grecos and Titians — all so mighty, so perfect and immense as to seem to be the handiwork not of human beings but of great, solemn gods — he stumbles, once more, upon the Impressionists. Adit watches uneasily as his face is illuminated by reflection. Taking care to speak only in a curt, almost grudging tone which will not betray his perfectly childish sense of joy and liberty, he says it is as though a window of a medieval castle has been flung wide open all at once and, in a flash, the grey dawn is over and it is high noon!

'Don't make so much noise,' Adit hisses, 'the attendant is looking at us.'

Giving him a furious look, Dev is happy to walk off alone and revel, without any fear of betraying himself, in the delight of seeing the originals of what he has so far only seen reproductions. He is not so much discovering those well-known South of France landscapes, the greens and oranges of Cezanne, the cornfields and olive trees of Van Gogh, and the muscular ballet girls of Degas in their ethereal tutus, as recognising them. He stands comparing the yellows of the original sunflowers to those in the print hanging on his wall at home when Adit comes up, a little reassured by his quiet behaviour.

'That Renoir,' begins Dev.

'Pronounced Ren-wah, old boy.'

'Renoir,' insists Dev, 'I've seen his pictures in books and they only looked like chocolate boxtops to me. But these ones, they're not, they're not at all, —'

'I should think not,' cries Adit indignantly, hastily glancing over his shoulder to see if anyone has overhead this piece of heresy, and then they both gaze in silence at the rays that dripped from Renoir's brush as from the crystals of a chandelier. The dancers are as rosy as he had known they would be but not, he is joyful to see, with paint but with rich blood and good health and he believes he can almost hear their castanets and their tambourines. He has been reading *Renoir, My Father* on the boat to England and he is able to inform Adit, proudly, that she is Gabrielle the maid, in one of the many costumes the painter kept for his models. 'She used to cook and wash and mind the babies in his house,' he is able to inform Adit. Now he has met her, the original, and she is smiling and blushing and he can hear the silks of her skirts rustle. Everywhere there is this joyful, magnificent light, like the first advent of light upon earth.

As they go out, reluctantly, Dev allows himself a groan. 'How will I ever go back to looking at prints after this?'

'There's always Shantiniketan,' says Adit, making Dev growl with discontent.

Out in grey-blue Trafalgar Square, they stand at the foot of Nelson's column amongst the fountains. Everything about them is in the colours of a gay-necked pigeon's feathers. The buildings are slate grey, the sky blue-grey, the shadows deep and violet. The fountains spout and sparkle about the grey column and the grey lions, and the spoilt, overfed pigeons tumble above the welter of red umbrellas and blue mackintoshes. Red buses rumble down grey streets and, here and there, at the foot of tall grey pillars or on quiet grey windowsills, stand tubs of pink and blue hydrangeas. At the corners are stands where Dev buys bright postcards with pictures in red and blue.

By the time they find their way to Lyons Corner House for lunch, it is drizzling. In the rain the smile of da Vinci's St Anne lingers, lingers like a wisp of mist grey-blue and tender.

Suddenly Adit said, 'Why go home already? Let's be devils and do the Victoria and Albert as well, Dev. I want to show you the best collection of Moghul and Rajasthan miniatures there is. And the Kangras —'

'Don't be funny. Do you think I've come to London to see Indian paintings?' snaps Dev, and looks out of the window where St Anne's smile wavers in the rain.

Adit sighs and helps himself to more potatoes.

'This could be one of our bazaars,' says Dev, standing stockstill in the middle of Petticoat Lane. 'It is a bazaar, Sarah, really it is.' Out in the open, between grimed walls, there is an Oriental turmoil of shove and bustle, push, pinch and pickpocket. There are jugglers of china cups and glasses, there are hangers displaying coats with secret rents and dresses with crooked hems, hot dog vans streaked with mustard, toffee, apples and ices, prams and pearly kings, guitars and mouthorgans. To make it all the more authentic, there are even Indian traders with little trays of Moradabad brassware and Kashmir papiermache. One or two of them sidle up to Sarah, seeing her in the company of two of their countrymen, and hiss sibilantly, 'Madam, are you interested in sari ?'

As Dev and Adit steer her out of their clutches, she tells them, with characteristic wryness, 'It seems to me the East India Company has come to take over England now.'

Dev is delighted with the idea. He is exhilarated by the rowdy, libertine Indian atmosphere about him. His guard is lowered and 'Topping!' he shouts, remembering the phrase from some schoolboy comic and finding it appropriate. 'Let history turn the tables now. Let the Indian traders come to England — the Sikhs and Sindhis with their brass elephants and boxes of spice and tea. Let them take over the City, to begin with — let them move into Cheapside and Leadenhall and Cornhill. Let them move into Threadneedle Street and take over the Bank, the Royal Exchange and Guildhall. Then let them spread over the country — the Sikhs with their turbans and swords and the Sindhis with their gold bars and bangles. Let them build their forts along the coast, in Brighton and Bristol and Bath. Then let our army come across, our Gurkhas and our Rajputs with the camel corps and elephants of Rajasthan.' Getting more and more carried away by the glitter of the pearly king's buttons, the cheap tin goods and glazed china and, above all, his own highly coloured vision, he goes on like a flood. 'Let us abolish the British Railways! Down with Beeching, down with Bradshaw! Let us set up our elephant routs, and let the people travel in camel caravans. Let us abolish the vicarages and rectories and parsonages and build temples and mosques and gurdwaras. Let us bring across our yogis and gurus, barefoot and robed in saffron. Let us abolish the British public schools. Down with Eton, Harrow and all that bunkum! Let us replace Latin and Greek with the study of Sanskrit classics and Punjabi swear words. No one shall cook stews any more, or bangers and mash. Let us feed them all on chilli pickles, *tandoori* chicken and *rassum*. Let all British women take to the graceful sari and all British men to the noble *dhoti...*'

Sarah laughs, losing her self-consciousness in her amusement, but Adit glances nervously at the crowd gathering around. Nothing he hisses at Dev stops him but finally, two old men in filthy greatcoats who have been watching and staring put an end to Dev's inspired outburst. They do this by paying no attention at all to Dev's harangue — quite possibly they have not understood a word, Dev's Bengali accent having thrown them off completely till they think he is speaking some heathen gibberish. What interests them is the bag of roasted chestnuts in Dev's hands and, seeing that Dev is too occupied in his vision and his speech to eat any, they shuffle up in front of him and say, 'Oi, oi loikes hot chestnuts too, oi, do.'

Dev smiles at them vaguely but is disturbed in his vision of the Indian hordes sweeping across an England of fortresses and waterways and Roman roads, by the sight of the two ragged, bearded old men. He imagines they are being friendly, recoils from their friendliness and, made suddenly aware of the crush of onlookers, moves away with Sarah. To his astonishment, Adit stops and gives them some chestnuts from his bag.

'What, are they beggars?' he cries.

'What did you take them for — friends of mine?'

'But there are no beggars in England. We are always told that in India — that no one needs to beg in England.'

'Oh, there are a few,' says Sarah, 'one sees them here and there.'

'Hardly any. Just stray misfits,' snaps Adit. 'Nothing like the swarms in India certainly.'

'I know. Everyone knows that. One expects them in India. But here — beggars!'

Another thing to which Dev cannot grow accustomed, in all his walks and bus rides through the city is the silence and emptiness of it — the houses and blocks of flats, streets and squares and crescents — all, to his eyes and ears, dead, unalive, revealing so little of the lives that go on, surely must go on, inside them. The English habit of keeping all doors and windows tightly shut (fresh air fiends — wasn't that what he had been told they were?), of guarding their privacy as they guarded their tongues from speaking and their throats from catching cold, cannot quite be explained to him by the facts of the cold and the rain. It remains incomprehensible to him. He walks down the street, thinking surely somewhere a child will cry, somewhere a radio will be playing, but the houses might be uninhabited if it were not for the windowboxes of geraniums, freshly watered, here and there, and the lights that come on in the dark. Such is the emptiness of the city that he finds he can be startled by the sight of a woman emerging from a shut, silent house, with a shopping bag or a baby in a pram, as though she were making a casual and bizarre appearance in a bombed-out street in wartime. It never fails to make Dev uneasy to walk down a street he knows to be heavily populated and yet find it utterly silent, deserted — a cold wasteland of brick and tile.

May Day, May Day. A bell swings from side to side somewhere inside him and peals out the sideways swinging words — May Day, May Day. He has never seen a green like the green of Hyde Park in that Sunday sunshine — never seen such a sheen, such a gleam, such a freshness of green in grass and leaf-inlaid sunshine. It, too, sings in a ringing, trilling peal — May Day, May Day! As do the minute wildflowers in the grass (and it is a wonder to him how so many shoe-shod feet of so many picnickers, strollers, sleepers and jumping children allow such a wealth of wild flowers in a city park) — the minute cups, stars and clusters of pure white, pure yellow, pure blue. Each sings and rings — May Day, May Day.

'And this,' says Adit, 'is Rotten Row.'

'Of course. I know,' answers Dev scornfully. 'You don't have to tell me. And here is the Serpentine.'

'What makes you so sure?' asks Sarah, amused. 'I have always known them,' he assures her. 'Always. Ever since I could read,' and stands with his hands in his pockets, watching the professionally attired riders canter past, their heads bent low beneath the bright foliage, on their sleek Sunday-spirited horses. Beyond them, the Serpentine, ruffled by the breeze, stirring and waking to the summer sun. The wind bellies out the red and white striped sails of the boats, and swans compete with them, graceful and languid. Expectantly, Dev stands on the edge, waiting for a boy to come and skim a flat stone upon the water. The boy in shirtsleeves, comes and flings, exactly as Dev had known he would. Satisfied, he wanders on behind the Sens who are making purposefully for the refreshment pavilion. The park is littered with Londoners at leisure, sprawled upon the daisy and buttercup embroidered grass, under the chestnuts and flowering May. Dev stares at them from under lowered lids, recognising and labelling the familiar types — the comfortable, middle-aged housewives in their floral print cotton dresses worn evidently in a doomed effort to keep in tune with the season, who call each other Mabel and Ada and speak of the Sunday joint and the summer sales; the men in shirtsleeves, or even stripped to the waist, their pale, piscine flesh looking delicate and pathetic, exposed to the unpredictable and windworn sunshine, newspapers spread over their faces, dreaming of cricket played in school long ago, or sitting up to watch the girls walking by the water in their bathing suits, wondering if they dare plunge in. There are butter-and-cream fed children, apple-and-cherry-cheeked children, Sunday exuberant, rolling enormous red rubber balls. Dev waits for one to throw a stick for a dog. In no time a little ginger-haired boy flings a stick up into the air, shouting 'Toby, catch it, Toby!' and a clumsy brown cocker leaps to catch it and Dev is content.

He notes, also, those elements that now serve to remind him he is not reading glaze-eyed, Henry James or Galsworthy, but is walking inside the original of the scene he knows in descriptions and pictures. There is a young Chinese father who plays ball with his round, slit-eyed son while his thickly pregnant Saxon wife dozes in a striped deck chair. The father bullies the child, makes him run up and down, shouts at him for his clumsiness till the child is reduced to tears, then kicks the ball right in his face and goes off, without a word, for a beer in the pavilion. The howling Mongolian child is at last picked up and comforted by the placid mother plunged deep in her chair. The slim young woman of fashion, often coveted by Dev in stray copies of *Harper's Bazaar* and *Vogue* at barber shops, now appears in person, clad in some pyjama-like costume that is the fashion that summer in a print of those orange and pink shades that are the favoured colours that year. She poses haughtily under the trees and the two young men, equally fashionably dressed, photograph her from this angle and that.

'Come on, come on, stop staring at the girls,' Adit admonishes him, coming down from the pavilion with great mugs of beer frothing from his fists like foaming cornucopias.

'Isn't that what one comes here for?'

'Come at night and you'll see many other reasons for coming to the park.'

So Dev spends an evening studiously observing, he claims, the lovers of Hyde Park as they sprawl on the grass in the summer dusk, lost to the world about them. Beating a hasty retreat to the Sens' commonsensical kitchen, Dev wants Sarah to explain.

'How can they!' he demands and, ignoring Adit's facetious explanations, asks, 'Don't they really notice the people walking past them? Or the children playing around them? Do you really think they are too busy with each other to notice anyone else ?'

'Yes,' says Sarah, thoughtfully washing a colander of rice. 'English people aren't as selfconscious as they are supposed to be. They are really quite unselfconscious when it comes to things like that. Unlike Indians who are not in the least bit selfconscious about their persons but very much so in their relationships. I think the English are just the other way around.'

'I don't, I don't,' says Dev, still too agitated to sit down. 'You know what? I think those people are really a bunch of exhibitionists. I think, I think they like to *flaunt* themselves, their sex, their prowess, just the way our beggars, our Indian beggars, enjoy flaunting their filth and their mutilations at one. If these people catch your eye, they leer exactly the way our beggars do.'

Sarah is a bit startled, she has never thought twice herself about the dark Siamese twin heads obscuring half the screen at the cinema, or the couples under the lampposts at night.

Adit puts down the knife with which he is cleaning out a fish, and declares, 'I predict that in six months no, three months from now, it will be Dev himself who will be rolling in the grass in Hyde Park with some blonde landlady's daughter — I mean some landlady's blonde daughter. And it will be I who will come walking down to catch your eye and leer.'

Dev is about to make a rude rejoinder when the poor taste of the remark strikes him, and, glancing first at Sarah's long, bright hair, newly washed, spread over her shoulders as she turns her back to them and bends over the sink, he merely glares at Adit.

'Can you imagine an Indian couple behaving like that?' he asks, a bit later, unable to let the subject drop.

'No,' says Adit, promptly. 'There aren't any. Not unmarried ones, and the married ones aren't in the parks, they're at home, quarrelling.'

'Oh, don't pretend there isn't such a thing as romance in India. There are lovers enough but you don't see them carrying on like that in a public park or — or under a lamppost. Why under a lamppost, for God's sake? Why not in the dark where no one would see them and leer at them?'

'Why not under a lamppost? Why not in the light?' Adit shouts fiercely, chopping off the fish's head, and then its tail — bang, crush. 'Why always in the dark? In India, too much goes on in the dark.'

'There are things one wants to keep in the dark — for privacy,' insists Dev, just a little surprised at his own vehemently righteous tone, and more than a little at a subdued giggle from Sarah.

'Then you had better go straight home and ask mother to find you a suitable bride, "skilled in household affairs, wheat complexion and vegetarian," for "young, England-returned soapbox orator, Krishna complexion, height negligible." Meet each other over the wedding fire. Have twelve undernourished children for Oxfam to bring up for you. An ideal match. Unless, of course, as I predict, in three months time you meet the blonde landlady's daughter — I mean the landlady's blonde daughter — who will think you a maharaja in disguise, marry you for the family jewels and then find herself keeping you on a typist's pay and feeding you fish and chips in a furnished room in Brixton.' He flings the fish into a pan of bubbling fat so that the fat springs up and hisses in surprise. While Dev mutters, Adit sings.

'When I was a bachelor I lived by myself,
  And all the bread and cheese I got, I laid up
   on the shelf.
The rats and the mice, they made such a strife,
  I had to go to London to buy me a wife.'

Adit and Dev, brought up as they were on dogeared copies of Palgrave's *Golden Treasury*, chant,

> 'Earth has not anything to show more fair:
> Dull would he be of soul who could pass by...'

till Sarah, holding her hands to her ears, sends them out to 'do' St. Paul's and Westminister Abbey, to see if that too will not silence them.

In the case of Dev, her prescription has wonderful effect. So awesome he finds them, so overpowering, that he tiptoes around on mouse toes and gazes at the marble statues of great British warriors and builders of the Empire, lifting his eyes up, up to the unwinking splendour of the stained glass, shivering slightly to hear the resonant organs play, and taking his first breath only upon emerging from the great oak doors to stand on sunlit steps and hear the Sunday bells peal.

What has silenced and subdued him is not the expected sensation of humility and inadequacy in the face of the might of a religion and the expression of its passions for which these edifices have presumably been built, for there is remarkably little religious aura about them. Even on a Sunday the worshippers are few and scattered and seem either distracted by the tourists or sunk into the muttered routine of the service. The Cross itself is almost obscured and certainly overshadowed by the monstrous white mushrooming of marble statuary. Dev has an uneasy feeling that these are no temples of Christ, but temples dedicated to the British Empire. They seem not to celebrate the Christian concept of God so much as the British concept of God, King and Country. These form the Holy Trinity of the British and not God the Father, the Son and the Holy Ghost. By populating their temples with these massive marble memorials to their admired warriors and statesmen, they proclaim their belief that it is not piety that makes a man worthy of honour, but service — dedicated, ambitious and, above all, successful service to King and Country, *in the name of God.*

He peers around to see if he can find a memorial to a priest, a dean or a bishop in some shadowed corner but the only ones he sees are those who have also been great political figures. Of the people who swarm in, there are more tourists than worshippers and they come with guide books, gaze into the white, unseeing eyes of Pitt, Burke, Wellington, Cornwallis and Hastings, and whisper of history, not piety. They do not seem to come to worship Christ at any austere altar, but to pay homage to the might and power of the Empire.

Adit, who has been experiencing all the proper sensations expected of him, cannot understand Dev. 'You stick. You stone. You clod of mud,' he called him. 'What else can you be if you say you feel nothing — here where "Earth has not anything to show more fair" ?'

'I am the dull soul who passes by.'

'Look up at the stained glass!'

'I can't — it's too bright, all those reds and yellows glaring in the sun.'

'Look at the altar, the Cross. Doesn't it make the Bible come alive for you?'

'Certainly not. Nothing could be farther from the Bible in spirit — farther from the spirit of religion. All I see is the great, solid gravestone of the British *Raj,* that's all.'

'You don't. You only say you do because that is what you have decided to think and say. The trouble with you, Dev, is that you are too Westernised.'

Dev thinks this could only be a slip of the tongue and is about to point it out when Adit, still clasping his Kashmiri *fez* in his hands piously, goes on, 'In the worst possible way. You've made yourself over — already had done in your Calcutta days — in imitation of these smart Western cynics who are in fashion these days. Now I, I'm a romantic, an old fashioned romantic and I don't feel ashamed of it — not here on the steps of St Paul's with all the bells ringing.'

'A romantic Oriental in love with the cynical West — beautiful!' laughs Dev, sitting down on the sunspread steps. 'Very, very appropriate to see you standing here bareheaded, bowing, before a memorial to just that — the romanticisation of a history of cynical greed and aggressiveness.'

Cities in India are tight, insular clusters, built like fortresses on plains and seacoasts — houses, streets, windows, lives all turned inwards, with rarely a slit left from which to gaze outwards. But, in London, built on hills and with its roads curving and dipping, Dev is caught up, again and again, by the swift wonder of a vista suddenly opening out where he has expected nothing but city. In Greenwich Park he trudges up to the bare hilltop, his head bent to a biting gale. He huddles under some low, rough hawthorns, trying to shelter from the bitter wind but turning quickly blue and envying the small children with their blood-red cheeks who race uphill and then roll down. He feels that as he has come to Greenwich he must see the Line of Meridian and stares down at the white chalk line in foolish disappointment. Then, looking up, he sees below and around him one of those vistas that one comes upon so delightedly in England. At one moment one finds oneself level with neat garden walls and brick houses in rows and tiers and decks and suddenly, one is transported above the rooftops to be faced with a wide sweep of town or landscape, blue-grey and shadowy or gold-freckled with sunshine, making one catch one's breath with the sudden, unsuspected awareness of space and depth. The river, the spacious elegance of Wren architecture on its banks, the city coiled about with its own smoke and vapours, and he above it, encompassing it all in one glance, gives him the expanding, soaring sensation of an explorer on the verge of discovery.

With its open-air booths, its leisurely crowds and loud brass bands, Portobello Road has the air of an Indian bazaar though not its appearance, and Dev, accustomed as he is to the Indian trader's obsession with the newest, the 'novelties' — in plastic and tin and nylon, wanders glaze-eyed at the profuse manifestation of the young English people's obsession with the past — the collections, in crowded bow windows, in booths and on barrows, of trumpeteared gramophones, Victorian posters, birdcages, painted porcelain jugs, crystal marmalade jars, bent toasting forks and pewter teapots, yellowed christening gowns, charred and grimed firearms from the First World War period — pieces which the British covet and cherish like fetishes, as though they believed that as long as they kept their grandmother's silver polished and their grandfather's pistol safe from rust, the world will continue to be as cosy and secure as it is at present. It is not the older generation that performs these rituals of faith, Dev is surprised to note but the young beatniks and fashionmongers who throng the street — long-toed, tube-jacketed young men plucking tuneless guitar strings, the more shabby ones in rugged sweaters and sandals and long hair, and girls in white lace stockings and peep-holed boots, all with a lean, searching look peculiar to them. There is one who carries a sitar with a self-conscious air of achievement, another wheels along a barrow full of tattered old books. In a window, swarming with period furniture and pewter, lies a round baby in a cradle, rocked by a mother with a smiling, feline face. The Salvation Army band goes tum-tum-ta-ing down the road.

Dev is drawn by rays of gold to a booth hung with dusky, glinting icons from Russia. A natty young man in charge of them notices that Dev has stood in contemplation before a Madonna and Child for fifteen minutes together, and stands watching him so suspiciously that Dev wakes up to ask, 'How much?'

'Oh,' says the young man, smiling with an infuriating kindness, 'it is expensive.'

'Yes. How much ?' repeats Dev, more heatedly, on fire to possess an object which he has so far viewed with a detached and objective ardour.

'Very much,' the man bites on the words as though they were thin threads, snap-snap, still smiling like a jocular alligator. 'Oh, very much. I wouldn't even name the price to you.'

For a moment Dev is too thunderstruck to move. He stands there staring at the man whose smile interrupts his view of the icon which has begun to glow more alluringly than ever in its dark corner, and suddenly he feels himself melting away, melting to pieces, flowing on several different currents at a time, trying vainly to collect the pieces and hold them together with inept fingers. The man — he said — but did he? — how? — why? — the picture — Adit grasps him by the arm and Sarah is smiling and cradling a painted china duck in her arms at which Dev stares in confusion. A china duck? A painted china duck?

'What's the matter?'

'That man,' he hears himself gabbling shrilly. 'Do you know what he said? I asked him and he said — but why? Do I look that shabby? Do I look any shabbier than any of these people around here? I don't have any holes in my clothes, do I?'

'What are you talking about ?'

Dev waves his arm in the direction of the icon booth and the saurian icon peddler, and now his outraged pride has returned and is building inside him, block upon block, like a tower that has been assaulted but has not fallen. 'That man there, he refuses to tell me the price of the picture. What does he think? Does he speak only to maharajas? How does he know I'm not one — in *incognito?* Sarah, do you know what he said to me ?'

Adit fluffs out the silk handkerchief in his pocket. He gives his ring a little quick polish on his sleeve. He sets his hat at a tilt and saunters into the booth where the icons shine like so many candles on some dark altar. In a few moments he is back. The alligator smile has transferred itself to Adit's lips like some child's transparency. It flaunts itself at Dev.

'Charm, my dear boy,' he minces at Dev. 'A little superior charm is all you need to impress these clots.'

'Did he tell *you?*'

'Of course, my boy, of course. As he said, it is no good telling *you* the price. Have you fifteen pounds on you?'

'Of course not.'

'Just what he thought.'

'Yes, but why couldn't he have told me? That's all I asked.'

'He probably thought you were a petty pilferer. You must admit, there is something shifty about your twitching mannerisms, your beady eyes, your —'

'Shut up ! What made him tell *you?*'

Adit sighs at his ring again, gives it another little rub of a clean white cuff, puffs out the red silk handkerchief like a coxcomb and takes Sarah by the arm.

'Come along, Sarah, Dev. I shall stand you a cup of tea — you need it.'

It is the beginning of Dev's obsessed search for signs of imperialist insolence in the bland manners of the British. Coming through the green door into the kitchen one afternoon and seeing Sarah having tea with a girl friend at the kitchen table, he is struck by what he instantly takes to be a blatant expression of it on the young woman's face and, also, by the instant recognition of her as the Christine Langford of whom he has heard much banter between Adit and Sarah and their friends. She is the Christine who introduced Adit to the English female sex and even to Sarah herself. It was Christine who discovered him, a clerk in a little tourist agency to which she had gone in search of pamphlets on Greece — or, perhaps, Spain (Christine the sunworshipper), and invited him to lend a touch of colour (as she humorously said, behind his back) to one of her cocktail parties. Sarah, a schoolfriend, was invited too and her shyness and rectitude brought out the protective in Adit whereas all the other guests, and the hostess, had only made him feel uncertain, possibly even humiliated. Humiliation and uncertainty were not sensations in which Adit felt at home, and so he chose Sarah for company. ('You are like a Bengali girl,' he told her. 'Bengali women are like that — reserved, quiet. Maybe you were one in your previous life. But you are improving on it — you are so much prettier!')

Now Christine, who had started a tourist agency of her own (she had visited Adit's to spy on it, not to collect pamphlets on Greece or Spain) and made it far more prosperous than Adit's, so that it sometimes appeared to him in the dazzling form of a Christmas tree decoration that he might have had but didn't get, walks about Adit's kitchen tapping tins of things and saying, 'How *very* curious, Sarah.

And you say this is what goes into a curry — not dear old curry powder at all?'

Sarah is explaining to her the properties of the different spices. 'Each curry is made with a different combination of spices. Adit won't have curry powder in the house. He flings it out of the window if I get any.'

'Ohh?' Christine draws one fine eyebrow like a bow drawn in battle. 'How *violent* of him,' she remarks and turns, with the bow still drawn, to study Dev who has come in from the rain, as if to say *Another* member of the Indian multitudes that surround poor Sarah?'

Sarah gets snarled in the fuss of introductions and, defeated, turns to the stove to make more tea while Dev and Christine study each other coolly across the table. Dev, while taking in her handsome, brutal face, her navy-blue tailored suit and the jangling metal bracelet on one wrist which is the uniform of women of her class, wonders how far she went with Adit — all his friends maintain they went far — for she is gazing at him in a manner that makes it seem the pages of the *Kama Sutra* are fluttering through her mind. When at last she turns away and strikes the match she has been holding in readiness against the box, he decides it is all a myth about her and Adit and therefore her curiosity was left unsatisfied, and is still roused by him and his friends.

But Christine pays no more attention to him. Swinging one leg over the other — and Dev is definitely stirred by the sight of those large muscles encased in sheerest nylon — she turns around in her chair to face Sarah and begins to talk to her of their early adventures in London. Dev, who has been led by Adit to think of Sarah as a woodland creature he discovered, lost and astray, in the city, wonders how to match her background to Christine Langford's.

'Priscilla's divorce is coming off, did you hear, Sarah? Uncontested. Can you imagine Priscilla contesting anything? I always thought her such a drip. But you liked her, didn't you, Sarah?'

'It was her house I liked, really, and her family.'

'What that old Anglo-Indian colonel papa of hers? You liked *him?* Sarah, what discoveries I'm making about you — they simply astound me. And even that poor little suntanned memsahib of his, you liked her as well?'

'Well,' Sarah begins to explain and makes a great hash of the Lyons ginger cake which she is trying to slice with a bread knife, 'they had such interesting things to tell about India, and their house was full of the most curious Indian things.' Turning to Dev, she confesses, 'That house first made India real to me, you know, and interesting.'

'And then you met Adit,' smiles Christine, making a little circle in the air with the narrow toe of her long white shoe, 'and so your marriage to him was — a foregone conclusion?'

'It is funny,' agrees Sarah, 'perhaps,' and feels too ashamed to pass the plate of hacked blocks of ginger cake to her tailored friend, and leaves it on the table.

Christine reaches out and picks up one butchered piece of cake, her bracelet making loud what might have been performed more unobtrusively. 'You really do astonish me, Sarah — *Priscilla's* family! Why, my uncle might have been more interesting to you surely. You know he was a Governor — or something — in Madras — or somewhere. He has *such* interesting things to tell of the widows burning themselves on their husband's funeral pyres, and about the holy men — we always tell him he should write his memoirs. They'd sell like hot cakes,' and she licks the crumbs off her lips and takes out a compact and lipstick to make them up again.

'Your uncle?' asks Dev. 'Or did you say your grandfather?'

'Uncle! Why should it be my grandfather?'

'Because, if it was your uncle, he couldn't possibly have seen any widows burning themselves on funeral pyres,' says Dev in a tone of flat conviction.

'But he did,' and this time both of Christine's eyebrows are drawn in bows. 'I am afraid he did. He has the most appalling things to tell...'

'Perhaps he only heard them from other people,' Sarah says, glancing unhappily from Dev to Christine.

'My *dear,*' says Christine, reaching out to pat Sarah's hand, 'now *you're* not to get upset. *You're* not a widow yet.'

'She's not, but do keep her safe and sound here in Clapham,' shouts Dev through a mouthful of cake he has quite suddenly and savagely snatched up and eaten — he hates cake.

'I will,' retorts Christine. 'I would hate to lose little Sarah —'

'To the Bengal tigers and funeral pyres of ruddy Hindoostan,' shouts Dev.

'My dear !' exclaims Christine, with pointed mildness. 'I do believe this — this young man doubts me.'

'Only your uncle,' says Sarah hastily.

'Comes to the same thing.' said Dev.

'Well, in *that* case,' says Christine, slowly uncrossing her splendid legs and rising, 'in *that* case...'

'But do stay. You said you would wait for Adit.'

'Did I? Oh dear. I must have forgotten my appointment with the airlines chap when I said that, Sarah. I am so sorry but — duty, duty. Nose to the grindstone,' and, tapping the tip of her nose, she picks her way through the kitchen and down the passage. Stopping by the door to stare at some letters the postman has just slipped through the slit, she cried, 'My dear what darling little stampkins!' and then marches — if one can at all be said to march — down the stairs, crying, 'I wish it wasn't raining — I'd invite you to a little spin in my Jaguar. Such an *amusing* little car — but only on a sunny day.'

'There aren't many of those !' shouts Dev, determined to have the last word, however weak.

Christine glances over her shoulder to make one more effort of her well-exercised brows and Dev stands watching her draw her long, muscular legs into the bright blue car that stands at the gate. The little Sikh children stand aside as the engine starts and smile delightedly as mud spurts up from under the wheels at them.

For weeks Adit has been agitating for an annual visit to his former landlady in Harrow. For some reason he insists on visiting her once a year. Sarah is strangely reluctant. Out of curiosity to discover the reason for her more and more obvious reluctance, Dev agrees to accompany them one Sunday afternoon when no one could think of anything better to do, to Harrow where, at the end of a very straight road lined with white villas, each with a garden flaunting roses in technicolour, is the house to which Adit points excitedly, shouting, 'That's where I lived for three years, Dev. That's the only landlady I stayed with for more than a fortnight. The others all threw me out, but I stayed with them, with the Millers, for three years.'

Sarah's feet begin to drag.

'Miller,' says Dev in a whisper, as they wait for a response to their ring. 'Does that mean there is a miller in the family background, Sarah?'

'I don't know. They come from Germany. Their name was Muhlstein. They changed it when they came to England just before the war.'

'Such brave people,' says Adit, pressing the bell again. 'What they have been through!'

The door is pulled open by an old gentleman in slippers who is still quite fuddled by his postprandial forty winks. But he courteously leads them into a parlour and, in a little while, Mrs Miller limps in — her short grey crop of hair tousled from the deep pillow and her eyes red-rimmed from disturbed sleep. Everyone sits up very straight, thinking — with either annoyance, regret or embarrassment — of the interrupted afternoon nap.

Adit is, of course, the first to throw off such antisocial thoughts. He leaps up, flinging an arm towards a picture on the wall — a Teutonic landscape of windmills, clouds and grazing sheep in meadows, framed in scrolled and convoluted gilt.

'Sarah, look,' he shouts excitedly, 'there's the picture that used to hang in my bedroom. Mrs Miller, you have brought it down from my bedroom.'

The old Millers exchange looks that make Sarah sink into the deepest well in the sofa. 'I beg your pardon,' says old Mrs Miller, as dryly as dust. 'I should never have touched it without your permission, of course. What a terrible thing to do!'

Adit laughs, too pleased to see the picture again that has obviously given him much pleasure during his dismal bed-sitter days, to notice anything else. 'Isn't it a beauty, Sarah? Dev ? I always loved it. I used to lie on my bed — after taking off my shoes, Mrs Miller, I never forgot that, ha ha — and stare at it till I forgot all about the cold and the rain and everything else. What a beauty it is,' he says with proprietory affection, examining it from close. 'You brought it with you from Germany, didn't you?'

'How do you know?' snaps the old grey lady.

'You told me,' Adit reminds her, surprised. 'Don't you remember? About how the frontiers had already been closed, and you left Westphalia in the last train with one crate of books and one of pictures, and the guard opened them and said—'

'Remarkable memories you Orientals have,' chuckles old Mr Miller, twiddling his toes inside his slippers, suddenly quite happy again inspite of the rude ringing that had shattered his sleep.

Mrs Miller, looking drier and more brittle every minute, rises and says, 'I suppose I had better make you some tea. You'd like some tea, I suppose, Mrs Sen?'

'Please don't bother,' says Sarah, in a smothered voice, from her cushioned well.

'Bother, what is bother? We need a cup of tea, I'm sure. It is no bother,' and she limps away on legs streaked with varicose veins, painfully, self-sacrificingly.

'Memory,' smiles Mr Miller, now comfortable and kindly-eyed. 'It must be a result of the training you have in memorising those long Sanskrit verses. Did you receive instruction in Sanskrit, Mr Sen?'

'Oh yes, yes, all Indians do, Mr Miller. Every Indian child, by the time he leaves school, has read most of the *Mahabharata,* the *Ramayana* and a good portion of the *Vedas* as well.'

'Dear me. Can you still recite any of it, Mr Sen? I should very much like to hear some Sanskrit verse.'

'Ha ha,' laughs Adit who, to Dev and Sarah, has appeared quite unhinged since the moment he sighted the Millers' house. 'Mr Miller is a philologist, you know, Dev. He teaches philology at Harrow you know —'

'*Ach*, philology is a big word. It is only simple grammar I teach, and not at the Harrow,' twinkles the old man. 'Only at a girls' school which happens to be in Harrow.'

Dev is not going to let Adit escape, he is too furious with him. 'Then Sanskrit must be of great interest to you, Mr Miller,' he says. 'Do recite some, Adit, and let us have Mr Miller analyse it for us, philologically.'

'Oh, that is only one of Mr Miller's interests,' cries Adit in panic. 'He has so many, Sarah. I remember your study with all its collections, Mr. Miller — I used to love pottering around in it when I would go in to pay the rent. Stamps and matchbox labels, you know, Sarah.'

'I used to be something of a phillumenist but I've given it up now. You never did get me any Indian matchbox labels, Mr Sen, though I am told you have a very good variety in India,'

'Sarah, I told you to write and ask my family for some, didn't I? I *am* sorry, Mr Miller, I shall write myself. You'll have a packet of them next week —'

'Can't possibly go that fast,' Dev interrupts.

'Next month then — oh, definitely. Tell us about the girls' school, Mr Miller — it sounds like fun. Are they nice?'

'Very nice, Mr Sen,' smiles the old gentleman, twiddling his toes inside his slippers. 'So much more conscientious and earnest than the boys. Not as clever though, I'm afraid,' with a sideways glance at Sarah, shy and sharp.

Mrs Miller brings in the tea. When she says tea, she evidently means tea, not bread and butter or cake as well. Handing a cup, half-filled, to Sarah she scrutinises her with eyes growing opaque with age. 'So you are still here,' she says at last. 'You told me you would be going away to India.'

'We will. I'm not sure when we can manage it, but we will.'

'Remember what I told you,' says Mrs Miller, lifting a long grey finger in the air. 'It would be very, very unwise to pack all your things and emigrate, Mrs Sen, without first making a trip exclusively for looking around.'

'That is what I always tell her myself,' Adit breaks in triumphantly. 'You are so right, Mrs Miller. You used to tell me that, too, when I was engaged to Sarah, and I haven't forgotten.'

'I feel I know India well already,' Sarah ventures, turning for comfort to old Mr Miller. 'I feel if I went, I wouldn't find it strange at all.'

Mrs Miller draws out her lips into two thin grey lines like a stretched rubber band, and says, 'Hummmm.'

'What about Joanna?' Adit asks suddenly, with a little jump on his embroidered footstool. 'Where is she? Did she go away to Scotland ?'

'Joanna? Scotland?' Mrs Miller raises both hands in the air and looked ceilingwards. 'How do you know about Joanna going to Scotland please ?'

Adit is dumbfounded. 'But she married a Scotsman. You sent me a card, a notice, don't you remember, after the wedding? And I used to meet him when he came to visit Joanna here. They said they would live in Glasgow after they were married.'

Mrs Miller makes a dramatically disbelieving face but Mr. Miller corroborates Adit's story. 'Yes, yes, you were with us in the days when Angus was courting our Joanna. Yes, Lizzie, he was — I remember.'

Inspite of this Mrs Miller does not seem to like any personal questions about her house or family. It is as though she wishes to reject the fact of Adit having lived in their house for three years. If he keeps insisting on it, it is very unmannerly of him, she implies. 'Joanna is very well, thank you, and in Scotland,' she says very emphatically, pulling up her shoulders. 'She has two very handsome boys — both have blonde hair and blue eyes.' She pauses to let the room fill with her emphasis and her pride, then asks, 'What about you, Mrs Sen ? Have you no intentions of starting a family — or do you think it is wiser not to, in view of—' she stops, letting the silence make a series of long, straight dashes towards Adit.

'We want a big family, yes, certainly,' says Sarah suddenly, to everyone's surprise, it is so rarely that she says anything so positive and personal. 'As soon as we are able.'

'Hmmm,' says Mrs Miller. 'Hmm — mm.'

They leave soon after and, while saying goodbye and once more promising Mr Miller his matchbox labels, in a small hall webbed with the green roots of air-fed plants, Adit makes a quick dash into the dining room. 'Oh, I remember the meals I've had here, Mrs Miller — veal cutlets *par excellence*!'

Mrs Miller does not seem particularly pleased with this compliment. She says, 'I have an excellent lodger now — we are most satisfied with him. He does not take his meals with us, and he is very quiet, so he is *no* trouble at all. We are *very* satisfied now.'

As they come out, neighbours stare curiously from behind their technicoloured rose trees and a dog barks and barks. They walk down the rose tree, garden gate and cottage lined road and Adit reminisces. 'Do you know, when I answered their advertisement, and turned up at their door with the newspaper folded in my hand, Mrs Miller gave me *such* a stare — she hadn't expected an Indian to turn up, you see — Sen is quite a pronounceable name, even for the English. So she left me in the hall and went into the study and I could hear her whispering with Mr Miller. Then she came out and said I could have the room but *not* meals. So I said, "look, the ad doesn't say that and where, in Harrow, can I go and get a meal on a rainy night?" Then Mr Miller came out and said, "*Ach*, Lizzie, he is right, perhaps he should eat with us at least till he finds a place nearby for meals." She didn't look at all pleased — she is such a funny, prickly old thing, isn't she — but she had to agree, so she said, "All right, for one week then, till you find a place." But at the end of the week, she didn't say another word, just went on calling me down to dinner every night. You see, she must have thought Indians eat with their hands and burp and when she saw I wasn't doing that, she let me continue.' He laughs nostalgically. 'Later she became quite fond of me — she really did, you know.'

Sarah now makes her second positive suggestion of the day. 'Let's go up Harrow Hill,' she says and takes Adit's arm. On their way up the twisting, leafy lanes that wind uphill, past schools tucked away in intense, silent, wooded glades, she refuses to talk of the Millers and draws Dev's attention to the little schoolboys in their tails and boaters and the sixth-formers in their top hats, walking in pairs 'down to the tuck shop,' Dev imagines. 'But how the devil do they have fights or play games in those mad hats and with tails between their legs?'

Sarah laughs. 'You don't have the prerogative of preserving quaint customs. We like to indulge in them, too.'

'They look like Tenniel drawings,' observes Dev. 'It does look quaint, of course — to outsiders, but I would hate to be on the inside of *that* custom.'

Adit protests, 'You have no feeling at all for tradition.'

On top of the hill Dev observes that the English have a genius for preserving beauty and keep it somehow fresh and vivid, miraculously safe from the ravages of time and decay, so that it affects generation after generation in precisely the same manner — and even outsiders from the far corners of the world. The silent grey church on the hilltop stands in mourning amidst its ancient gravestones. Rose vines are in crimson bloom, rhododendrons flutter with pale blossom. Wandering in misty happiness amongst the cracked, faded stones, the tufted grass and nostalgialaden violets, they come upon the great elm tree beneath which Byron's ode is engraved on a tablet and standing, all three, in that chill blue shade in the old and silent graveyard and looking out at a faintly stirring frieze of summer greenery to the sunlit city of London lying far below them — its green commons and red roofs and sweet, insistent tone of pigeon-blue — and thinking, all three, of Byron lying in this tall grass, chewing a sap-filled stalk and composing an ode to be preserved in rough stone, they experience, all three, that shudder down the spine that only the cold, unhesitant fingertip of time can give.

Deeply moved, Adit asks, 'Could you really leave all this, Sally, and go away to India to live?'

'Yes,' she answers promptly. 'I could. When I think of all the Millers of England, I could leave at once.'

He turns upon her with such a face, so aghast at her perversity and wilfulness, that Dev hastily slips away, from the engraved tablet, elm and friends, and goes at a tumble down a lane on fire with scarlet roses and wild daisies and birds and butterflies fly up from the grass at his step.

Whenever chance takes him past Hyde Park, he stops to walk up to and stare at the Albert Memorial. Its ballooning grotesquerie, its fantastic black-magic brew of marble, bronze, mosaic, brass, black and white colours, all drawn out, beaten and billowed out into the most fearful shapes — like a piece of architecture having a nightmare following an ample Victorian repast — recall to him similar nightmares of stone and marble in India: the Victoria railway station and the University, the Clock Tower and Flora Fountain in Bombay; the Victoria Memorial and the Marble Palace in Calcutta; the big-thighed, deep-lapped, pigeon-nestling statue of Victoria outside the Old Delhi railway station — all these pockets and stretches of Victorian India which continue to have a life of their own, a dream life out of touch with the present. In India are still to be found those provincial clubs hung with yellowed hunting prints, missionaries still clutching their Bibles and dissolving crystals of pinkie in their drinking water, regimental functions still ringing and clanging with brass and barks of moustached laughter. The Albert Memorial contains the spirit of that era — bulges with it, balloons with it, groans and sighs with it. Standing before it in the rain, or squatting on its steps in moments of precious sunshine, Dev is not sure whether he comes to it, again and again, in order to look upon the face of England as it had existed in his imagination when he was a child — years before he had begun to plan to come to England — or because it reminds him of that Victorian India that formed a part — unreal and, therefore, all the more haunting, omnipresent and subliminal — of the India he had known. He stands there, or squats, for many hours, in many seasons, with a frown on his brow as though he were trying to piece together a jigsaw puzzle of which the pieces are antique flakes of mosaic, marble, bronze and brass, velvet and lace.

And so he walks the streets and parks of the city, grateful for its daffodil patches of sunshine, loathing its sooty, sodden dampness. Eats toffee apples in Petticoat Lane and fishes limp sausages out of pools of fat in Lyons Corner House. Lies in the grass under the green canopies of Kew Gardens, and narrowly escapes being run over and crushed to death twenty times over in Piccadilly Circus. Stands in the dark, wistfully gazing at the peacock-blue and rose-red paper flowers in a Mexican boutique, then is enthralled by the massive, blank bulk of Battersea power station. He watches, covertly, the girls impatiently pounding up the escalator on their way to work, unable to quench his amazement at their well-developed leg muscles and the free, brisk swing of their walk, and is fascinated by the warty old men in Laurel Lane who dig like moles through patches of turnips and cabbages. He stops to let pass a gigantic marmalade cat in Russell Square, and watches it stalk regally and soundlessly towards the British Museum, a veritable don of a cat who makes all of picture book nursery rhyme England come alive with one twitch of its pink nose, one wave of its marmalade plume. His heart expands and fills with warmth at the sight, from a rainshrouded window in a bus, of a crescent of Georgian houses, their long windows and graceful stairs, their spindly railings and grave silence etched in black on grey, and then is stifled to sadness as the bus continues over the river to Brixton and Lambeth where the great roads are lined with those strangely lifeless houses of liver-coloured brick and soot. He is intoxicated to think that of all the long programmes of music, theatre, cinema and art exhibitions that he sees in the papers, he can choose any to go to on any day at all, and then is bored to a headache by the endless hitting of ball with bat, pounding of horses hooves and athletes' feet, twitching of hips, twanging of guitars and flashing of outsize smiles on the television screen. It is a strange summer in which he is the bewildered alien, the charmed observer, the outraged outsider and thrilled sightseer all at once and in succession.

And the summer winds on, slow and sweet as the Thames, and there is no more talk of the London School of Economics or of any other college. There is more and more talk, instead, of finding employment in London. To Adit he explains, glibly, that the streets of London are an education so rich that he can't possibly cut it short by entering the stuffy halls of some ancient college. It is partly the reason. The other part is something he cannot explain, even to himself, for it is only a tumult inside him, a growing bewilderment, a kind of schizophrenia that wakes him in the middle of the night and shadows him by day, driving him along on endless tramps in all weathers while he wonders whether he should stay, or go back. In this growing uncertainty he feels the divisions inside him divided further, and then redivided once more. Simple reactions and feelings lose their simplicity and develop complex angles, facets, shades and tints. He is in too excited or agitated a condition to hold the weighingscales with a steady hand and see whether his pleasures outweigh his disappointments, or vice versa. There are days in which the life of an alien appears enthrallingly rich and beautiful to him, and that of a homebody too dull, too stale to return to ever. Then he hears a word in the tube or notices an expression on an English face that overturns his latest decision and, drawing himself together, he feels he can never bear to be the unwanted immigrant but must return to his own land, however abject or dull, where he has, at least, a place in the sun, security, status and freedom.

He is perfectly aware of the schizophrenia that is infecting him like the disease to which all Indians abroad, he declares, are prone. At times he invites it, at times he fights it. He is not sure what it might be like to be one himself, in totality. He is not sure. Any longer.

4

Emma Moffit, in a dress fashioned out of a Madras sari of lavender silk shot with a crimson shimmer, stood at the door, waiting for her chief guest. He was already half an hour late but she had managed, so far not to wring her hands or crack her finger joints. Only the agitation of the long onyx chain on her bosom could not be controlled and her eyes were like puddles of disturbed water. The room full of her Indian guests aroused an excitement in her that she was not made to cope with, and her chief guest's unpunctuality gave all the excitement a hollowness, a hole at the bottom that was draining all the triumph out of her first Wednesday.

Forty minutes. She withdrew to the kitchen to knot her lace hankie tightly and consult a stoical Sarah, a giggling Bella and a resigned Mala. They urged her to let them pass the refreshments to the guests, now beginning to buzz restively, and she gave in eagerly.

The gathering grew coherent again. She felt she was, after all, capable of moulding it into a circle — the circle of which she had for years dreamt and was now gathered in her large attic under the electric bulbs she had covered with red crepe paper, on a floor marked with the rice-paste *alponas*[1] some of the ladies had come and painted that morning, while the rain streamed down the windowpanes and drummed on the eaves just as she has predicted it would on Wednesday evenings.

---

[1] Decorations made on the floor within a room with rice paste — normally near the skirtings of the walls or even in the middle of the room.

She could not quite suppress a grimace on discovering that Mala and Bella had already poured quantities of milk and sugar into the tea they were passing around in slopping cups, but the oldest Mrs Singh from downstairs, who had been persuaded to mount the stairs despite her rheumatism, smiled at her over a cup that she held between her two hands, with a fold of her *chunni*[2] forming a protective layer between her palms and the hot china. 'Good,' the old woman muttered, 'very good.' It was the full extent of her knowledge of the English language. In a little while she was blowing on the steaming tea and sucking it up with loud, appreciative noises and had drawn up her legs under her comfortably. Emma was not sure whether to be happy to see her guests relaxing and making themselves at home or to fear a certain dissipation, a laxness in the air which was beginning to threaten the formality and importance of the occasion.

Had the Swami lost himself in the Underground? Did Swamis not possess watches? Had he gone into a meditative *samadhi*[3] from which he might not rouse himself for hours, even days?

Dev, disdaining the carpets on the floor on which most of the Indian women and some of the Indian men were sitting cross-legged Indian style or sprawling, Western fashion, sat on a kitchen chair in the corner, his arms folded in a definitely antisocial posture. He was watching, with veiled eyes, two elderly Indian ladies seated on the carpet at his feet. They had very dark and luminous eyes set in sad and leathery faces. They held their arms about their knees, clad in dazzling silks of mango green and banana yellow, the effect of which was rather spoiled by the woollen socks they wore (their square toed walking shoes had been left neatly at the door so as not to spoil the carpet). He listened — and his mouth twisted with amusement and scorn — to their glib mixture of Bengali and English.

'Mother should go home now. Her heart is so bad, she needs nursing, and where have I the time for it? She doesn't realise what a

---

[2] A piece of fine cotton or silken cloth (approximately 2 × 1m) used by women to cover the head, shoulders and bosom.
[3] State of intense concentration.

responsibility... At home she would have her sisters and servants. But she won't go.'

'But what will you do when she falls really ill? Our people are not used to the nursing home idea. What will she say when she has to have a nurse to look after her? Wouldn't she rather be at home?'

'She says no — the disgrace of having an unmarried daughter living alone in London is too unbearable at home!' The woman — of forty-odd years Dev surmised — made eloquent gestures with her hands and shoulders. 'As if one were a child. And I tell her it is not the same as being an unmarried woman in India. She agrees but she says that people at home don't understand that.'

'Perhaps she is right. I will never forget that year after I left Oxford to go home and work with All India Radio, Minakshi, I never will.' The woman in yellow shuddered and Dev could not hold a visible twitch of curiosity. He was not disappointed. 'Those horrible men, those *ogres,*' she hissed, unaware of Dev behind her, leaning forward like a gargoyle. 'All at least fifty years old and with a dozen grandchildren at home, but if they saw an unmarried working girl — *toba* !' she exclaimed. 'They just go mad. They think that if you are working and not married, it must be because you are...' her voice dropped. The two womens' voices fell into the soft, fluttering pit of feminine Bengali.

Dev turned his attention to another interesting pair in the corner: a young Indian artist of dark, Byronic appearance who, he had been told, was exhibiting his pictures at one of London's lesser known galleries, and his girl friend who, with her long black hair swinging to the waist and her orange silk shirt worn above black tights, might have been Italian, Spanish, Greek, had her powerful Punjabi accent not given her away as soon as she opened her mouth. She was twisting about on her chair with impatience, crying, 'Man, it's time to get back to civilisation now — why don't they start the show?'

Emma came to Dev and perched for a moment on the chair next to him, with her teacup balanced on her trembling knees. 'Dev, Dev, what am I to do?' she quavered from a full throat. 'Whatever can have happened to the Swami ?'

'Indian Standard Time. Don't worry — he is just observing Indian Standard Time, that is all,' Dev said, as reassuringly as he could, but Emma jumped up, spilling tea on the front of her shimmering shot silk shirt, and cried, 'I don't know why you people keep saying that. What do you mean? You shouldn't say it, it is so degrading. Oh my, here is my musician now — but *who* is that with him?'

She streaked away to receive a dainty young man in white who had entered with his sitar in his arms and was followed by a woman dressed in a heavy brocade sari that she had drawn over her head and down to the tip of her diamond-studded nose, and was carrying a silver filigree box in her hands. Behind them came the drummer, of a contrastingly shabby, unclean and dropsical appearance, bearing the two drums, like two globular pendants, with his fingertips at the ends of his two extraordinarily long arms. Mostly he kept his eyes on his feet as he shuffled along but now and then he looked up and sideways with a shifty, glowering roll of his yellow eyeballs.

'Crumbs,' whispered Bella, from the kitchen door.

Once again there was a distinct shift in the atmosphere, an audible alteration in tone, a visible stir in the order of the gathering. From resembling a group of office workers relaxing after work with a cup of tea, the gathering was now marvellously touched with the purple bloom of the exotic. The musician with his long, oiled locks of blue-black hair curling about his ears, dressed in long white leggings and a fine white Muslim Lucknow *kurta*[4] covered only with a short waistcoat of raw silk, his lips stained crimson with betel and his long fingers caressing the fine sitar strings, looked too authentic an Indian to be able even to breathe and survive the London air. Indian women in London generally manage to retain their genuine native looks — but only above the ankles: their thick woollen socks and heavy shoes, so British and practical, give away their discomfort, as do the chilblained hands plunged into coat sleeves, and dumb, even unconscious yearning in the eyes. But the young woman who followed the musician like a strident shadow in her heavy brocade sari of rose-pink daubed with a gold mango motif

---

[4] Loose pullover shirt traditionally worn by Indians.

and lined with a border of corn-yellow and violet, looked as though she had never stepped on any soil but that of her native Benares. The very atmosphere thickened and twisted itself into sensuous coils as her rich perfume of jasmine wafted through it. An aura of a *nawab's* court in Benares or Lucknow, of Mughal leisure and music and colour surrounded her in rich, rustling folds. Her manner of settling down on the carpet — a little behind the master — of peeping briefly, brilliantly from under the glittering gold *pallav*,[5] or opening her silver filigree box and getting to work with expert, gymnastic fingers on the betel leaves and areca nuts, aniseed and cardamoms that she found there, showed flamboyantly how she had preserved herself from all contact with modern England, how successfully she had carried with her, her own aura — a brilliant ruby set permanently in gold.

The musician turned to take a geometrically folded *pan*[6] from her fingers and smiled at her languorously, caressingly. She dipped her head, smiling contentedly, placidly, with an answering caress. He turned back to his sitar, refreshed by this visual draught of her Benares manner, inspired by her wholly native glory.

The old Sikh grandmother from downstairs leant forward eagerly and said, 'Where does the prostitute get her *pan* from — tell me that, eh?' in a voice rough with envy and curiosity.

Emma watched in a panic-struck silence, completely out of her own depth. While her guests were drinking in the sight of the musician and his muse with thirsty, greedy eyes, taking in great draughts of that especial air and poetry that nothing in England could ever yield to them, she clutched her hands together and murmured, 'Oh my, this wasn't what I — oh my, I never planned — Oh *Christmas,* what am I—'

The musician tuned his sitar, turning the knobs, tightening the wires, strumming them, smiling to himself a sweet, feline smile.

---

[5] End of the sari which hangs from the shoulder.
[6] Betel leaf.

The drummer tapped his drums and tightened the thongs, uttering low bestial grunts as he did so, and darting his strange underworld look at the guests.

One of the two Bengali ladies at Dev's feet whispered suddenly, '*Toba*, Minakshi, isn't he just like that goatherd in *Virgin Spring*?'

'The rapist?' whispered the other. 'You're right — horribly like.'

At last the sitar player turned to his muse and asked, 'What shall I play for you? Tell me what your choice is.'

'Play me the *raga*[7] *Shree*,' she murmured huskily, in a perfumed voice, and he gazed at her, his assent glowing in his eyes.

Hell, thought Dev, where had Emma Moffit picked them up?

Emma suddenly darted across to them, bravely, like an unarmed amateur daring the arena. 'Oh, could you please wait, could you please wait a little while, only till our chief guest arrives? He will be here any minute —' and then she stopped short, seeing her mistake, her dreadful, rough, heavy British mistake, the insult she had unthinkingly dealt this pretty lotus of a man, this exquisite ivory figure of a musician and, through him, to his painted, bejewelled, tintinnabulating muse.

Exquisitely Oriental, he said nothing. His upper lip curled up to meet the lines at his fine, pale nostrils. He half-turned his head so that his expression could be caught by the woman who looked up, startled, unable to understand Emma's words but quick as monsoon lightning to sense their meaning. They exchanged a look and it was like a dull silver, jade-handled dagger being passed from the fine white clothing of his bosom to the gleaming golden vestments of hers. Then he faced Emma and the gathering with an inscrutable and impressive face, his hands resting, stilled, on the trembling sitar. After a few minutes, the drummer, too, realised that something had happened and, ceasing to tap and tighten, scowled at his feet, now and then darting a swift, glinting look at some woman or the other in the room.

---

[7] Musical mode of Indian classical music.

'Oh, dear, oh dear,' moaned Emma on Sarah's square and sturdy shoulders. 'I never thought, I never imagined — I had only been told they tour the north of England and play in the factory towns for the Indian workers. I thought he would be like one of the folk artists who play at harvest festivals and things. Oh Sarah, they make me feel like — like — an old bone, like — a peasant.'

'Ssh, Emma,' Sarah comforted her a little wearily, tired of brewing tea in the tiny kitchen and too diffident to venture into the crepe paper hung attic which only depressed her. 'Haven't you heard how temperamental they can be? And Indian artistes must be even more temperamental than European ones, seeing what ordinary Indians can be.'

'Do you think so?' asked Emma, raising her wrecked old face, and then — it was a blessed moment, like the beginning of the monsoon after a summer of heat and drought — the door bell rang and it was the Swami at last. Like the long awaited monsoon, like the yearned for call of the *koel*[8] in spring, like the moon rising in the dark, expectant sky, the great Swami of Hampstead arrived.

Adit, who had been held up at his office, came pounding up the stairs, two at a time, just behind the Swami, and gaily waved and winked at Sarah from over his shoulder.

Robed in saffron, with a shawl of the finest cream *pashmina*[9] about his massive shoulders, his vast head like a gleaming globe unmarred by a single hair, the Swami was a sight majestic and exotic enough to please the most homesick Indian in London. Yet his manner — notwithstanding his observance of Indian Standard Time which had led to such anguish on Emma's part — had the brisk efficiency, the commonsensical air of an affable City man or, at least, a totally successful expatriate. Seventeen years in a well-established, respected office in Hampstead where his disciples held yoga classes two evenings a week which were widely attended by shortsighted men in dark suits and rimless glasses and middleaged women with thick bodies and fine souls, the mystic instruction he

---

[8] Cuckoo.

[9] Fine quality wool made from goat hair.

himself gave to a large, handpicked class once a week, the lecture tours he went on regularly and which had taken him as far as California, the funds he was now accumulating for the building of a temple — seventeen years thus successfully employed had given him the air and speech of a professional man of some status. Yet his appearance and his lordly, kindly gestures of extending his palms in blessing and half-closing his somnolent eyes in speech made it quite clear what profession it was in which he had achieved such wealth and renown. It was a very great honour indeed to have him visit Miss Moffit's attic to speak to a gathering too unofficial, too informal even to be called a club. He was truly an Oriental after Emma's own heart. She had to restrain an impulse to throw herself at his sandalled feet.

Waving aside the cup of tea which was wafted to him with speed over the heads of the gathering, he went immediately to settle down on the carpet — his impressively solid thighs symmetrically crossed — and began, 'My children—'

Here Emma made her heroic bid to play the gracious hostess for whom it was impossible to allow one guest to feel less than the other. 'Swami,' she interrupted hurriedly, 'we are going to have a little music to introduce your speech. The great artiste, Ustad Sultan Ahmad of Benares, has graciously agreed to play for us.'

The Swami nodded with his kindly air and, fanning out his hands on his knees, drooped his head low and closed his eyes, as if to let the sweet wings of music fan him into an appropriately inspired mood in which to deliver his set speech to yoga initiates. It soon became evident, however, that he was taking a little catnap, perhaps with the same intention.

Emma's knowledge of Indian music was confined exclusively to Adit Sen's records, none of which played for more than twenty minutes at time. This had led her to believe, naturally, that a *raga* takes no more than twenty minutes to play. She had no way of foretelling that once the Ustad Sultan Ahmad of Benares began to play, he would play himself into a state of creative ecstasy in which it was impossible to stop short for the sake of something as unimportant as a programme, and in which new ways of embroidering the basic theme, of adorning and explaining and expanding it would occur to him at every turn, inspiring him with greater, and still greater powers of invention. He began gravely and serenely enough, appropriate to a *raga* that belongs traditionally to the evening, but once his introductory and solitary *alap*[10] was over — (here Emma rustled her teastained silk skirts, preparing to applaud and make way for the Swami who also woke gently) — the drummer joined in the swifter and more rhythmic *gat*[11] and the sitar player became carried away by the onrushing tide of his mood. In this he was aided by his jewelled muse who had now crept up to his elbow and would, now and then, burst into a wordless phrase of song in her husky voice, so impassioned that it would break on some notes, thrilling the whole audience but no one so much as the sitar player who would turn to her after every phrase of music, tossing the blue-bottle black locks of hair out of his eyes and exchange with her a soulful look that belonged to some highstrung, private realm of their own. On and on the wild music spiralled, creating great whorls and coils in the twilight, now translucent and amber in their sweet glow, then peacock-coloured and glittering in their brilliance and fantasy.

At an hour when Emma had expected to clear the attic of her guests and to be settling down to a cosy cup of soup and an evening of triumphant ruminations, the musicians had barely presented their theme, there was no prospect of the Swami being given a chance to speak and there was a distinct look of displeasure and resentment on his darkening face. The sitar player was used to being the star of the show on the northern England circuit of factory towns where he played to highly impressionable and loudly appreciative workers' audiences. He knew how to put a mere Swami from Hampstead in his place.

Many of the ladies on the carpet were glaze-eyed as the music poured over them like showers of mango blossom, of the jasmine-scented night that they recalled with a deep, unburied passion, extravagantly glorified and thrice romanticised by long memory.

---

[10] Introduction/introductory piece of music played/sung to a slow tempo.
[11] Piece of music played to a medium-paced tempo.

But the Bengali lady in green who kept darting looks at the drummer rather than at the beautiful sitar player, whispered suddenly, 'He keeps staring at me, Minakshi. Or perhaps it is I who keep staring at him. I can't take my eyes off him, Minakshi.'

'The evil fascination of a cobra!' hissed her friend in yellow who was staring too.

Next to Dev, the Indian painter's girl friend was twisting, restlessly, on her chair and grumbling, 'Man, he gets my goat,' and 'He's giving me a bellyache. Can't we get away, man?'

Dev himself was engaged in fighting the powerful tide of emotional music with every nerve, and wondering why a second-rate musician giving the most syrupy rendering possible of a *raga* he had heard played better in India, should arouse reactions on this alien soil so utterly different from what they would have been had it been a concert and an audience in India. In Calcutta the sitar player and his muse would have drawn at least a catcall or two.

Emma, twisting her hands about her rattling onyx chain, darted frightened looks from the Swami's thunderous brow to the inspired sitar player's lustrous eyes to the drummer's lecherously rolling eyeballs, and wished herself dead.

The two Bengali ladies suddenly burst out into agitated whispers audible despite the music that had mounted to an extravagant climax, and the one in green rose creakily to her feet, gathered up her shawl, coat, umbrella and shoes and hurried out. The other, after some embarrassed hesitation, followed her, bowing her head low before her shoulders in the hope of avoiding notice. The drummer's furtive look of lechery followed them to the door.

Their departure made a break in the highstrung atmosphere of the concert and, in a little while, too abruptly, the sitar player wound up the *raga* and brought it to a flat end. His muse drew out a large red silk handkerchief from the depths of her brocade blouse and held it to him with her long, scarlet nails. He took it and wiped the glistening perspiration off his face. The drummer did not bother to wipe off his own copious perspiration but sat there, dripping and panting like a driven beast.

Emma found herself so stiff, that it was only with the most painful and audible creaks that she could unfold herself from the upright kitchen chair and go to rouse the Swami for his speech. She found him asleep, with his head bowed low, his hands planted firmly on his knees to keep him from toppling onto his face. Waking, he shot a loaded look at the musicians who were being refreshed with betel leaf and, rising slowly to his feet, he made the briefest speech of his entire career.

'My friends and countrymen,' said he. 'I came here to introduce you to the mystic joys and the very real and practical uses of *hatha* yoga. We have, instead, given our time to the music of the great Ustad Sultan — Sultan of — of Bradford, Leeds and Manchester fame — I think,' he whispered in an aside to the quaking Emma. 'Let me only say that, at your next meeting I shall send my chief disciple, Pandit Gobindram, to help you begin your yoga instruction without further delay. I wish you happiness, health and good luck,' and he sat down and called loudly for tea.

Sarah had been able to guess some time ago, that many of the guests would need another round of refreshments before they could be sent on their way in the pouring rain of a Wednesday night, and she had dashed downstairs for a fresh packet of tea while Bella and Mala washed cups and spoons and now, before Emma's astonished eyes trayloads of steaming cups began to circulate.

Warmed and revived by the hot, sweet tea, the young Sikhs on the carpet began to praise the sitar player in their floweriest Urdu, and in no time managed to persuade him to play on.

'We are strangers here,' they told him, 'It is so long since we have heard our own music. To listen to it is to have our own Indian sun shining on us again, warming our frozen blood. You are a magician, Ustad. Your magic has brought our homeland to us here in this foreign country...'

The sitar player smiled sweetly and modestly, his eyes downcast, but his fingers began, almost inspite of themselves, to strum the fine wires. The drummer began to tap and tune his drums. They put their heads together in consultation and, after a bit, the Ustad

Sultan Ahmed of Benares turned to his audience and announced he would play a *Kajri*[12]. There was frantic applause.

Sarah came to Emma, waited till she had said goodbye to the Swami who had suddenly remembered a dinner party being given in his honour by the First Secretary of a Far Eastern Embassy, at which he ought to have presented himself an hour ago —'But it doesn't matter, doesn't matter at all, everyone knows our Indian Standard Time,' he laughed affably in the doorway — and then took her gently by the arm and suggested, 'Why don't you go down and sleep in our flat tonight, Emma? Adit says this is likely to go on till dawn — the musicians are in the mood and most of the people are willing to listen all night. Do go and sleep on the divan. We'll look after the party and may be sleep on your divan after everyone's left.'

Emma put up a little, hostesslike resistance, but very little and obviously simulated, so Sarah helped her collect her toothbrush and nightie and led her downstairs. Emma tottered on the steps and had to be supported. Very soon Sarah had her flat on the divan and left her in the dark. But the passionate and restless music of the sitar penetrated the ceiling and kept her awake till three o'clock when, in the midst of the most astonishing noises, the party — for so the first gathering of the Little India Club of Clapham had undeniably become — broke up.

Happiness is egg-shaped

Nevertheless, a mere fortnight's convalescence later, Emma asked Dev to become Secretary of the formal Club she had decided to form.

'I asked everybody for suggestions and they all advised me to take in regular subscriptions and use the money for the club!' she said in gusty astonishment. 'Here I am with all this money — and a special contribution from those darling Singhs downstairs — and I have to quickly plan what to do. Isn't it *exciting?* Well, I thought the very first thing I would do is to employ a secretary.'

---

[12] A lively form of light Hindustani classical music.

Dev, kept in by a morose spell and caught moping in the flat by Emma, pleaded preoccupation with college entrance exams. Emma laughed him off, shaking a finger at him coyly. Embarrassed, he then pleaded preoccupation with employment problems.

'Ahh,' she breathed with deep understanding. 'I understand perfectly of course. Sarah has told me all. But that is just what led me to think a little occupation like typing out invitations and writing a few letters, which won't take up more than one or two mornings a week, will be the very thing while you are waiting for *the* job to turn up.'

She gushed on with such animation and conviction that Dev, whose good day it was not, found himself weakly agreeing to come up that afternoon and see how much work there would be. When he caught her discreet hint that the job would be a paid, not voluntary, one as he had feared, he felt a little less morose. His money was running out fast, and five pounds were, after all, five pounds. He did not want to be reduced to asking the Sens for his bus fare. Occasionally — as when he stepped into the bathtub and found a row of nylon underclothes dripping down on him from the shower rod, or when an animated conversation came to a guillotined end as he entered the drawing room — he had the unhappy sensation of being the fifth wheel of the carriage. He knew he could not stay on and on. Sometimes — as when he stood in the tube, gazing at the girls in their jaunty office clothes, or when he listened to Samar, Jasbir and Adit discuss their bachelor days in London — this sensation was not an unhappy one: it seemed wholly desirable then to move out of the enclosed confines of the Sen household to the freedom of a bachelor bed-sitter life. Miss Moffit's five pounds a week were a step in that direction. With five pounds in his pocket, he could stare calmly in the face of those civil cards, slyly beckoning to him from the shopwindows along the roads he walked:

Launderette assistant wanted. Night duty, they said, and
Waiter required. Experience not necessary.

Two mornings and one afternoon a week at Miss Moffit's father's typewriter (he had been an officer in the Crimean War and there was a photograph of him on the mantelpiece, between a brass camel and a sandalwood elephant from India), typing very formal invitations to a demonstration of yoga by an expert, a lecture by the visiting Professor Binode Kumar Chatterjee, MA on the terracotta temples of Bengal, a recital on the *veena*[13] by the visiting artiste Srimati Indulekha Menon of Malabar, the opening of the young Indian painter Prem's exhibition in a private house kindly lent for the occasion by Mrs MacGregor of Kensington... Letters to be sent to academies and colleges in Baroda, Bombay, Shantiniketan and Madras. Letters to be received and read from Liverpool, Southampton, Delhi and Travancore. Neat cardboard shoeboxes began to fill with neat index cards and files swelled and fattened most satisfactorily. The cardtable grew too small. The dining table was brought into use instead. Miss Moffit brewed coffee, opened the biscuit tin, brewed tea. Thank you, Emma, thank you but pray do not insist on my presence at your next charming Wednesday afternoon — a headache, an important engagement, an interview with prospective employer, you will understand. Also a certain embarrassment. An alarm and a depression. But the five pounds — if you remember — you said — ah, thank you, thank you very much indeed, Miss Moffit and Little India Club of Clapham.

With five pounds in his pocket, London looked a summer city from the top of the 139. The Thames looked narrow and sweet enough to wade across with one's trousers rolled up to one's knees. The grey buildings rustled with the rainbows shed by pigeons' wings. With five pounds in his pocket, the door of every coffee bar in London opened to him. *The New Statesman* on the tabletop folded to the Appointments Vacant column, a cup of coffee to one side, a plate with a fat-soaked hamburger to the other, and London's history shrank and crept closer to him, cosily, familiarly, with Dr. Johnson and Boswell tripping down the road to their coffee bar next door and Dryden having a session of his own across the road. Sunshine fell crackling like an ice cream wafer across his table every

---

[13]Musical instrument of the stringed lute family.

time the door opened to admit another student or unemployed musician. Lazily, he glanced at the column before him, and hummed over its contents. If the appointments offered by the Universities of Leeds, Sussex and Durham, of Wellington, Melbourne and Ghana all required of him a PhD in Russian literature or, at least, an MSc in nuclear physics, no matter. Not much anyway. He had five pounds in his pocket and the universities were full of degrees waiting to be picked up when he was ready to bend down and pick. Carelessly, but with a private sense of timeliness, he got up to have his cup refilled from the ready spout.

Up with the pigeons in the Royal Festival Hall watching Sir Malcolm Sargent draw a groan out of a tuba here, a snort from a trumpet there, and a heart-spinning, top-spinning sweet and silver whip of lyricism from a violin out in front. Rain, slush and queues for everything in Oxford Street left behind as he entered the Academy Theatre and saw a Swedish film about the white flesh of Nordic women and the sombre ways of their men. Every leaf on every tree clapping, clapping till they almost dropped, all in a bright green flutter, upon Queen Titania tittering, Bottom stumbling and Puck leaping on a stage beneath a primrose sky.

An afternoon nap on the steps of the Albert Memorial, dreaming bulbous dreams in bronze and marble, then a shuffling wait in a queue at Albert Hall and an evening of hilarity inside while beatnik poets from America intoned Sanskrit prayers to the clanging of cymbals, English poets in black turtleneck sweaters recited poems about the docks and dens of Liverpool, and Russian poets with springing hair sang about Siberian wastes and elderberry jam.

Portobello Road — he was drawn to it Sunday morning after Sunday morning by a fascination not unconnected with the alligator smile of the icon peddler, but had also to do with a girl in long white boots and long, almost white hair about her round and feline face, who sold wineglasses and candlesticks in a booth. He watched and listened till he saw her tilt her face in answer to the boothowner's call, 'Rose,' and saw her face reflected in the oval mirror behind her, then obscured by a sweep of her glistening hair, soft as a child's, to pick up and display a Venetian glass the colour of a green grape. Frightened, he left — and dreamt at night of Rose, white-armed, extending a grape-green wine glass to him, on a green summer night. He woke and suddenly thought that five pounds a week were not enough.

Floorwalker in self service store. Coloureds need not apply.
Waiter for Indian restaurant, Five pounds.
Wanted, shop assistant. Seven pounds.

With a slight shiver, he turned from the cards in the shop windows to the Appointments Vacant column in the papers. They seemed to require, exclusively, professors and managing directors. Both kinds of employment were impossible, barred to him. But surely there must be something in between the two extremes, something temperate, something accessible — wasn't there?

'...Isn't there?'

'There are very few of those,' even Adit, the overoptimistic, admitted. 'The truth is, we *babus* get it neat. People like the Singhs manage to find a place in any society, even if it is on the bottom rung of the ladder. At least they have a trade, they are useful — even the British recognise that and admit it. But not us. We haven't studied for any profession, we want to gatecrash into one. We haven't the time, money or patience to acquire one in a school, we want to grab and learn in a week what others take three years to master. Cheek, that's what. It's the ageold *babu* dilemma — executive temperaments linked with worthless qualifications.'

Dev crumpled up a pile of Sunday papers and flung them on the floor. 'Dammit, there must be something a willing young man can find to do. There must be something.'

'Nothing — except to insert a neat ad in the agony coloumn of the *Times*: "Young man, non-public school, non-University looking for adventure. Will travel — westwards. Anything lucrative considered." But don't mention it's Indian public schools you didn't go to and Indian universities. Adventures just aren't offered to the like — not on a Spode china platter, the way you want them served.'

Dev held his head in his hands. 'I can't go to college, not now. I want freedom, not restriction. I want enterprise, not discipline. I want money, I want life. But I don't want to take a secretarial course. I don't want to take a correspondence course in radio engineering or social service or any bunkum. I just want a job, that's all — a real, paid job. I can't sit around like this any longer, Sen.'

'You're not as indiscriminating, my dear chap, as you pretend. Want a job badly enough to be the ticket man in the Tube? To be a postman? To be a waiter in the local Indian curry shop? You can pick up one of those jobs any day you feel like it.'

'Yes, I know — I've come to the land of golden opportunities, this England, this teapot, this shining flannel mat.'

'Don't be bitter, *yar*. If there's one thing the Englishman likes to indulge in overseas but can't stand the smell or sight of at home, it's bitterness. They'll not stand for bitterness. Not even my Sarah. So mix us a pot of tea with plenty of sugar and wait for Monday morning before you let yourself get bitter. There's always a fresh start and a clean page and a shining Monday morning to live for.'

'You can talk, you're sitting pretty,' said Dev, with envy. When he had arrived in London, he had been amused, in a superior way, to find his old friend Adit Sen, who had lived in rambling ruin of a *nawab's* palace in Calcutta and been much pampered by parents and sisters, none of whom would have minded had he never lifted a finger to work, here in London working as a small clerk in a tiny tourist agency off the old Brompton Road, arranging bus tours of Yugoslavia for groups of school teachers from the north of England, booking flights on obscure East European airlines for seedy freelance journalists, handing out lists of rundown pensions and boarding houses in Milan and Normandy and the Black Forest to superannuated government officials from Torquay and Bournemouth. But now already he had grown to regard as enviable Adit's position in the little office in a mews, with the kettle always on the boil, its multicoloured and sanguine posters and pamphlets, and his colleagues, all cheerfully unambitious and comfortable in an atmosphere of perpetual holiday induced by the very nature of the work they did. It had begun to seem to Dev the proverbial warm nest, the place in the sun, the homely haven and covertly desirable goal. He was slowly, regretfully letting drop and melt away his dreams of adventure, seeing now quite clearly that he had left the true land of adventure, of the unexpected, the spontaneous, the wild and weird, for a very enclosed part of the world, a pigeoncote in which it was necessary to find an empty and warm niche before one was pushed over the ledge into the sea that lapped the island's stony shores. That small, warm niche, in the beginning so scorned and despised became more elusive the more it was desired and pursued.

'Yes, I'm sitting pretty,' said Adit, patting his dressing gown draped stomach with a self-congratulatory gesture. 'I'm very content as I am, but I know I'll be Director one day. My employers are very pleased with me — recognise drive and flair and imagination when they see it, you know. But,' he said fixing Dev with a stare, 'remember I have also had to work in a post office in Coventry, to begin with. Not as a postman, never did I descend to that, but I did work in the sorting office during the Christmas season. A perfectly respectable thing to do, of course, even collegians do it — in the hols, you know — and I always regarded it as temporary. But I've had my ups and my downs, as they say. The post office was one of the downs. Then there was that camping equipment business. I didn't exactly pack the bloody boots and tents, just sort of checked them. I used to take a correspondence course in shorthand at that time. My God, it was depressing — hob-nailed boots and first-aid boxes by day and shorthand by the wireless at night, in one damp room in Coventry. That's when I decided I had enough of the provinces and came to London. I stayed with Jasbir and Mala for six months, picking up occasional jobs of teaching English to Indian bricklayers. Then I did a stint in an Indian agency office that handled things like sandals from Kolhapur and ashtrays from Moradabad, but I hadn't come to England to work in little India, so I went on searching — till I found my little job at Blue Skies. What a relief it was to have a desk of my own, a secretary to make me tea and the feeling that I had found something I would like to make permanent at last. I moved in with the Millers and the lovely room they gave me, and then I met Sarah. It was luck, *yar*. And I wish you the same. Without it, England isn't worth living in.'

Guinness is good for you.

Monday morning. The *Times* folded to a small square inside his pocket, a red circle drawn around the lines:

Vacancy for a young man of initiative in well-established concern facing expansion. TED.

A walk drawn out into slow motion by the drip-drop of rain. Long rows of trees weeping down his neck. High walls and dense shrubbery making his errand more and more obscure and somehow sinister. Moments of disbelief when the newspaper had to be taken out and another look taken at the strangely indefinite address before he could continue. Miles of high railings, dense damp greenery within, till he arrived at the wrought iron gateway, immense and forbidding, with lettering in a great black arc over it that at last revealed the reason for the discretion, the obscurity of the address. He had arrived at a cemetery.

Panic and confusion. Dismay and disbelief. But there was the vague possibility, he felt, that the vacancy had been advertised by someone who happened to live here but had nothing to do with it at all. And who could that be? A marble angel requiring someone to water the basket of frozen lilies in its hand? A beakless dove with a wreath of violets round its neck, wanting a man to bring it its daily breadcrumbs? He laughed with hollow bitterness and went in.

In the silent, ivy-shrouded office in the lodge, he found the advertiser — no granite dove or marmoreal angel, but a red-cheeked, purple-nosed man, small and rotund, nursing a horrendous cold with Vicks inhaler, Kleenex, scarf, nose-drops and hot water bottle. While Dev felt steadily stranger and stranger, as though he were being magically transformed into a creature with wired bones and plaster wings, fit for some silent realm other than this one, rudely rent as it was by coughs, sneezes and snorts, the manager — as he called himself — seemed too wrapped in his cold to find Dev or the situation in the least bit strange.

'We've had a number of applications already — such a reputable cemetery ours is, you know' — a cough and a blow and a rustling of Kleenex — 'but somehow it has so far attracted —' sneeze, sneeze and blow — 'somewhat elderly people, and we are determined to have a young salesman.'

'Salesman ?'

'Ah well, that is what he will be, really, although Public Relations Officer is the more fashionable term —' a catarrhal laugh.

'But what am I to sell — graves?' Dev had an instant vision of himself ringing doorbells in Lambeth greeting housewives in flowered aprons with a, 'Good morning, ma'am, will you be needing a grave today? Anyone dying on the family hearth? Pack him in this pretty coffin, hoist him into the hearse, bring him down to us and we'll find him six feet of beautiful earth under violets, yews and dove droppings. Plenty of room for all relations to come and join him when they feel like it. Lovely atmosphere, real deathlike you know. Do your heart good every time you come to visit the dear departed...'

The man studied him with something more bothering his eyes than a streaming cold — the faintest, most elusive twinkle, or so Dev thought.

'You sell the cemetery — the idea of burial in our cemetery rather than in another.'

'But how?'

'Oh, I don't suggest door to door calls of course. You will deal mainly with funeral parlours and vicarages — visit the local vicars, you know, and ask them to put up our advertisements on their notice boards. The funeral parlours can influence the local public by advertisements in their windows and advice to the bereaved ones. We're already doing very well down here of course — such a beauty of a cemetery, aren't many like it in the City — and you will have little to do south of the river. It's north we wish to go now, cover the City, bring people down from Wembley, Hampstead, Finchley — bring 'em to our gates, show 'em all we have to offer: beautiful cypresses, funeral flowers, peace and quiet — and sell 'em the idea of burial here...' Exhausted by this long speech which inspiration had led him to pursue despite his streaming eyes and nose, the twinkle in his eyes fanned to a mad blaze, he suddenly sank down into the recesses of his brown leather chair, peeped at Dev over the top of the desk with those cunning, knowing, if bloodshot eyes of his and waited to see his reaction.

Dev sighed. His alarm was quickly dissolving into grey depression. He was also trying to ward off the germs that hung thick in the air by breathing as little as possible. 'And what are the — the —'

'What's in it for you? Tell you in a jiffy.' The manager refreshed himself with inhaler, nose drops and a long blow into a handful of Kleenex, then glanced at a paper on his desk. 'A good income,' and he named it. 'Possibility of accommodation on the premises,' and he twinkled up at Dev quite naughtily, noting Dev's sudden, compulsive jerk. 'Transport and lunch allowance when on duty. Regular pension and —' he clasped his pudgy, pink hands together on top of the piece of paper and, despite the tortures of this cold, managed a broad Cheshire Cat beam — 'the guarantee of a small plot of ground all your own in our lovely cemetery.'

Dev licked his lips. 'How much? Six feet?'

'Dead right! You're a smart lad, you are. Now tell me briefly about yourself. Education?'

Dev licked his lips again — they were extraordinarily dry. 'St. Xavier's School, Calcutta. St. Xavier's College Calcutta. B.A. — Eng. Lit. No experience.'

'Ahh,' beamed the little man, growing more and more jovial as Dev shrank and shrivelled. 'Mission college, eh? Does that mean you are a Catholic?'

'No,' said Dev, deciding to leave. 'Hindu.'

'Oh dear, oh dear,' lamented the little man. 'Not Catholic? Not even Christian?' He looked as though he had just remembered his woes and felt his forehead with the back of his hand, then looked at his watch and went through the routine with nose drops, inhaler and Kleenex again. 'I am sorry. Dear me, I ought to have mentioned it at once, oughtn't I? We simply must have a Catholic, or at least a High Church man. It's public relations, you see? It wouldn't do, no, I'm afraid it wouldn't do to have a Hindu gentleman in this job.'

Dev found it difficult to maintain decorum in his walk as he left the office and made for the gates of the cemetery. Once outside, he stopped in the middle of a large puddle, sneezed mildly and felt his forehead with the back of his hand. Then he hurried through the rain to the nearest bus stop, throwing the folded *Times* into the gutter on the way. He had a morbid feeling that his first interview, with an angel of Death, would prove to be symbolic of his search for employment.

You get there faster by train.

'Good morning, Madam. Without holding you up in your work of the moment, allow me to introduce myself as the Fleur Cosmetics man, here to tell you to await the morning of the fifteenth as the great day when Fleur bursts forth — Yes, hullo, hullo, I can hear you, can you hear me, madam? No, no, this is not a crossconnection. Are you aware that, on the fifteenth, you will be able to buy, at your dealer's a wide and stunning new range of lipsticks, eyeshadow in six glamorous new shades... No, madam, I know you do not know me. I do not know you either. I am merely introducing you to the great new world of Fleur, the cosmetic company that knows what youth wants, what feminity needs, what — hullo, madam? Please do not be alarmed. Be aware of what is going on in the fresh summer world around you. Be eager, be joyful. Fleur Cosmetics will bring you the newest — Hullo? Hullo? Madam? Dammit, two minutes, I said, just two gruesome minutes, that's all.'

'...Lipsticks in twelve new shades, eyeshadow in six, mascara in three — er, no, one — and a new, scented deodorant in a novel container in the stunning Fleur shades of lilac and — Madam? Hullo? Ah, hullo to you, too. Allow me two minutes of your precious morning and I will introduce you to a thrilling new world of fragrance, colour, glamour and allure which will give you a new outlook on life. On the fifteenth, at your local chemists', you will be able to buy the stupendous — hullo? Hullo? What? Dr. Dickenson, you say? Mr Dickenson there? Sorry, so sorry. But you do speak very softly, you know.'

'...All in the distinctive Fleur containers of lilac and rose. Twelve new shades of lipstick — Lemon Sherbet, Pear Compote, Rose Jam, Petunia Petal... Madam? No, you do not hear right. I know you are not decorating your house. I am not selling you paints or linoleum. I am bringing you glad tidings of the fabulous new Fleur Cosmetics which have invented a new range of colours to bring the hues of spring flowers to your cheeks, of autumn leaves to your hair, of dewdrops to your eyes... Madam? Hullo ? The police? Whatever for? I'm not burgling your house. I'm not holding you up at gunpoint. All I'm doing for God's sake, is bringing you *tiding — tidings,* I said! Hey you — you, *woman,* you —'

'Dev,' warned Miss Moffit in a whisper from the sofa where she sat enthralled, watching his agitated dance around the telephone of which he held the two halves in his hands, growing more and more enmeshed in its wires as he progressed through the telephone directory. 'I think, Dev, a slightly more personal approach would be less alarming for the poor ladies.'

'Personal? Hell, what's more personal than talk about a lady's armpits? Anyway. Mrs. Rogers — hey — ho — Mrs Rogers, here I come. Hullo? Madam? Are you going to shampoo your hair today? Forgive me for being so personal, madam, but may I ask you if you are fed up with your old shampoo, if it does nothing for your dandruff — oh madam? Are you there? Ah, hullo to you, too. I am the early bird that is chirping the big news of the summer of '65. A new shampoo to bring out the firelight in your hair. Try Fleur's Starlight Shampoo and see the rockets shooting out of your ears...Don't worry, Emma, she rang off two minutes ago, I'm just practising.'

'Have a cup of tea, Dev. You sound so hoarse, it must be a bit frightening for the poor ladies at the other end.'

'Thank you, Emma, thank you. Allow me to dial just one more number before I collapse on your carpet. Ring, ring, ring, ring. Ah, madam, good morning to you. Today is the fourteenth — ha-*choo!* Excuse me. Good morning again. No, no, this is not Jimmy, this is Fleur Cosmetics bringing you glad tidings — ha-*chooo!* Damn. My hankie! Just a minute, madam, just a minute. Do you need an aspirin — sorry, a blue-black mascara today? One that doesn't come off in the rain — hullo? Oh, God, I can't, I can't — ha-*choo!*' He wrapped his head up in his handkerchief and would not take it off till Emma had removed the telephone from his knee and quietly put the directory away.

Drinka pinta milka day.

At the door of the India Tea Centre, he tried to hold himself out of the push and shove of pedestrians and to peer at each passing face without catching anyone's eye. It was the lunch hour and lunchers were streaming in and out of the restaurant — a few Englishmen with the lean explorer look, amidst a mass of Anglo-Indians who looked both hungry and hunted, and Indians with that sadly inappropriate air that their dark skins and their brilliant clothing had in the grey-and-dun setting of Oxford Street in a drizzle, moving with that slow, lingering walk of the Oriental so distinctive amidst all the purposeful bustling about of the British. One of them drifting round and round a lamppost like some sodden streamer, finally came up to Dev and enquired, with a confidential air, 'Can you recommend Indian-style hotel?'

'No,' snapped Dev.

The man glared at him, then resumed his slow-motion dance about the lamppost till he gathered enough momentum to rush up and accost another Indian he had sighted.

Dev found many Indian eyes turning to stare at him — perhaps they had expected someone else standing in the doorway and waiting for them — and when he had begun to feel himself lost and without destination, he glanced again at the newspaper in his hand with the red line drawn around the lines:

Wanted: Indian contact to help establish export-import business. Good connections, enterprise essential. Rich opportunities for right man.

Or he looked across the pavement at the strawberry man with his barrow of ripe, conical fruit that people were buying and eating straight out of the paper bags, much to his amazement — he had been brought up to believe fruit inedible unless first dipped in a dark rinkie solution. The strawberry man caught his eye once and raised a little basket of berries invitingly.

'Two and six?' he said, as though asking Dev how much he had in his pocket.

Dev shook his head and brought out his newspaper in defence.

'Good for the complexion, y' know,' shouted the barrow man encouragingly, and Dev gave him one startled look, unable to decide whether this was an impertinence or not, and then walked to the other side of the door, turning his back to the cheerful strawberry man.

He nearly bumped into a large Indian in a blue suit who was bearing down on the door with a big laugh, but it was only to greet yet another Indian, a small man in a green suit. Jovially, the large man shouted, 'How you are, I hope?' Simpering, the other replied, 'Oh yes — simply' and, clasping hands they went to their Indian lunch.

At this point Dev decided to abandon his post and go and telephone the number given in the advertisement and find out what had become of the advertiser. Just then he felt a tap on his shoulder and turned around to find what he had somehow not expected the advertiser to be — another Indian. The smooth Oxbridge accents that had slid down the telephone wires earlier that morning had led him to expect someone sleek, pink and British, an adventurous City man seeking to extend his empire to the fabled India of silks and tiger skins. Instead, here was a young Indian of distinctly Dravidian complexion, dressed ostentatiously in many shades of blue, a bowler hat set at the correct angle on his crisply curling head and a quantity of rings on the fingers that tapped Dev's shoulder.

'I see the newspaper in your hands, folded to the correct square,' he smiled silkly. 'Come in Mr Dev, let us discuss things over lunch. I hope they give us decent grub. Never been in here before — have you?'

Dev was given another half hour in which to study the young man and assess his qualities as a man of business and enterprise, for they had a long wait in a slow queue before they could get their trays filled with helpings of rice, *dal,* mince-and-peas and *chutneys* of their choosing. Then there was another wait till they could get two seats at an occupied table, and another till the others seated at it had finished their trays and left them to discuss business in relative privacy.

'Disgusting,' said the young man who had introduced himself as Mr. Krishnaswamy Krishnamurthy, B.A. Cantab. 'Never imagined we would find ourselves in such a serum.'

'I suppose it means the food is good.'

'Hmm, quite decent,' said Mr Krishnamurthy, shovelling in rice and *dal* at great speed. 'Now, Mr Dev, let me put all my cards on the table and then let's have a look at yours, and we shall see what game we can play.'

Dev felt a bit uneasy at this figure of speech — he had no idea of business except that it should not be played as a game, at least not by amateurs. His uneasiness grew as Mr Krishnamurthy sketched for him what seemed a bizarre design. Sardines, said Mr Krishnamurthy, were the one decent thing to be had in India, cheap. So the British dealers thought. Sardines were to be had in plenty in Kerala and Malabar, Goa and Mangalore. Everyone knew this, as all tins of imported sardines were marked with the names of these abundant coasts. But there were other, yet untapped seas, bays and coastlines in India. What about the Saurashtra coast? What about the Bay of Bengal? What was being done about the sardines hauled in there? There was surely scope for cold storages and canning factories. All they had to do was buy some trawlers — the Japanese were said to make very decent ones — hire a fishing fleet, so easy to do in the land of the unemployed millions, set up a cold storage and a canning factory and — why, export sardines by the millions to the British Isles! 'No better market in the world. Not only does the British proletariat live on sardines, but so does the entire cat population. There's a fortune to be picked up, my dear chap, a fortune.'

Dev had kept his eyes on the shimmering play of ring that hovered over Mr Krishnamurthy's tray of rice and *chutney,* as he tried to visualise these fingers at work — pulling trawlers across the seas from Japan to Bengal, constructing a cannery and a cold storage, handing out copper coins to barebodied fishermen with famine-carved figures, labelling and packing, storing and exporting... He ventured a few questions to break the monotony of Mr Krishnamurthy's English accent and Indian abundance of speech. 'How much do the trawlers cost? From where does one get the capital...'

'We shall float a company of course. There are thousands of wealthy *banias*[14] in Hindustan who haven't the brains to create a scheme like mine but will be grateful for the opportunity to invest. They simply haven't any imagination — that is why I never returned to the coral sands. It really is an impossible country, my dear Mr Dev — the smells! But a short reconnaissance will reveal a whole queue of these stinking rich moneylenders, I know, and then we must find the best bays and coasts for our cannery to be set up...'

'And who is to go on this reconnaissance?'

'Ahh,' said Mr Krishnamurthy, putting his fork down and smiling brilliantly at Dev. 'That is precisely for whom I am searching. I have all these contacts here in England and am prepared to handle all the business at this end. What I expect you to do is return to India, go to Bengal, to Gujarat, to Saurashtra, give me a detailed report on their fisheries, contact interested investors, collect

---

[14] Merchants.

tenders for the construction of an on-the-spot cold storage and cannery, report back to me.'

'I see. Then who is to run the business end in India?'

'Naturally, you. I shall leave the entire business in your hands, giving you the fullest freedom possible. Complete delegation of power, my dear chap, that's my motto. You must admit the opportunities are staggering.'

'Decent,' said Dev, after a pause, 'very decent.' Mr Krishnamurthy cocked a dark eyebrow in recognition of the phrase, his very own. 'You are interested in returning to India and finding something to do there?'

'No,' said Dev, thinking he lost nothing by being frank and putting an end to the waste of a morning. 'Frankly, no. I am looking for employment here.'

Mr Krishnamurthy appeared to be in some consternation for a few minutes. He twiddled his large opal ring somewhat exasperatedly. But his decency got the better of him in the end. 'Don't blame you at all,' he said at last. 'Perfectly understandable. I've been avoiding it myself for the last five years. The point is — no one in his senses would go back to that land of the dead and the dying, but if one is offered such an excellent opportunity to wake up the sleepyheads and set up such a promising business with, of course, plenty of travel to Britain — what objection can one have?'

'I don't see myself trudging the Saurashtran coastline, interviewing naked fisherman, old chap, simply don't,' said Dev.

'My dear boy, of course I don't expect you to do that. You will get yourself an airconditioned car and simply make forays into the wilds, setting up headquarters in some halfway civilised place like Bombay or Calcutta.'

'I'm sorry, but it's London I want to set up headquarters in. You haven't thought of doing the reconnaissance business yourself, have you?'

Mr Krishnamurthy shot him a look like that of an offended storm god, thunder and lightning combined in one roll of his eyebrows. Then he rose and declared the interview over.

As they stood collecting their umbrellas and briefcases, their table was taken by two Sikhs with loaded trays who immediately settled down to wolfing their lunches, though one paused long enough to say, in a tone of some disgust, 'What can you expect? The mince is from a cold storage, the peas are frozen, the potatoes from Woolworths, and they call it *Indian* food!'

Dev laughed out loud, suddenly relieved and refreshed as by a good, strong gust of India's own dustladen, odour-laden air. He did not want a job alongside one of these vigorous, undampened and authentic compatriots of his, but far less did he want one that would put him in contact with the Krishnaswamy Krishnamurthy, B.A. Cantabs of England.

Keep Britain Clean.

Pausing on the gravel path to get over a fit of sneezes and blow his nose, Dev was ensnared, one day, by the matriarch of the Sikh family downstairs. So far he had always managed to slip away quickly if anyone of the family looked like making advances as he hurried in or out of the gate, having been warned by Adit who had sometimes been accosted, so he claimed, by the women who were, like all good Punjabi women dedicated needlewomen. Walking briskly down the path, Adit had felt some powerful hand grip him by the back of his sweater, pull him up, shoot a hand under it, right up his chest and examine the fairisle pattern closely. 'Your wife made?' they asked. 'No, readymade,' Adit snapped huffily, and then they looked at him in pity, saying 'We can make for you.' But he drew away from them haughtily, twitching his shoulders in distaste. So Dev was made aware of them mainly by the noises and smells that filtered past their closed windows and through the cracks of their ceiling — pungent smells of Indian cooking, sounds of radio and television, babies and quarrels, singing and banter. Dev would sometime tease Adit about landing himself in a three-in-one cake with layers of white, black-and-white, and black

— in that order. Adit would look put out and say the neighbourhood had been quite different before the Sikhs moved in and that Emma Moffit had been a fool to take them in. He kept them at a distance with his hostile air, but they were friendly people, eager to be neighbourly and, occasionaly, on a wet Sunday perhaps, one of the young men would come upstairs for a little *'gup-shup,'* which consisted of a discussion of Indian news that had appeared in the English papers, but soon the discouraged Sikh would leave, saying politely, 'Why don't you drop down sometimes? We'll give you a good Punjabi meal — my mother cooks in pure *ghee* only.' Even this proved of no attraction to the Sens who never would 'drop down,' but now Dev found himself beckoned by the old lady, enveloped in her white garments from which she extended one arthritic hand.

She made him a special brew for his cold. 'Haven't I heard you cough, cough all night? Isn't that landlady of yours doing anything about it ? Poor boy, alone in a foreign land, and this sinful climate...' she muttered as she mixed and churned and pounded, inside a large metal tumbler. 'Cinnamon, clove, pepper, hot tea and sugar. Drink it down quick. It will burn your throat but I have a spoon of honey here to take the burn away.' She stood over him with the stolid, martial air of many Sikh women and he, cowering on a pillowstrewn bed that played the part of a divan, tried not to splutter as the fiery liquid went scorching a trail down his throat although he could not keep the tears from springing to his eyes.

'In and out, in and out the whole day, I see you,' she said as she put away the spoon and tumbler with a satisfied air. 'Not even a muffler about your ears. What is the matter? Haven't you been able to find work yet, son ?'

'No,' he admitted, finding himself growing weak in the powerful presence of that combination of bullying and tenderness with which mothers in India manage their sons. He saw in it a reflection of his own mother's quieter, more reserved and subtle Bengali version of the matriarchical power complex. The metal tumbler, the ritualistic churning and pounding and brewing of a special family remedy, the bustling about of women around the weak and pampered figure of a man, so much cared for that his obligations weighed on him like a fat and stifling cushion — these were all familiar and therefore insidiously potent.

'And you did not come to us for help? What is this — are we not neighbours? Am I not like your own mother? It is bad you have not thought of coming to me and calling me mother. I am here to be mother to all our poor Indian boys, lost and alone in this cold country. And my sons — such strong young men — can't they help you? Each one of them has a good job, a good pay. Every week they bring their full salary to me. I divide it into three parts — one for their own pockets for they are my sons and I must keep them happy, one for the household, and the third, the largest, for our family and our land in Punjab. How many Indians have come to us for help and my sons have found them all jobs. Did you never think of asking them for jobs?' She shook her head and twittered inside her mouth. Then, sitting down crosslegged at one end of the divan, she wrapped her hands up in her shawl so that all of her was covered with the white widow garments, except for the sharp lines of her face and her bright black eyes under the bushy white brows.

Dev began to struggle up from the pillows and bolsters, from the coddled pit of this intense community feeling like an insect trapped in cottonwool. 'Thank you,' he said, 'thank you. But your sons are qualified men, they are trained workers, it is easy for them to find work anywhere. I have no training. I could not work in a factory.'

'Factory? Training? What is all this talk? Who is saying a *babu* from Bengal should work in a factory?' She laughed. 'A *babu* can only do a *babu's* job, whichever country he might live in. But my sons will find you a job at a desk in their factory. There are many such jobs in England too.'

'Also many English *babus* to do them.'

'*Babuji*, why do you talk like that? Have courage. You are a young man, younger than my sons. This is the time of your vigour, your youth, and here you are talking like a sick old woman. *Chhee chhee,* what bad talk. This is not right. You must come to us oftener and I will feed you Punjabi *roti* and *dal* and pure *ghee,* and then let us hear you talking like that! You *babus* have brains, we all know that, but courage you have still to learn from us. Look at me, old woman, all teeth gone, hands useless, but when my sons called me, I came. I packed two tins of pure *ghee* made from my own buffaloes' milk, and I came to cook for my sons. You have seen how strong and handsome they are, my sons? I sent for wives for them from my own village, and now our house is full of children. You have heard them singing our Punjabi songs? We may live in exile here, but we work hard and we eat well and live in our own way. Come to us, we will show you. No English landlady can look after you as I can, son.'

The mention of buffaloes' milk *ghee* proved more than Dev's Bengali stomach could stand, and his revulsion gave him enterprise to get up and make for the door. She stood at the door, calling up advice to him as he fumbled up the stairs: 'Don't listen to these English men — soap you can do without but an oil bath you must have daily — ginger juice and lemon in hot water for your throat — two scarves, one round your neck and one round your ears—'

But he heard in the croak of her rasping voice the call of *'Factory hand, colour no bar,'* and he shut the door upon her in a shiver of panic.

Go To Work On An Egg..

The next morning, as he was trying frenziedly to cook his breakfast before going out to follow up an advertisement, Sarah stopped him.

'You are not going out,' she said as she stooped to pull on her shoes. 'You go back to bed. I heard you cough all night, I don't think you slept a wink. You'll get pneumonia if you go out in the rain again.'

'Let me go, Sarah. I'll come back and get into bed but I have to follow up this ad. See, it sounds good—'

'It sounds useless,' she said, glancing at it. 'Go to bed now. I'll tell Adit to take in some tea for you before he goes to work. I'll bring the doctor home with me.'

'Now don't be silly.'

'I'm not silly, I'm worried. Back to bed now, at once please. Goodbye! I'll fetch the doctor. Goodbye!'

Dev, staring at the green door slammed in his face, saw and heard the green door of London itself slamming shut — briskly, decisively, as British doors do slam. Why? Because London invited courtship, admiration, flirtation, enjoyment — but not conquest. Because London would not be conquered! Why? Willingly England had conquered his own country, then why — he sighed incoherently, feverishly — would she give nothing in return? With a blurred vision of a toffee tintop he had seen in a Calcutta shop long ago before him — a garish picture of St Paul's dome, flushed but unscarred, amidst the flames of the Blitz — he trailed back to his room, slugged by defeat and, flipping the quilt off the hideous turmoil of the bed in which he had had no sleep, he got in gingerly, found it happily still warm from all the kicking and wriggling and turning over of the night, and sank down, thankfully giving himself up to the pleasures of being mildly ill.

He dozed. Adit opened the door fearfully and handed in a cup of tea and, when asked for some reading material, a book on thugs by John Masters which Dev hurled back at him in disdain, croaking, 'Have I come to England to read up on India?' The door shut. Then another. Adit was gone. The house, after a quivering moment of disbelief, began to take on those colours, those shadows and sounds that did not intrude upon it when it was occupied by people but now came dancing up to Dev's bed — as if he were not any longer people — and draped about him such silent, unfathomable visions as those seen upon a stained wall, through an opaque pane of glass, at the bottom of a stagnant pond, in unpierced darkness. Turning towards the wall, Dev saw upon it a barrow piled with such fruit as can only be seen in an Indian market — pomegranates, guavas, loquats, litchees — and he twisted his fever-dried tongue about his mouth in an effort to taste one drop of juice from this faraway fruit. Turning to the window, he felt certain it was a parrot's flight that sliced a corner off the sky with its emerald scimitar wing, swiftly, dazzlingly. Laurel Lane dozed in midmorning somnolence and allowed such sounds to creep through its white eiderdown of peace as could only have travelled down all the way from India — those hawkers' calls, sing-song and piercing, those rough tumbling, droning sounds of cart and barrow wheels, that cacophony of wildly varied traffic. Burying himself beneath the pillow and quilt, he felt himself back in the company of Indian friends, in the relaxed ambience of uninhibited friendship in which jokes and taunts and banter needed no explanation, were understood almost before they were spoken. Beyond the prim walls of Laurel Lane, surely his own family bustled as they would have bustled had they known him ill — he saw faintly the figures of mother and sisters, of servants and relations in the veranda, on the terrace, murmuring, laughing. moving so close to him yet quite apart from him, divided by white walls that were melting into grey streets, grey lanes, grey squares and bridges over a river, a sea of black water: *'kala pani.'*

It was the greyness of London in which buses moved brilliantly like the red beads on a child's grimy abacus. Dev's journey into sleep and fever was made inside such buses, to the tune of West Indian voices calling such charmed London names as Old Paradise Street (but where were the parrots and pomegranates of paradise?), Lambeth High (accompanied, all down its length, by some raucous Cockney tune of which he could not remember the lyrics), Tooting Bec (a schoolboy bent over a rail, spitting on the top of a passing, roaring, smoking train), Pepys Street (newspapers flapping about a coffee stand, the odour of roasted coffee and newsprint mingling with untroubled naturalness), Holywell Road and Ploughwell (trumpets and carillons ringing out of bronzed history), and he awoke, muttering, 'Bewitched! Bewitched !'

A clock striking, a key turning. Footsteps and voices. The door opened and a hot rum toddy was handed in. Sipping it, he felt himself steady, felt the landscape steady, grow coherent and coloured again, while 'Bewitched!' sounded gently as an echo. The rum and lemon juice glowed with clarity between his cupped hands, set his blood moving in his veins again, and he wondered, with an extraordinary precision of thought, how it was that so many people in his country, of so many generations and so many social and economic classes, had been brought up on a language and literature completely alien to them, been fed it like a sweet in infancy, like a drug in youth, so that before they realised it, they were addicts of it and their bodies were composed as much of its substance as of native blood. They were the people who had been called — who had called them that? — 'Macaulay's bastards.' This was his label too — Dev's. And why — he asked himself, sipping the hot rum — had he not remained content with the taking of the drug (available on every pavement, in every stall, in bright paper covers, for a few rupees), but had travelled so far in search of the origin, the fountainhead of the vision induced by this drug, that enthralling, bewitching vision that had lived in him so long, so that now both drug and vision, copy and original, held him in a double net? Sipping a little more, he asked himself if this net did not cut into his flesh, maiming him, or whether enslavement were not sweet, heady, rewarding, more fantastic than abhorrent, more true than untrue. Bewitched, he moaned — but was it not a mad, secret job to be so bewitched?

Sarah came to warn him that the doctor had arrived, but Dev never saw him. Adit gave him a whiskey in the drawingroom, and started him talking of his rich women patients, gave him another and started him talking of the opera, gave him a third and... Finally Dr Baker had to be helped out to his car and Dev fell asleep without being examined at all.

He woke — that night, another night — and found a cheesy moon staring at him out of a curds-and-whey sky, casting his room into an exact reproduction of a draughtboard, square of white placed precisely beside a square of black, demanding of him a similar precision of logic. Answer the question, he told himself, sitting bolt upright in his bed — honestly, logically. Black on white and no hedging.

Why was he here, coughing and keeping awake the strangers in whose house he had lived all summer?'

Why was he here, wasting the last of his father's money, and not studying politics, philosophy and economics in some secure stepping-stone of a college?' What were, he asked himself with growing sternness, his intentions?

He thought of a pretty, a fancy answer with which to placate the beady-eyed moon. With some inspiration, he gave it what he felt sure was a stunning reply: I am here, he intoned, as an ambassador. I am showing these damn imperialists with their lost colonies complex that we are free people now, with our own personalites that this veneer of an English education has not obscured, and not afraid to match ours with theirs. I am here, he proselytised, to interpret my country to them, to conquer England as they once conquered India, to show them, to show them.

He was shouting, his tongue clattering silently inside his dry mouth, so loudly that his skull echoed with unsaid words and they bounced from wall to wall, growing louder, loner, more garbled all the time, till he was brought up short by one look from the moon — no romantic flower this — which shot him a curdled stare, waited a while in between grey leaves of cloud, and then reappeared.

Lies, lies, admitted Dev, cravenly, for he was growing sleepy. All I want is — well, yes, a good time. Not to return to India, not to marry and breed, go to office, come home and go to office again but — to know a little freedom, to indulge in a little adventure, to know, to know.

The effort to explain what he wished to know was too great, at that hour of the night, and he fell back, fell asleep and woke only when Sarah brought him his morning tea, to find his cough altered in tone, thinner and emptier, so that she said at once, 'You sound better today.'

'I am,' said Dev with some eagerness. 'I'm getting up. As soon as you leave the room I am going to jump out of bed and look at the papers.'

'You're not,' she said, and did not leave the room but stood leaning against the doorpost, thoughtfully, 'I had a letter from my mother yesterday, asking us to come down for the weekend. We didn't go at Easter as we usually do and she wants us to come now.

Come with us. I'd like to show you my home. It's different from anything you'll see in London, you ought to come. And then stay on for a bit, for a week. You need a holiday.'

Dev put down his teacup in alarm. 'In the country?' he asked in fright. 'But that's all downs and sheep and long walks, isn't it? You know, I don't feel quite hearty enough for that yet.'

'What rot,' shouted Adit, coming to stand safely on the other side of the door in his Hollywood blue robe. 'The country, *yar*, the English country — Morris dances and thatched cottages. The blacksmith under the spreading chestnut tree and trout streams and daffodils like — like what, Sarah?'

'There won't be any daffodils now,' Sarah said, 'but there is a trout stream at the bottom of the garden.'

'What ho! The country!' shouted Adit and did a little dance on his bare feet. 'Come on, *yar*, be a man, an Englishman, take a deep breath, put on your tweeds and get your riding crop out.'

'When ?' asked Dev, shrinking under his quilt.

'This weekend,' said Sarah. 'We'll take the train to Winchester—'

'Rot !' shouted Adit, dashing into and then out of the bathroom. 'What does one have friends with cars for? We'll get Jasbir and Mala to drive us down,' he announced, with a splendid gesture of a wide sleeved arm. 'Invite Samar and Bella for the drive. Get your mum to give them a cup of tea and then send them back to London while we stay on for the country air, country walks, country cooking...' Back in the bathroom, he locked the door and could be heard ecstatically singing:

> *'Wenn ich früh in den garten geh*
> *In meinem grunen Hut,*
> *Ist mein erster Gedanke,*
> *Was nun mein Liebster tut?'*

5

Following upon the symmetry of the little suburban houses with their chimney posts, their gravelled yards, their washing lines and bun-faced men in shirtsleeves digging — the symmetry of the countryside. Fields of tall, ripe hay and wheat and barley, swaying and murmuring in the breeze luxuriantly green and golden. No speck of dust, no patch of arid earth, no sign of blight for mile upon mile upon gracious, rolling mile. The neat hedged lanes sweet with poppies and foxgloves, roses and honeysuckle; the streams swaying silver and green with water weeds and trout, crossed by painted bridges; and, here and there, a village with the first thatched cottages Dev had seen in England. They were, he thought, like loaves of lumpy brown bread, standing in fields of yellow-cupped wildflowers that surrounded them like butter, and the summer sun pouring down on them like honey. The land about them was perpetually green and fruitful, the low hills tamed and rounded, the fields of such perfect grain, each blade symmetrical and rich.

In the car, the party sang the gayer and more rollicking tunes of Bengali folk music *'O red earth of my village home,'* they roared, beating time on their knees, as they crossed the greenest corner of the world, the sweetest and freshest.

But the highways leading out of London on this weekend afternoon soon became more and more of a sticky nightmare in which one had packed and prepared and set off on a journey only to find one self unable to move, to travel, one's feet stuck like those of ants to rivers of glue. Every road and lane an unbroken chain of cars, linked together by their obedience to the rule of weekends to be spent in the countryside, inching along, then halting for hours, unable to break up and speed away.

'Talk of Indians being copycats,' sneered Dev, beginning to feel cramped and bilious in the backseat of Jasbir's small Morris. 'Is there anythmg more regimented than life in England?'

'Why be impatient, *yar* ?' Adit said, lolling back and letting the tall hedges, embroidered with dog roses rise above him against the still sky. 'Look at the fields, listen to the birds, enjoy yourself for once.'

'But he is right,' said Sarah. 'I should think ninety out of every hundred people here live lives exactly alike. Every evening they watch the same programmes on the telly, every Friday night they go to the local for a pint, every Sunday have roast beef for lunch, every Whitsun and Bank Holiday stream down to the sea like lemmings...'

'Well, so do we,' said Adit, more grumpily. 'And enjoy ourselves at it, too.'

'But this is supposed to be the land of liberty, of eccentricity, of individualism,' Dev protested. 'Just look at them — the masses, like herds of cows — placid, bovine, above all stoic — neatly, obediently following the Way of the Masses.'

Whereupon Jasbir, who had been studying the map spread across the steering wheel while they waited for a particularly crowded and enclosed lane to make way for motion again, suddenly took his foot off the brake, backed his car past the momentarily astonished eyes of the drivers behind him, and escaped into a side lane he had just discovered on the map by a great stroke of serendipity. 'We'll go down the forest paths,' he shouted, and the wind whipped up, cold and refreshing, at their open windows, bearing the odours of new leaves and damp undergrowth.

In the car the party began to sing, *'The monsoon clouds roll over the paddy fields, my heart...'*

They were not exactly rid of the tourist traffic yet. Adventurous cars passed with camping equipment and even boats strapped to their tops. The less adventurous were drawn up at the roadside, their passengers disgorged on to canvas campstools placed in neat rows within safe distance of their cars and the highway. Many of the picnickers were buried deep in their newspapers. Others were heaping tins and cartons in the litter bins placed conveniently under the trees. When Dev saw that one youthful couple had put its child in a playpen placed in the centre of a smooth green meadow, he gave a snort of laughter, baffled by a mentality that found need of such precaution, restriction and obedience even in the midst of a land so sweet and safe, so gentle and sparkling. With their newspapers, their tables and chairs, their litterbins and playpens, what did they ever learn of this treasure they owned, this rich abundant beauty and green grace?

'Mad,' he snorted.

'Daft's the word,' Samar told him. 'English people love being told they are daft — don't they, Sarah?'

'Yes, they like being daft like the white Rabbit, not daft like the Mad Hatter,' complained Dev.

'There is no satisfying you,' sighed Adit.

'Standardisation can't satisfy, nor regimentation, nor mass production, nor —'

'India was the land for you, *yar*. Nigger, go home.'

Jasbir drew up in a lay-by in the curve of a ripe hay field and they piled out to stretch their legs by a broken stile beside a bonfire of wild poppies. Far away, a little stone abbey and a clump of elms broke the sunlit evenness of the hayfields. Matches grated, cigarette smoke spumed. Sarah got around the stile into the field. She walked a little way into the hay and stood there, clutching two fistsfull of crackling hay, staring across at the abbey with her grey, silent eyes. The men perched on the stile slid down to sit on the grass, and soon were lying flat upon it, arching their backs to accommodate the humps of grass, twisting to avoid pebbles, groaning under the brilliant weight of the blank blue sky.

Then Adit said, 'One could travel from Bombay to Calcutta and from Kashmir to Cape Comorin and not find two consecutive miles as rich and even as all the land here.'

His voice sounded strange. Some glanced to see who had spoken, but no one disagreed. Like speechless animals, they breathed audibly.

'There would be miles and miles of desert instead. There would be trees without fruit or even leaves. The cattle would be starved, their skeletons lying around the rocks. Vultures wheeling in the sky. And sun, sun, sun.'

Still no one spoke. Their cigarettes made idle, curvaceous replies of smoke in the clear air.

'Either that — or flood. Everything blotted out by mud and water. Mud huts, cattle, crops — all swept away, drowned. Then, cholera and typhoid.'

'What they call the Land of Death Everlasting,' said Dev, whether with irony or in agreement, no one knew.

'And here there is no death at all. Everything — animal, vegetable, mineral — is alive, rich and green forever.'

No one replied.

When Adit spoke again, as if compelled to by the pressure of their silence, his strange voice cracked open harshly, like an empty nut, brittle with pain. 'It seems unfair, *yar*,' he said. 'Nothing ever goes right at home — there is famine or flood, there is drought or epidemic, always. Here the rain falls so softly and evenly, never too much and never too short. The sun is mild. The earth is fertile. The rivers are full. The birds are plump. The beasts are fat. Everything so wealthy, so luxuriant — *so fortunate.*'

Silence. The wind ran through the hay, caressing it, admiring it, like a pleased farmer. In the elms around around the stone abbey a cuckoo called, called again, softly, melodiously. A flock of helicopters approached flying low over the rounded hills, like great dragonflies humming through the green summer sky, reducing the people lying beneath the hay to the size of crawling ants, and then busily disappeared.

Then Adit sat up and, flinging away his cigarette and stretching his arms above his head, he groaned,

'O England's green and grisly land,
   I love you as only a babu can.'

And, suddenly feeling very pleased, he repeated the words loudly, to a tune, which brought Sarah back to him out of the hay field.

'Come on,' she said. 'Mummy must be getting tea ready for us. It's too bad Bella couldn't come,' she added, to Samar, as he helped her into the car — rather hypocritically for she knew there was no place for Bella either in this green southern land or in her mother's drawing room.

'By now her sister might have had her baby, and those two boys of hers will be giving old Bella hell, they're proper *shaitans*[1],' he said of Bella's nephews whom she was looking after while her sister was in hospital. 'But Bella's scared stiff of the country anyway. She's like one of those people picnicking by the road — got to have her camp stool and her little bin and her cuppa, country or no country.'

'So do I, really,' Sarah said, feeling ashamed of her hypocrisy.

They passed villages of new red brick and villages of old. half-timbered cottages with thatched roofs like teacosies, their green doors and whitewashed walls splashed with red and gold roses. On willow-hung banks, picturebook children fished with bent pins for flngerlets of fish. Fruit trees dipped unripe fruit like promises over stone walls, curio shop windows glinted with pewter and brass and the mad, round faces of rag dolls. They drove past farmhouses and motels, teashops and inns, carts and motorbikes. They drove into glades of forest where sunlight slipped like rain through green mantles of foliage and small ponies scampered up tamely for apples and buns, then cantered wildly away into groves cast under magic spells by gauze-winged fairies. They passed small booths with large signs that said: *Fresh Strawberries 2/6*. Grazing in the meadows were hens as large as turkeys, sheep as big as cows, cows as big as barns.

---

[1] Devils.

There were lanes spattered with cowdung, horse chestnuts and dog roses, and cottage gardens in which cabbages gleamed like giant globules of dew. They lingered by an ancient, uninhabited farmhouse with bluebottle glass windowpanes set in crooked frames that blinked like peasant's eyes under the beetling brows of the thatched roof, and its courtyard of misshapen apple trees and dry water troughs. They drove on and crops were drawn like green gauze, soft and bright, over the rich earth. In the meadows streams overflowed with their bright abundance, and irises and willows bent over them, lazily in love with their own limpid reflections.

Adit, leaning out of the window, sang softly.

> 'Here no one can love or understand me,
>   Oh! what hard luck stories they all hand me.
> Make my bed and light the light,
>   I'll arrive late tonight.
> Blackbird, bye-bye.'

Then Sarah said, matter-of-factly, 'We're home.'

'Have a watercress sandwich, Mrs Singh,' said Sarah's mother, holding out a plate of delicate, flowered china heaped with these English delicacies to a tiredly lolling Mala, and Dev gave a small snort at the sight. It seemed a strange, an incredible twist of fortune that had brought this band of Indians, in their heavy overcoats, on a summer's day to a drawingroom so totally, so irrevocably English and conservative and country house, with its chintzes, its laces, its tiny ashtrays of rose pattern, its bowls of potpourri. its silver candlesticks, its medley of real and fake antique furniture, its framed photographs of people in wedding garments and people in cardigans cuddling furry dogs. It was not quite the country house of the stage or cinema, for Mrs Roscommon-James, fluttering her hands so that the heavy metal bracelet on one wrist jangled incessantly, had to get up every now and then to fetch this, that or the other from the kitchen. Sarah helped her in silence. Mala made not even the perfunctory gesture of a guest to rise and offer help. She lay back in her little chintzfrilled armchair, her thick fall of hair dishevelled after the long drive, the silk folds of her crimson sari crumpled badly, sighing in gratitude for a cup of tea.

'Oh no, no watercress for me,' she said with some horror, indicating that she had met with it before and did not care to renew acquaintance.

'But it is homegrown,' urged Mrs Roscommon-James, waving the plate more emphatically. 'Almost everything is in our house. My husband is such a gardener — I couldn't get him in from the garden even for tea, you know. You'll have to go and call him again, Sarah dear.'

Sarah nodded but sat down instead. Her face had narrowed and tightened with concentration on making this visit of her husband and her husband's friends to her parents' house, if not exactly a success, at least an uneventful and unmarred occasion.

'What, he gardens all this?' asked Jasbir, waving the watercress sandwich that he had accepted with somewhat apologetic fervour, at the window from which the lawn could be seen flowing down in tidy waves to the stream bordered with willows and meadow flowers.

'Oh yes, he put in every flower you see. It was all a marsh when we came here.'

'Listen to that, Mala.'

'Listen yourself,' answered his wife lazily. 'Do you ever mow the lawn?'

'No, you always tell me you will arrange for a gardener to come and do that,' said Jasbir. 'We wait for the window-cleaner to come and clean our windows, we plan to get a char to come and clean our house, and think someone will surely come and cut our grass for us some day. Mala doesn't mind waiting.'

'Oh, you will have to get down to it yourself soon,' said Mrs Roscommon-James, 'If you stay here long enough.'

'We've been here seven years already,' Jasbir shouted with laughter.

Mrs Roscommon-James gave a startled and incoherent exclamation. 'But in seven years one can surely learn to use a lawnmower. We had to learn ourselves, you know,' she said with a sniff. 'As children, our parents were still able to maintain a staff. Now we have to manage on our own — mostly.'

'Not Mala,' said Jasbir, and Mala rolled her head against the back of her chair and laughed.

'The house is a pigsty,' she agreed, and Mrs Roscommon-James replaced the plate of sandwiches on the trolley, put her knees together and pursed her lips. It was evident she was thinking that all she had heard about the filthy ways of the Asian immigrants was correct.

She turned to Sarah with a pitying expression. 'How is your cooking getting on dear?'

'Adit still does most of it,' Sarah said.

'Now that,' said Mrs Roscommon-James, 'is something an English husband certainly wouldn't have done for you, I must admit,' and she laughed, not with approval.

'Well, I always say English cooking is *wonderful,*' declared Adit, making everyone stare at him, 'if it is well done. But if it isn't — then I prefer to go to the kitchen and make myself a proper Indian meal. English women aren't all very careful about their cooking, though some make the most wonderful pies and stews in the world. Now my landlady, Mrs Miller, could do things to a piece of veal—'

'But she, I think you told me once is really German,' protested Mrs Roscommon-James.

'Yes, and Germans are wonderful cooks,' cried Adit. 'God, I remember the holiday I spent there one summer. I ate so much, I came back fifteen pounds overweight.'

Mrs Roscommon-James shot him a cold and disbelieving look. 'Have some walnut cake,' she said.

'Lyons?' he asked, reaching for a thick slice.

'Lyons indeed!' she snorted. 'I made it myself.'

'But they're not bad, Mummy,' said Sarah. 'I buy them a lot.'

Mrs Roscommon-James directed that cooled look at her daughter. 'As a mother, I am very shocked to hear that,' she said. 'Of course, I do understand how hard you have to work and I suppose you are tired when you get home.'

'But she loves the school!' Adit expostulated. 'How often I've said, "Sarah, give up your job, it doesn't look nice for you to work after you are married," and every time she says to me, "No, Adit, I love it." '

Even Sarah's expression registered a degree of surprise at her own words, and Jasbir and Samar, in an effort to cover their friend who had gone too far, began to speak simultaneously. Samar spoke louder — so loudly that Mrs Roscommon-James' very old and weak Pekinese got up from under the teatable and removed itself to a far corner with a grumpy expression.

'Did I ever tell you about the Sikh I saw having tea at Selfridges one day?' Samar shouted. 'He had a big piece of chocolate cake on his plate and then he called for tomato ketchup and poured it all over the cake and ate it up with knife and fork.'

Everyone shouted with laughter except Mrs Roscommon-James who had screwed up her face as though she herself were experiencing the Sikh's pangs of indigestion.

'Hah, it's always a Sikh in your stories,' grumbled Jasbir, when he had finished laughing. 'What about the Bengali who got onto the bus and asked for a ticket to "Qownsbury", and when the conductor asked him to spell it, he said "Qow-yow-yee-yee-yen-yes bury".'

'It must have been a Madrasi, not a Bengali,' said Adit, with dignity. 'The Bengali has the only correct English accent in India.'

'But *you* are a Bengali, Adit,' Mrs Roscommon-James said, pointedly, and Adit said, 'Yes, Bengal was the first province to have an English school. The missionaries had more effect on Bengal's intellectual life than anywhere else,' and having made his speech, he looked proud.

'Well, you must admit it was a Bengali who gave that woman on the bus such a stunning answer, Jasbir,' said Mala, and laughed so hard that Jasbir had to tell the story.

'We were travelling on this very crowded bus when an Englishwoman got on, carrying a whole lot of parcels. No one got up for her and she sniffed, "There don't seem to be any gentlemen on this bus." There was an old Indian chap on the bus, and he piped up, "Madam, there are many gentlemen, but no seats".'

'Of course it was a Bengali,' cried Samar with rapture. 'They're the Indians with the most wits, Mrs Roscommon-James, I can tell you that.'

Jasbir was incensed. 'Not all Bengalis can boast of wits.' he roared. 'What about your dance-hall days, eh, Samar, my boy?'

'What about them?' said Samar, embarrassed and haughty. 'You used to come with me in those days. Those were our bachelor days, in Coventry, Mala, when we were interns at the hospital there. It was our plan to explore *all* levels of English society, you see.'

'Oh dear,' murmured Mrs Roscommon-James faintly. 'Dance-halls in Coventry!'

'Haven't you heard about the kind of girls Samar used to pick up in those dance-halls?' asked Jasbir, beaming at everyone while Samar glowered like an insulted monkey, helpless behind his bars. 'I used to see him making a beeline for all the old, whitehaired grannies, frustrated spinsters, ageing tarts and the like, you know. Well, I just couldn't understand this. I mean, I'd never heard of any perversion that made *old* women appealing. So one day, after he'd danced a foxtrot with one of these grannies, I asked him, "Samar, *yar*, what's this? Why do you always ask such white-haired old *buddhies*[2] to dance?" And do you know what Samar said? He said, "That was no white-haired old *buddhi yar* — that was a platinum blonde"!'

Shrieks and yells exploded with such force of hilarity that the indignant old Pekinese rose and left room while Mrs Roscommon-James, one hand to her brow, looked as though she pined to do the

---

[2] Old women.

same though a horrid fascination kept her in her chair, open-mouthed.

Samar was protesting angrily and ineffectually but, as soon as the uproar subsided, he was heard to say, 'But just let me tell you about the Sikh fitters in a factory in Coventry. They're the ones who took the cake. Let me tell you about it, Mrs Roscommon-James. One day there was a riot in the factory.'

'Heavens, one of those *racial* things?' murmured Mrs Roscommon-James.

'No, it was just the Sikhs beating each other up. One of the Englishmen finally went up to one of the rowdies and asked him what it was all about. So he pointed at another Sikh and said, "That swine, he called me Blackie".'

Sarah, having smiled quietly at this story, gave her mother a glance of pity and perhaps sympathy for she had not seen her mother — so smart in her very pointed shoes, so assured in her tailored suit from Harrods, so in command of all the twinkling silver and porcelain, the dainty sandwiches and the cake forks — so flustered, so torn between outrage and horror since she had attended Sarah's wedding and seen Sarah in a sari of gold-flecked red Benares silk sent by Adit's parents in Calcutta, standing surrounded by Adit's dark and hirsute friends in a chilly magistrate's office on a still September morning.

'Shall we wash up, mother?' she said gently, beginning to collect the plates, but Adit shouted, 'What are you doing? Don't fiinish off the tea party so soon, Sarah. What's your hurry? We want more tea.'

'Yes, more tea,' Jasbir called.

'Dear me!' Mrs Roscommon-James exclaimed, looking uncommonly frail. 'Of course. The kettle's on — I'll fill the pot.'

Sarah let her go, understanding her need to escape from people, humour and conversation so many miles beyond the comprehension of her naturally restricted curiosity.

But Adit, Jasbir and Samar seemed almost deliberately determined to pursue her with their holiday exuberance.

'Mala,' shouted Jasbir, 'come on, woman. You're supposed to be an Indian wife, always serving her husband. Why don't you go and make us some *pakoras*?'[3]

'Yes,' roared Adit in delighted agreement. 'God, wouldn't that just make it a perfect party — a plate of hot *pakoras*?'

Mala looked lazy and unwilling. 'In Mrs Roscommon-James' kitchen? I couldn't, could I, Sarah?'

Sarah looked equally unwilling but Adit insisted. 'Why not, Mala? There's sure to be some potatoes and onions and perhaps spinach, isn't there, Sarah?'

'But what will I dip them in?'

'There may be some corn meal,' Sarah admitted. 'I could ask.'

They rose and went into the kitchen but with such obvious reluctance that their men felt they were not to be trusted and came after them, hungry, enthusiastic, loud.

Only Dev remained in his chair by the window, silent since he entered the house, wondering only how he was going to live in it for a whole week. 'I'm trapped,' he kept saying to himself, 'I'm trapped.' He felt entangled and suffocated by all the chintz draped around him, the little rugs about his feet, the rose-patterned ashtrays beside him, the atmosphere of precious narrowness, of cultivated restraint, of hard-won comfort. He gazed out of the window with unhappy eyes, and was comforted a little by the view of the immense cedar tree, the uneven turf tumbling down to a distant idyll of stream, willows, meadows and woods softened, as in a painting by Constable, by the glowing ripeness of the evening sun. Then he thought of having to walk there with the nervous and disapproving Pekinese, of lemonade and canvas chairs under the cedar tree, of Mrs Roscommon-James and her Tory country friends assaulting him with their astonished squeaks, well-mannered gulps, jangling metal bracelets and harsh high heels, and he croaked again 'Trapped, trapped.'

---

[3] Fritters.

In the kitchen, however, the atmosphere was one of a holiday at its golden peak. In the dainty drawingroom the visitors had felt somewhat hampered and inhibited by their embarrassment — although Mrs Roscommon-James would never have suspected it — but once in the kitchen with its large, uncurtained window looking out into a long, narrow, enclosed garden of wild roses and fruit trees, with its immense old-fashioned stove, its brightly patterned linoleum, its bowls of cherries and pears, they felt freed of all the restrictions that are subtly imposed upon guests and aliens by the very surroundings, if not the hosts. If Mrs Roscommon-James had thought their behaviour over the tea-table uninhibited, boisterous and tactless, she could now only blink and gasp and then sit down weakly at the table and surrender her cupboards, her pots and pans, her potatoes and onions, her composure and her kitchen to the dark waves of immigrants. Joyfully, they took over.

Vegetables were being sliced on the linoleum tablecloth with a sharp knife, batter being mixed in the salad bowl. Soon bubbles of hot fat flew up and spattered the wall behind the stove that had remained immaculate through the preparation of innumerable English stews and broths. Adit gargled *'Largo ife factotum'* with passion and an accent that led Mrs Roscommon-James to think he was singing one of his emotional native songs. Then Mala, stepping out into the narrow garden in order to leave the distasteful task of cooking to the only too willing male cooks, discovered a bush of wild mint under the jasmine vine at the door.

She gave a loud, dramatic scream.

Everyone dropped frying pans, choppers, onions and spoons in order to rush out and see what she had found, and soon a ritual ring of worshippers was formed about the plants that seemed to them to be transported, by magic, from their own land. For a moment they were hushed. The sudden, fresh odours released by the plucking and crumpling of mint leaves. and the soft, insistent fragrance of the tiny stars of jasmine aroused a thousand different memories in minds always open to tbe winds of nostalgia.

Sarah and her mother, who had remained seated at the kitchen table, watched them through the window in silence. Sarah's face looked oddly crumpled and shadowed: she was experiencing an unsettling wave of that intermittent schizophrenia that Adit said was a result of her having been an Indian in a past incarnation and that sometimes allowed her to feel herself into an Indian mood while still able to observe herself undergoing this curious transformation with her normal Saxon detachment.

Even Mrs Roscommon-James' dormant curiosity had been aroused. After watching them a while, wondering at the silence of their tongues and the stillness of their postures, she said, in a low voice, 'Do you know, I always thought Indians were — what do you call 'em — intro — intro—'

'Introverts?'

'Yes, yes. People say they are so moody and self-conscious. But my dear, your — your husband and his friends, they are the very opposite, aren't they?'

'Extroverts? Adit certainly is, and so are some of his friends, but not all. Dev, the one who is to stay on with you, he is moody enough to make up for all the others — at times. Then he can be very outgoing too, in spurts. Rather like us, Mummy, and your friends — everyone a bit different from the other but not too much.' An unusual speech for Sarah to have made, but spoken in a tone of doubt and exploration that explained it.

'Well,' said Mrs Roscommon-James 'Well, I must say I see a great deal of difference even if you don't.'

Outside, in the silent ring around the jasmine and the mint, Mala spoke up. 'You know, I am going to make you some mint *chutney,*' she said and, taking a fold of her sari to form a small sling, she began to fill it with leaves plucked deftly and neatly from the bush. Then she went into the kitchen put them on a wooden board and began to chop and pound them, humming with the pleasure of activity for once.

The men hung back in the garden that had enchanted them with its unexpected odours, both foreign and familiar and lay down in the tall grass between a border of rose bushes luxuriantly covered with red and gold and cream roses, crowned with intoxicated bees, and the high stone wall that separated the garden from churchyard. Low fruit trees climbed against the wall, their boughs nobbled with infant apples and pears, and over their tops the tall, fine spire of the Norman church rose in Saturday silence and ominousness.

Jasbir began to sing a song that had been popular in India when he was a child there. *'Sundar nari, pritam pyari,'* he sang, and the others, clapping their hands to keep time, joined in. *'Pyari, pyari, sundar nari,'* they sang, clapping their hands and swaying their heads to its innocent rhythm till Mala opened the window and called, 'Come and eat *pakoras* — they're nice and hot hot, and just taste the *chutney!'*

They flew up at her word and a soft, brown thrush flew frightened out of its nest in the pear tree, circled the silent spire and then settled back again, with little murmurs and squeaks of indignation, in her nest.

In the kitchen, no one could be bothered to pull up chairs or fetch forks; they stood around the table, devouring the hot *pakoras* and mint *chutney* with a voraciousness that Mrs Roscommon-James could not help taking as an insult to the ladylike tea she had provided for them. She refused to try one of the *pakoras* offered her — 'My dear I never saw anything to be *fried* in my life,' she told a friend next morning at church — but Sarah seemed to enjoy them.

Having munched as many as a dozen of them, Jasbir paused to sigh and say, 'Haven't had so much fun since my bed-sitter days in Coventry where that sweet old landlady of ours — Mrs Bee, wasn't she Samar? — used to let me into her kitchen on Friday nights when she herself used to go off and mind her daughter's children on her daughter's pub night, and I used to call the whole bunch of Indian doctors at the hospital to come and try *pakoras* and *alu-tikkis.* That used to be the best meal of the week.'

'Who did the washing up?'

'Oh, we washed up and put everything away by the time Mrs Bee got back. But her husband — he was a mean old brute — he used to say the kitchen stank for the rest of the week.'

They laughed and reached for a fresh lot of fritters that Mala brought to the table in triumph, her hair all dishevelled and her rich silk sari spattered with fat since she had not put on the plastic apron Mrs Roscommon-James had handed her.

Eyeing her, Mrs Roscommon-James said dryly, 'Isn't it time you went into British dress, Mrs Singh?'

'Never!' cried Mala, taken aback. 'Me, in a frock?' and she laughed at the preposterous picture.

'But it is much more practical,' Mrs Roscommon-James protested. 'How on earth can one travel or do one's housework wrapped up like that in yards and yards of silk? It is beautiful of course — on you dark women — but *not* practical.'

'No, but I am not practical,' said Mala, and repeated, *'Me,* in a frock!' and laughed again

Every scrap was eaten and when nothing was left on the plates but streaks of quickly congealing grease, they wiped their fingers on the embroidered tea towels and sighed and said it had been the most enjoyable meal in ages and sighed again to imply that nothing else on this holiday could match the fun and happiness of this cooking spree and, therefore, it was time to leave.

Sarah and Adit wandered out into the vegetable garden in search of her father who had remained unseen and unheard as long as the tea party was in swing. He did not appear even when he surely must have heard the noisy car start and spurt over the gravel of the drive through the big green gate and away through the meadows to the distant highway. Adit could not comprehend a parental relationship so cool that the parent did not rush out and embrace the daughter whom he had not seen since last Christmas, but kept himself out of her way as though he were avoiding her. He did not say this aloud — he had, in the past, sometimes mentioned his astonishment and disapproval of their colourless, toneless, flavourless relationship only to have Sarah say impatiently, 'Oh we can't stand cuddling and netting and all that!' to which Adit had protested, 'But your mother *loves* it when I give her a hug and a kiss,' and then was offended when Sarah gave a small snort of scorn.

He held Sarah by the arm, not so moved to romance by the still, poetic acres about them, the sudden singing calls of the harp-throated birds inivisible in the trees, and the soft rush and rustle of the stream, as made uncertain and tentative by these strange surroundings into which she fitted, to which she belonged with such obvious and graceful pertinence.

He said, 'He *does* know we were coming, doesn't he ?'

Sarah laughed. 'I wouldn't know. Sometimes 1 think he doesn't hear a word Mummy says anymore.'

Adit thought it would be impossible not to hear a voice so commanding, so large and demanding of attention.

Then they came upon him crawling about the strawberry bed, grunting and breathing fiercely through his hairy red nostrils, seemingly engaged in tying himself up with black thread to little pegs stuck in the ground. He had his back to them and his trousers, although fastened with big braces, were slipping low and his woollen vest was slipping out. He did not hear their footsteps on the soft, unturned earth between the vegetable beds and they stood watching him in silence — Adit with anxiety and Sarah with an uncertain and thoughtful wonder as if she had found her parent turned, like some hairy caterpillar, into an unexpected and surprising creature.

Strangely enough, when her father had been a successful physician with a large practice in Winchester, and they had lived in a house in which oak panels gleamed and porcelain sparkled, it was her father who had seemed to her a sophisticated, well-read and quietly distinguished man of the world — a man for whom the *Times* was especially printed — and it was her mother, moving about the *gemutlich* British prettiness of the house with little darts and rushes and jangling sounds, who had seemed shabby and out of place by comparison, too coarsegrained and clumsy. She had this unfortunate way of thrusting her tongue under her false teeth and making them protrude in a row and flap weirdly up and down between her lips as she stood outside the fishmonger's window, speculating upon the sole and the haddock. If, in company, she wished to reprimand Sarah for allowing her skirt to creep up about her knees, she would wave her hands to attract Sarah's attention and then exaggeratedly pull at her own skirt to show Sarah what she meant. Yet now, in the centuries' old house with its cedar tree and trout stream, its strawberry beds and pear trees, its copper beeches and French windows, it was she who played the Tory matron in retirement, busily organising church bazaars and cluck-clucking over a farmer's daughter who had become pregnant by no one knew who long after her own parents had grown to rejoice in the child, sending inedible cakes that had not risen to lame Mrs Dobson who baked excellent cakes herself, and planning shopping and dentistry expeditions to London, while her husband lapsed into the appearance, manners and speech of some forgotten peasant ancestry. With his head sunk up to its ears upon his shoulders, wearing a rough jacket that looked as though the dog slept in it every night, his boots with their soles peeling off and great nails painfully protruding, he shambled around the garden all day, now stoking up a bonfire of smoking green boughs, now squatting on the compost heap and investigating it with the congenital curiosity of a grub, now hacking at a dead beech tree and now hauling great lengths of pipe across vast beds of celery and lettuce. From day's break to nightfall he dug, bent, tied up, cut down, weeded, watered, dragged, carried and crawled. Now and then his wife darted out of the kitchen and called in a voice that carried across the trout stream and halfway across Farmer Coombe's hayfields. 'To-mmy! To-mmy! Remember to do something about those mo-oles!' He would give no sign, not so much as the twitch of an eyelid, as he went about his labour in the cabbage patch of having heard her. Every evening, as he came in, she went into a frenzy of irritation and alarm at the earth and manure that covered him from top to toe, leaking out of his sleeves and boots, falling upon her parquetry and her carpets. As she directed him to the sink, handed him a bar of yellow washing soap and scrubbing brushes, all the while standing at a safe distance from him, she scolded him in tones that would lead anyone not present in the room to think she was speaking to an unusually naughty and tiresome dog. He never answered. He had acquired the silence of a piece of log submerged in a water meadow, of a scarecrow in a cornfield. When he spoke, it was in the slurred accents of a peasant. He referred, strangely, to 'taters' and 'maters,' and attacked his plate, piled high with boiled mutton and potatoes, as though the fork in his hand were a farm implement, his mouth a waggon. Visitors and errand boys, seeing him about his land, took him for a paid labourer and ignored him as they walked, whistling, up the drive to the front door. Nor did he notice them. He was a source of no little embarrassment to his wife who had acquired so much social prestige with retirement and a country house. Most of the time it was easy enough to keep him buried unobtrusively in the back garden but he had an uncanny knack of trundling a wheelbarrow full of manure across the lawn just as she was handing out glasses of lemonade to a party of local Conservative matrons under the cedar tree. None of them thought of referring to an old, dumb gardener, of course, and she said nothing either, but could not restrain a look of bitter accusation at the line of smelly manure he had left behind him. On Sundays, when she liked to play the ruling gentry of the village by gracing with her presence the morning service at the little Norman church next door, she felt the need of a squire on whose arm she could make her appearance in petal hat and pearls. In preparation for this theatrical weekly occasion she sternly supervised his bath on Saturday night and had him dress 'decently for once,' then tried to ignore him as, tightly clutching his elbow and steering him into the best pew, she played her weekly role, smiling a serene and royal smile at which the farmers and their wives jeered, saying 'Who does she think she is, a bloomin' queen?' If the vicar made the foolish mistake of enquiring after his health as they filed out of church. she hastily replied for him unable to stand the huffs and grunts which went by way of speech with him. Otherwise he never showed himself to the village and not many visitors came to the house, so her attitude to him was less frequently one of embarrassment than of irritation and abuse.

To his daughter Sarah he was the memory of a well-dressed and portly man of Victorian speech and habits who had tried to cheer her dismal schooldays by unexpected little treats of muffins and scones at the God Begot House in Winchester, and for whom he always had a tender, if absentminded, smile when he saw her peeping mousily out of the window as he left for his chambers. When he retired and went to live in the house his wife had chosen for this new period of their lives, he retired from Sarah's life as well. On her occasional visits from London, where she was sent to take a secretarial course, she found him growing less and less recognisable. But, far from growing agitated about this, she accepted this transformation as merely a sign of his old age and adjusted quietly to the new stillness or even absence of their relationship. Adit often thought she was too careless of her aged parents and urged her to visit them more often, or at least write to them, but to this she had a ready and very exasperating answer. 'It's months since you've written to your parents and perhaps they would like you to visit them oftener too.' At times he thought she displayed more curiosity about and interest in his family than in her own and it perplexed him. He had begun by wanting to be an exemplary, an affectionate, an attentive son-in-law, but found that this picture of himself simply did not fit in with the pattern Sarah had made of her life in which family counted for so little. It never occurred to him that her marriage to him might be the reason for this severance — or, rather, the silent, barely percerceptible drift away from them towards an island independence.

Watching him shamble about the strawberry bed, tying up his legs with black string, Sarah saw suddenly that what had happened to her father was what happens to a garden bloom, carefully nursed and fed and pruned, when it is left out in the wilderness: it goes to seed, it rambles, its blossoms grow larger and looser, it lies down on the earth or collapses against a tree and can no longer be recognised as the crisp and upright and brightly groomed plant it had once been. Her father, in his country retirement, had gone to seed, had become an unwieldy, half-wild country plant.

'Whatever are you doing, Daddy?' she exclaimed in surprise at the simplicity of this revelation.

At last made aware of them, he slowly unbent himself and veered around to peer at them from beneath the earth-dusted bushes of his brows. He gave no sign of recognising them or of being pleased at their appearance, he simply answered her question. 'Savin' the last berries from the blasted birds,' he said. 'They've took most of 'em anyway but they're not — not...' his breath gave way, and his inspiration, and he stamped the earth to be rid of the knotted string. But Adit noticed how, for all his bullish clumsiness, he never stamped on a plant or berry.

'Strawberries?' Sarah's eyes scanned the bed. She bent down and her hair swooned about her face like a bird's wings. 'Are there any left? Couldn't we have some for dinner?' He gave her a sudden bright smile through the hair and bloated veins and coating of earth on his face, rather like the wink of a bird through its matted feathers, and said, 'All right, take 'em,' and all three of them began plucking berries onto a large leaf and were saved by their labour from the need of conversation. Yet, once the leaf was piled high with a hill of berries and no more richness or ripeness appealed from beneath a leaf or bush, they straightened their backs and, once more growing locked in the awkwardness of relationship brought on by this visit, they forgot the berries and walked back to the house in silence, watched by Mrs Roscommon-James and Dev who stood waiting for them under the cedar, with some impatience.

'Supper's on the table,' shrieked Mrs Roscommon-James when they were a few yards away and, when they came closer, 'You won't mind having the sandwiches left over from tea, will you, Adit? I'm afraid I was so busy with them all afternoon I hadn't time to cook the proper dinner I had *planned* to give you.'

After a ghastly moment of shock, Adit said, 'No, no — sandwiches are perfect, perfect,' and exchanged looks with a Dev whose face seemed to have grown several shades darker in the course of that afternoon.

'Then come along, *dear*,' she barked at her husband, 'wash up now and be quick, do,' and she led him off to the kitchen entrance, imploring him to keep off her carpets and not touch a thing till he had scrubbed his hands. 'And don't you forget your nails this time,' she was heard to say as she preceded him into the house.

"Well,' said Sarah, a bit helplessly, 'we had better go in then,' and found herself preceding her husband and his friend who trailed after her despondently into the dining room where amidst beautiful porcelain and heavy silver and a great bowl of sweet-peas, a supper of watercress and cucumber sandwiches was laid for them.

'I suppose I had better wash,' Dev mumbled as Mrs Roscommon-James strode in, now fully recovered from the shock and shambles of the tea party and, clapping her hands together, ordered them all to sit down, so he did. When the rude scraping of chairs and ripping open of starched napkins was stilled, Mr Roscommon-James came in, with the stoop of a servant unexpectedly called to dine with his mistress, and was told, 'Last again, Tommy.' He looked sheepish and crawled onto his chair awkwardly. Normally he was given his dinner in the kitchen while Mrs Roscommon-James sipped a cup of bouillon in the drawing room to rest herself, she said, from the long day's work.

While they rather sadly munched sandwiches that were already curling up at the edges, revealing greenery that had gone limp some time ago, Mrs Roscommon-James conducted the conversation with bright authority, enquiring after Adit's progress in his travel agency in great detail.

'I simply must come down and see it some day,' she chirped, 'I *did* hope to manage a little holiday, just a tiny one all by myself, in Sicily, or Venice, *this* year, but—' she shrugged.

'Why don't you go, Mummy?' Sarah asked. 'You haven't been anywhere for years.'

'Oh, I should love to, dear, but — well, perhaps if I can find someone to look after your father for a fortnight, I might manage it next year.'

Mr Roscommon-James' jaws worked hard on a cucumber sandwich and the business of keeping the slices of cucumber in between the slices of bread and not letting them fall from his mouth to the table seemed to occupy him wholly.

Then Mrs Roscommon-James turned to her guest and enquired politely after *his* job.

'I haven't any,' he said rather abruptly for he had finished with the sandwiches and was longing for a cigarette. 'Haven't found one yet.'

'Dear me,' she murmured, looking at Sarah in pity. 'But I thought you weren't allowed into our country unless you had a — what d'you call 'em — a work permit or something. Such nonsense of course, but isn't it the rule?'

'No, I didn't have one,' said Dev.

'He came to study, you see,' Adit anxiously explained, not liking to appear either the breaker of British law or the friend of one. 'Economics, wasn't it?'

'Oh, you are a student! Sarah did not tell me. Where are you studying — Oxford or Cambridge?'

'Neither. I'm not studying. I gave up the idea.'

Mrs Roscommon-James again looked across at Sarah who was carefully parting the petals of a sweet-pea she had plucked from the bowl and kept her grey eyes concentrated on them.

'London is the best education of all, you see,' laughed Adit. 'He's discovered it's more educational than any college could be.'

'A dangerous idea that can be,' Mrs Roscommon-James sniffed. 'I would suggest a job, Mr — er. There could be no greater education than that, as we told Sarah when it came to a choice between going to college and taking a secretarial course.'

'Oh, I would very much like a job,' Dev said. 'I have nothing against jobs.'

'I imagine they are bit difficult to find,' Mrs Roscommon-James admitted a bit mollified.

'For Indians, yes. There are many for people with the right complexion, of course, but not for Indians.'

Suddenly Mr Roscommon-James muttered aloud. They all turned to stare at him as he heaved himself out of his chair, growling, 'Left them berries out, I'll go get 'em.'

'What on earth is he talking about?' cried his wife as he shuffled out like a farm dog that feels uncomfortable indoors and makes for the open spaces as soon as his meal is done.

Sarah explained that they had planned to eat strawberries and cream for dessert which Mrs Roscommon-James immediately took as a slight upon the supper she had given them, and, sniffing said it was just like Tommy to pick all those berries and then leave them out. Rising rather haughtily, she said she was going to make coffee and drink it in the drawing room and they could join her when they liked. A little later Mr Roscommon-James returned, empty-handed, and informed them that the blasted birds had got all the berries. Mrs Roscommon-James was heard to give a loud sniff.

In the night, Dev lay on his back, smoking a cigarette and watching the moon fill the pool of the ceiling with its thin polar light in which the long weeds and fronds of garden shadows languorously swayed and danced. The rush of the stream, grown louder now in the stillness of night added to the illusion of being afloat in a water world as a shadow island — light, unanchored, disembodied as the mere shadow of a round wet leaf.

In Sarah's old bedroom, Adit opened a cupboard to hang up his suit and found it filled with the stuffed animals, the Beatrix Potter books and jigsaw puzzles of an English childhood. Enchanted, he squatted on the rug and began looking through them while Sarah glared from the bed.

'I've never seen such enormous puzzles in my life!' he exclaimed. 'Come on, Sally, do one with me — this little cottage with the hollyhocks. Let's do it tomorrow, shall we?'

'Don't be crazy,' she snapped. Despite the totally English tone of her childhood, she cast back no look of English nostalgia upon it. Was this dismissal another result of her unEnglish marriage? It was as though she had chosen to be cast out of her home, her background, and would not be drawn back to it, not even by her husband.

Adit was now cradling a large panda with bright button eyes and one ear missing, its red ribbon faded to pink on its furry neck. 'And did you use to go to bed with this, Sally?'

'Oh throw it away!' she cried, jumping out of bed to snatch it away from him. 'I don't know why Mummy keeps these torn old, broken old, smelly old things.'

'But it is charming of her,' he protested. 'Sally, I love to think of you as a little girl on a rainy day, playing all alone —'

'Adit,' she said, very sharply, 'stop being so *sentimental.*'

He was deeply offended and stamped off to bed. But whereas sleep quickly overcame the offence and had him matching snore for snore with his father-in-law next door, Sarah lay awake, face turned to the window where she could see the branches of the cedar tree lifting and falling and turning in the breeze against a moon-milky sky. She listened to the stream rush and an owl cry and felt herself cut loose from her moorings and begin to drift round and round, heavily and giddily, as though caught in a slow whirlpool of dark, deep water.

In the next room a great brown hill of hairy blanket rose to cover the vast stomach of the sleeping father, like an active mole-hill quaking and jumping with his horrendous snores, snorts, whistles and grunts. Everytime his wife jabbed him in the ribs with an elbow and hissed, 'To-mmy! For heaven's sake, Tommy!' the mole-hill shook mightily as though threatening to erupt, then gradually subsided to its own prehistoric and animal rhythm. She had dreamt she was borne upon the back of a mighty water mammoth that suddenly rose out of its underwater lair to start burrowing and digging through banks of black mud that flew back into her face no matter how she fought it off protesting, and very nearly choked her.

Outside, the moon illuminated the rushing stream to transparency, cast the cedar tree into black shadows of forest nobility, and the owl called, flew farther, and called again.

When Dev came down, swathed in the folds of his brown Bengali shawl, he found Sarah frying eggs for Adit who was sitting at the table, reading the Sunday papers. There was an air of sun-tinted contentment which highlighted the bowl of cherries and sweetened the bird sounds at the window. Sarah and Adit looked up with the mildly astonished expressions of fish in a sunlit aquarium.

'You look like a shepherd in search of his lost flock,' said Adit, and Dev grunted as he sat down to a cup of tea but, inspite of himself, he soon began to enjoy the pleasant quiet, the soft freshness of the house on a Sunday morning with the Roscommon-James away at church. The three ate their breakfast with the delighted relaxation of children left alone by their elders. Sarah piled the dishes in the sink but, instead of washing them, turned to lean out of the window, smoke a cigarette and feel the sun stream over the high stone wall and the crooked fruit trees to warm her back and glisten on her hair. Dev had another cup of tea, another cigarette and was content with the luxuriance of roses, the incessant hum of bees about the honeysuckle and the scent of sap-filled grass and twigs and freshly bloomed flowers.

Adit sat reading the Country Properties page in the *Sunday Times,* licking his lips over every two acres of fine meadowland, munching the insides of his cheeks over every Georgian facade and five hundred-year old wainscoting, wiggling his eyebrows up and down at the parquet floors and dormer windows and promised views of the New Forest, the Sussex downs and the white cliffs of Dover.

Dev and Sarah, turning from the window watched him in silence, like an audience at the silent films watching a scene they were not sure would end in farce or disaster.

'It's his favourite reading,' Sarah said, at last striking a match she had held aloft for the last five minutes.

'Next to *Mother Goose,*' said Dev, drawing out a cigarette from his packet.

Sarah gave an amused snort which disturbed Adit.

'Mother Goose,' he said. 'Don't you run her down, Sarah. *Mother Goose* is the Holy Mother of you Anglo-Saxons, whether you admit it or not, *Mother Goose* is the Anglo-Saxon's milk and water — I beg your pardon, your milk and sugar. Your milk and porridge *and* sugar, all mixed up in a Bopeep pattern bowl. She's meat and drink to every new, young, rising generation of Britons. She's beef and broth, bangers and mash, fish and chips, tripe and onions to them. They grow up on her, they grow strong on her.'

'Remarkable to what extent you've Anglo-Saxonised yourself, Sen.'

'I am a man of parts. Many parts,' said Adit modestly, and then shook the thin sheets of the newspaper in ecstasy as he discovered in them a Victorian parsonage with twenty rooms, a barn and five acres of dank forest.

'I know how you picture yourself in your happiest dreams, Sen. You see yourself as a country squire marching through his woods with his gun and gun dogs at heel, admiring your pheasants and your trout and horses while, in the distance, the walls of your Tudor mansion show through the leaves...'

'Oh *no*, that is much too hearty for him. He sees himself as a city man dapper in his Saville Row suit and bowler hat,' Sarah said with one of those rare outbursts of laughing volubility. 'Lunching at Simpson's on the Strand. Going to the opera with a carnation in his buttonhole. Making people look at him and exclaim, "Oo, look, there goes that successful man of the City, A. Sen, Esq"...'

Adit lowered the papers and broke into her joke roughly. 'Rot! Rubbish! Wrong — both of you; I see myself as an ambassador — an ambassador from India showing the English what a gentleman an Indian can be.'

'Oh ho! Oh ho!' roared Dev. 'An ambassador no less. A retired maharaja turned ambassador, I suppose. Tell me, Sen, if you were really the Indian High Commissioner here, would you acknowledge the fitters and mechanics of Leeds and Manchester as your countrymen?'

'No,' said Adit promptly. 'I wouldn't acknowledge them even at home.'

'There's a true Gandhiite for you,' said Dev, flourishing his cigarette. 'Just the man Gandhi would have chosen as ambassador — a man on whom the poor can depend for uplift, the wronged for justice, the hungry for food...'

'I never called myself a prophet or a saint. I only said I would occupy India House with some style, dining on the richest *murgh mussallam* and *chicken biryani,* serving liquors from Jaipur brewed of pigeons' blood and pearls, and dazzling everyone with my Oriental wit and fluency.'

'Like a Nizam. Well, no one can call you unambitious, Sen. Only a bit lazy. A bit handicapped. A bit retarded.'

'Who's talking?' growled Adit, returning from his too dazzling dream to the slightly more realistic newspapers. 'The worthy professor on his way home to bring the light of a British education to the aborigines of Bihar and Orissa?'

Dev got up from the table, not liking it turned upon him, and joined Sarah at the window where they stood idly smoking their cigarettes together. 'There's something about your house that makes one dream golden dreams, Sarah — too golden.' he said. 'It is unreal. It is so completely peaceful and beautiful and abundant. Life isn't really like that at all. Yet, look at that rose bush — I've never in my life seen so many roses on one bush. And the colour!'

Adit gave him a puzzled look, wondering what could have happened to lift last night's monsoon cloud from Dev's brow and reveal this sunburst.

Sarah said, 'Well it's very different in winter of course. And it means a lot of hard work, living here. Mummy has a lot to do and most of the rooms upstairs are kept shut. Then Daddy works like a slave in the garden.'

'Yes, of course, it could be horrible — all this sweeping and cleaning and weeding and digging. Yet, when one sees the results, it seems worthwhile. It must seem a reward.'

'You'd never do it yourself, *yar*, don't try and fool me,' said Adit. 'You'd let it all go to wrack and ruin in no time. A typical Indian has illusions of grandeur, takes an enormous house and garden, then sits back and applauds while the weeds grow high and the house topples down.'

'But it would be a beautiful life,' mused Dev. still gentle — seeing himself, with an inward eye, as author, painter, philosopher, living in a lonely tower, an old windmill, a Cornish cottage — wasn't it there that those blissful English authors, painters, philosophers were said to live? He could, too — perhaps.

'You two,' said Sarah, going to the sink and turning on the hot water tap full blast. 'I can hardly recognise you. Imagine the English countryside having such strange effects on you two.'

'I never would have imagined it myself,' Dev admitted, picking up a duster to dry the dishes. 'But all night I've been repeating whatever I could remember of Tennyson and Wordsworth and Browning.'

'You don't know any!' Adit shouted, outraged — *he* was the connoisseur of English literature, of English history, not Dev, the sarcastic iconoclast. 'You Bengali, you, you know nothing and feel nothing for England. That's been clear to me ever since you arrived. Now you suddenly put on this long-haired, bird-feeding country poet act. What a fraud.'

Dev realised he had gone too far in self-revelation and was a bit taken aback at Adit's perspicacity. He laughed. 'I was only trying to match illusion with you. But I see I can't keep up with you — you've gone completely over the horizon. How do you manage to keep his feet in his boots and send him off to work on the eight-thirty bus every morning, Sarah?'

Sarah shrugged and drew off the long rubber gloves with which she had been washing up. 'I'll leave you two to find out who knows more Wordsworth,' she said dryly. 'I'm going up for my bath.'

'Leave some hot water for me,' Adit shouted and then got up himself, dazzling in the resplendent new silk dressing gown he had bought especially for this week-end, and stretched and yawned before the open window. 'Let's shut the window, *yar*. These breezes in the treeses are all very well for memsahibs, but I just freezes.'

'Hah!' snorted Dev. 'And you were just telling me you belonged to the class Macaulay wrote about and helped create — "a class of persons Indian in blood and colour, but English in tastes, in opinions, in morals and in intellect." If that were true, you'd run out and do your deep breathing exercises on the lawn. It might lighten your complexion too.'

Adit gave such a dangerous roar that Dev decided to let himself out into the garden. The church bells began to peal and he stood stock-still in the high grass, looking up at the fine Norman spire, shaken inspite of himself by the sweetly insistent tone of the small, gentle bells that were so exactly appropriate to the old grey church and the landscape of meadows and streams and farms, that they seemed to peal from within the earth itself, the notes issuing from the white hearts of the calla lillies by the stream, and from the green grottoes of the cedar tree foliage, as clear and fresh and sweet as the water of the stream, the limpid sky and the hushed, resting Sunday air.

Adit stood leaning his elbows on the windowsill and watching him wander about delicately and not very surefootedly in the tangled grass, and was amused by the sight of his old Calcutta coffee-house friend in these alien surroundings. What urge, what miracle had brought about this meeting of incongruous elements, of discordant natures and backgrounds? Adit knew the answer so well, so personally. It was magic of England — her grace, her peace, her abundance, and the embroidery of her history and traditions — and the susceptibility of the Indian mind to these elements, trained and prepared as it was since its schooldays to receive, to understand and appreciate these very qualities. It was because of the whole heroic and remarkable history of the Elizabethan ships setting sail for the coral strands of an unknown land, because of the less heroic but equally adventurous East Indian Company and the missionaries who bore the Bible and Palgrave's *Golden Treasury* under one arm and a bottle of whiskey under the other, that Dev was padding contentedly about this enclosed garden in Hampshire and Adit, at the window, was smiling at the reconciliation of two cultures hovering in the air like a thrush with a laurel leaf held in its beak.

The thrush he saw was a very real one, although the laurel leaf was not, for just then it flew out of its nest in the pear tree which Dev had unintentionally disturbed and, in a panicked windmill of brown feathers, it flew in at the window, past an astonished Adit's nose, and began to circle the high-ceilinged kitchen in a whir of hysteria.

After a moment of shock, Adit leapt into activity and, snatching a duster off the rail, began to pursue the excited bird, leaping up in the air, then charging round the table, overthrowing a chair in an effort to bring down the bird with the wildly flapping duster.

The door flew open and Mrs Roscommon-James charged in, her face as flushed and her eyes as big as though she expected to find murder being committed in her kitchen. Adit, after shooting her a quick look, jumped up in the air just a second too late and the thrush flew into another corner with a twitter.

'Whatever are you doing, Adit!' Mrs Roscommon-James screamed. 'Whatever are you trying to do?'

'Trying to catch the lark,' he panted, coming to a stop in order to get back his breath. 'Thought I'd have it on toast, for elevenses, ha ha.'

Mrs Roscommon-James put her hands to her temples and slightly lifted the green tulle petals of her hat from her ears in order to hear properly for, surely, there was a mistake. Or, had Sarah's husband gone stark, staring mad just as she had predicted he would the very first time she set eyes on him? 'Lark?' she croaked. 'Toast? What on *earth* are you talking about?'

He waved his duster at the flapping bird, but a sheepish look had begun to seep into his face when he noticed her horror. 'It is a lark, isn't it?' he said a bit uncertainly. 'I've heard they are awfully good on toast.'

'A lark !' she croaked. 'My *dear* man, you must — why, it's a thrush as anyone can see. But even if it were a lark — well, I *must* say!' she glared at him like an injured macaw, through the splendid flowers of her Sunday dress and the green foliage of her Sunday hat. 'I never heard of such a thing in my life,' she snapped. 'Let the poor bird out of the window at once. Eat it on toast indeed — that's the cruellest thing I *ever* heard of.'

Adit opened his mouth as he thought of asking her what she thought she was doing to the chicken that was sizzling in the oven that very minute, being motherly to it perhaps? But another look at the unsabbath like ferocity of her face made him close his mouth, drop the duster and shuffle off for his bath while she clucked and fluttered at the bird till it found its way out of the window.

'I always imagined you people are vegetarian and nonviolent,' she continued over the lemonade under the cedar tree, trying to make her tone playful but continuing to look like a ruffled macaw. 'Well, you are different from anything I had imagined, *must* say. Nonviolent!'

'That's only to our cows and monkeys,' Dev told her. He had watched the whole episode from the garden and decided it was amusing enough to carry him, on its flapping wings, right through this sticky week with the Roscommon-James.

'Now why, why—' Mrs Roscommon-James began to ask, then thought better of it and lay back in her deck chair to gaze tiredly into the canopy of branches above her where the wood pigeons were resting from the sun and cooing themselves into violet-tinted sleep.

They all lay still then. Some had their eyes closed to the honey sun that draped a brilliant sheen across the sky, the earth and garden. Others watched, through half-closed eyes, the tumble of fat, striped bees from one drooping blossom to another, like thirsty drunkards falling from pub to pub. They listened to the pigeons dreaming aloud and breathed in the scents of seething earth growing grass and wild profusion of roses. Dev, sighing, felt these droplets of sound and smell drip, drip, drip into him like drops of golden syrup, filling him with an intense sweetness that ached through his whole body, made it throb and illuminated it with delight so that, supine and half-asleep as he was, he was as brilliantly alive and receptive as an insect on a twig, its antennae trembling with latent adventure.

Only Adit squirmed under the glare of his mother-in-law's eyes and finally said, 'I have an idea. Let's walk down to the local for a beer before lunch.'

'But lunch will be ready in half an hour,' Mrs Roscommon-James protested.

'We'll be back in half an hour.'

'You can't possibly — the nearest pub is a mile and a half away.'

'Perfect! Just the right walk to help me work up an appetite,' he roared, jumping to his feet.

'Who is coming along? Jump.'

Sarah, to her mother's surprise and disapproval, felt compelled to rise, although she sighed a little with unwillingness and said, 'Well, let's hurry then — it's nearly closing time.'

Dev, seeing it was a choice between the Roscommon-James' and the Sens, hurriedly joined his friends although he was perfectly aware that they could neither get to the pub before closing time nor return for lunch timed to be ready and edible at a definite hour, half an hour from now. All three were aware of the glare from Mrs Roscommon-James piercing their backs but, once out of the gate and in the village, they could not repress a sense of release, of adventure, of the buoyancy of freedom. Like schoolchildren playing truant, knowing perfectly well they would be missed, caught and punished, they enjoyed the flavour of freedom with a limited and, therefore, more intense sense of pleasure.

They walked through the village which was nothing more than a tiny village green canopied by an immense single chestnut tree, exactly as in the poem, although it was not a blacksmith who stood beneath it but the sole telephone booth of the village. At one end of the green a bright-eyed cottage postoffice dispensed stamps, boiled sweets and, if ordered in advance, tea at one of the two small tables by the window. At the other end, a thatched cottage, painted over with crimson roses, stood as in a child's picturebook. They walked past the abbey, discreetly screened by the great trees of the park, and a farm-house or two, reeking of cow dung, and clinking with milk pails, their yards full of brown hens and long-necked geese that came scurrying up to the hedge to stare and hiss and cluck at the strangers picking their way through the cow dung pats and puddles of the lane. Then they were out in the fields, walking between the high, thick hedges, now and then pressing themselves into the brambles to let a herd of cows loll past. Adit claimed he had been pressed into a bush of nettles, and Sarah laughed and plucked dog roses and foxgloves and Dev munched a long stalk of sap-filled grass. The lane led them over the river Test and they leaned over the bridge to watch an eel twist and untwist amongst the languid weeds and to cheer a galleon of swans that sailed past, with the speed and ease of racing yachts, to rest in the shade of low dipping willows at the bend. They walked on through meadows woolly with soft, white sheep, to the highway.

Here there was little to pause for, to linger over and enjoy, it was filled with the rush and hurry of holiday cars that approached shrilly and disappeared howling, and at each passage the three had to back down into a ditch or into a barbed wire fence and were rewarded with clouds of dust for their timidity. Once they saw a pheasant dart out of a field of corn, then — frightened by a roaring lorry — dart back into it. They were startled enough but no one remarked on its splendid tail of fire although Adit suddenly began to talk to Sarah about the peacocks in the Indian jungles.

The midday heat rose in a haze from the flatness of wheat and cornfields, the highway seemed long, straight and endless and it was long past the hour when pubs close down for the afternoon. Yet, when Sarah suggested turning back, Adit felt impelled to play stubborn and insisted they struggle on till they came to the closed doors and empty yard of the Bear and Rugged Staff. Defeated, disappointed, they hung around as though expecting the doors to open by some smiling act of mercy, some act of sweet, unaccustomed hospitality to dusty, thirsty strangers who had walked from a land so far away.

Nothing happened and the door remained shut. As they turned to go back, a man with red hair came to wipe and clear the tables under the tree and stared at them with open curiosity.

'Pub's shut?' Adit asked despondently.

'Sure it's shut, it shut an hour back,' the man replied and something like derision twisted his lips as he bent to mop up a tabletop — or so Dev thought, and he swore as they turned into the highway to plod back to the house where Mrs Roscommon-James stood with a face of blighted wood, over a roast that was overdone. potatoes overboiled, a salad gone limp and a husband fallen asleep from hunger and boredom.

'That's the whole damn snag,' Dev said from the depths of his deck chair after lunch. 'You rush out shouting, "Look, this is what Milton wrote about! Look here's Tennyson's poem in real life! Isn't it fine? Isn't it splendid?" and out comes a man with red hair flings his duster in your face and says, "It's not for you, buster. You ain't on time." Out you get.' Phoo!' he snorted and kicked at a chair leg violently. He could have continued his tirade, giving more vivid examples perhaps more real and justified ones, but his tongue was held by Sarah's presence. She lay back with her eyes shut, her face turned to the shade of the tree, but he knew she was as tense as he was, as wrought to quivering disappointment and indignation. It would have been cruel to continue then.

'But we weren't on time,' said Adit, lazily, agreeably. 'You must admit that is the trouble with Orientals — we don't really believe in watches and clocks. We are romantics. We want time to fit in with our moods. It should be drinking time when we feel like a drink, and sleeping time when we feel like sleeping. How is the Englishman to understand that? He's been a clock watcher since the day he was born. Do you know, English mothers even feed their babies and put them to bed according to the *clock?* So you can imagine how sloppy and foolish we must have seemed to that pub keeper, Dev, turning up after closing time and still expecting drinks.'

'Yes, thanks to you,' snarled Dev. 'But it happens all the time, everywhere. Everything tells you you're an outsider and not entitled to the country just because you happen to have read and enjoyed its literature, or because you belong to something called the Commonwealth. You can't see into the fields for all the hedges of nettles and brambles. You can't fish in the trout stream without a license. You can't shoot a pheasant without one. Dammit, you can't walk down a country lane without a goose staring at you and hissing "Hey, you stranger, what do you think you're doing in my lane"?'

Sarah lifted her hands off the arms of her chair and said, mildly, as though to herself, 'Oh, that is true for English people as well, Dev. The English feel restrained and deprived and discontented too. Few of us can enjoy the many things there are to be enjoyed.'

'*O England's green and grisly land,*' intoned Adit, '*The babu loves you — even when no one else can.*'

'It's not the same at all,' Dev snapped. 'You people are entitled to your own land and eventually Socialism will divide it up into neat green lots for all of you — or, perhaps, just brick and concrete ones. But I'm not asking for so much I'm only asking to be allowed to enjoy and admire without being kicked in the pants and told, "Wog, keep off the grass." '

'Like hell,' said Adit. 'You want nothing more than that, eh? Except of course, a job, a house, a car and plenty of sterling in your pocket.'

Dev was so incensed, he climbed out of his chair and Sarah opened her eyes to him standing over Adit with a look all the more fierce for being wildly confused.

She immediately rose, her English practicality quickly deciding upon an English solution, and said, 'Come on, it's time for tea. I wonder Mummy hasn't called us in yet. We have to start for Winchester in another hour if we are to catch the five o'clock train.' After exchanging ferocious looks, the men followed her into the kitchen where she was setting out the teacups, trying to rattle them as gently as possible so as not to disturb her parents upstairs, but they could not let the argument drop, and did not think to lower their voices.

'Bootlicking today!' Dev was soon shouting. 'If the British were still in India, you would be one of those *babus* who used to go crawling after them, drooling if they noticed you so far as to give you a kick. You'd be quite content to be thrown the leftover. "O thank you, sir, how kind of you. A bone for me — really? May I really sleep here, on the floor? O thank you, kind sir." But I wouldn't be content with that, I'll take no man's leavings.'

Adit showed himself to be outraged but he was really hurt to the quick. 'Leavings?' he said blinking 'I don't call my home or my job another man's leavings. In my office I am equal to the palest Englishman there, and I'll top them all yet, no one can stop me. I don't call my share of London *leavings.*'

'Oh, you're talking about your telly, are you?'

'Yes, I *am* talking about my telly. And the Covent Garden Opera and the pub down the road. I'm talking about my desk in the office and about picnics in Hyde Park. I have every right to enjoy them — because of my education, my tastes, my interest in them. No Englishman can deny them to me.'

'Oh no ?'

'No. If they do you, then it's because it's easy to see you don't care for such things, you want them only in order to throw them to the ground. I'm different. I love them. I love England. I admire England. I can appreciate her history and her poetry as much as any Englishman. I feel a thrill about Nelson's battles, about Waterloo, about Churchill —'

'Churchill!' screamed Dev, leaping half across the room in frenzy. 'Don't you mention Churchill to me or I'll vomit. I'll spit. That — that —'

'Shh,' hissed Sarah, looking up at the ceiling frightenedly. The name of Churchill was sacred in her parents' house. To denigrate him would be as to denigrate St Paul. And, after all, Dev was to spend another six days here. 'My mother,' she tried to explain remembering how Mrs Roscommon-James had dabbed at her eyes before the television screen while watching Churchill's funeral, and thinking of the little record in the cabinet on which could be heard Churchill's famous speeches which her parents liked to listen to ,on especially Christmas Eve.

'How dare you even speak of Churchill?' Dev interrupted her. 'Have you forgotten how he treated Gandhi? Gandhi — he was probably another incarnation of Jesus Christ — and Churchill sneered at his clothes, called him a "naked fakir." Why, Sarah, he — he's the man that ordered the miners of Tonypandy to be shot. He had no heart. He was no human. He was a statue — a statue made of tobacco. If anyone tells me I should admire Churchill, I'll just, I'll —'

'Yes, I know, Dev, but my mother thinks Churchill —'

'Churchill?' enquired Mrs Roscommon-James brightly, opening the door just then. 'Talking about Churchill?' She looked even brighter, not wanting anyone to think she had been asleep in the middle of the day. 'He was a naughty chap, he was — I remember the Christmas he stole a turkey from Farmer Coombe's yard.'

They all stared at her, openmouthed, the noise and confusion of their argument cut short as though the needle had been lifted off the crackling gramophone record. Then Sarah threw herself into a kitchen chair, dipped her head into her lap and laughter began to ring from her as from a bell gone hysterical.

At last raising a red face, she hiccuped, 'Mummy means the dog. We had a dog called Churchill once !' and she hung her head and shook with laughter again.

Her mother, still dulled by sleep and pricked by a vague feeling that she was being made fun of, clucked at what she considered Sarah's vulgar display of risibility and went about pouring the tea while Adit and Dev stood at opposite ends of the table, gaping at each other and at Sarah. Adit pulled himself together first and laughed, a bit weakly, as though he did not quite understand the joke but was willing to have explained another piece of odd British humour. But Dev shook his head and muttered, 'Crazy! A dog named Churchill — crazy!'

'Oh, he was, he was,' Mrs Roscommon-James agreed. 'I'll show you some snaps of him romping with Sarah — when I get back from dropping these two children at Winchester. Come on, Sarah dear, do stop giggling and hurry up with your tea.'

For the Sens, the weekend ended in a mottled grey fadeout of regret and apprehension as they drove off to Winchester beneath the thunderous unrolling of a summer storm, but for Dev the adventure had only begun. He considered it an adventure, not of discovery, but of recognition, and, however much Mrs Roscommon-James hampered and restricted him he believed he succeeded in having it.

Mrs Roscommon-James thought he should visit the abbey — it was a famous one — but he would not. She asked him — rather self-sacrificingly, she thought — to accompany her to tea at Lady Bendsworth's — or Boxworth's or Bandbox's — but he refused. She tried to make him call on the Vicar, to go to Winchester to see King Arthur's Round Table hung upon the Town Hall wall like a dartboard — but he wouldn't. She gave him peas to shell and sent him to buy postage stamps — neither of which he could refuse to do, but he did them in such heavy silence that she did not repeat such requests.

It was not that he was not interested in this country household and the lives of these self-styled squires — merely that he preferred to watch them through a protective pane of glass, with curiosity but not involvement. He even regarded it as an anachronistic Utopia and could not suppress his astonishment when she told him that, in autumn she would put a sign on the apple tree on the gate, saying 'Help yourself' because there were more apples than she knew what to do with, and that very few people did help themselves. He was amazed to see her leave the money for the bread and milk in the letterbox: it could not be done in India, but he did not tell her this. On Wednesday morning he was obliged to help her put the rubbish out for the van to collect and although he did not consider it pleasant to have to pile up and carry rubbish down the drive, he marvelled, inspite of himself, at the courtesy with which Mrs Roscommon-James did it up in neat paper bundles and the thoughtfulness with which she weighed down with stones the stacks of old papers to keep them from flying all over the green countryside.

More uncertain now that he was on his own, he dashed out of the room whenever Glynis, the charwoman, entered it, but could not help being interested in her. She was the first servant he had met in England and he looked in vain for some sign of servitude in her plain but staunchly held figure, her fresh cheeks and mild cornflower eyes. He could not help but notice and admire the perfect, unplanned and instinctive organisation with which she moved through the house with vacuum-cleaner, bucket and broom, leaving order and freshness in her wake. She treated the house not as if it were an unfamiliar, capricious and unpredictable mess to be dealt with in an attitude compounded of perplexity and resentment, as Indian servants will the house and possessions of their employers, but as though she pleased herself in swiping the dust off a tabletop or beating up a lumpy cushion. When she had done with them, she would give them the briefest pat, as to a satisfactory pupil's head, before moving on to the next object requiring her attention. She was as shy of Dev as he of her — he could imagine how she described him to the village — but once she brought her towheaded son with her and Dev could not resist handing him a bit of money. His mother, folding her boiled arms about her, said, 'Say "thank you" to the gentleman and run along to the shop for a lolly then.' Dev, forgetting himself in seeing the amazement on the child's face, took the opportunity to speak to Glynis at last.

'D'you live in the village?' he asked, carefully not looking at her.

'Down at the farm, a mile off,' she nodded, still looking down at her son.

'D'you go to Romsey or Winchester ever?'

'No, I've never bin,' she said, and then in a rush, while her face grew rapidly pinker, she told him, 'But I bin all the way to London once, to see the Queen. I was invited, you see. I was the only one from our village club to go.'

'No!' exclaimed Dev.

She blushed poppy-red but could not stop the happy tumble of her words. 'Yes, I saw the Queen and the whole Royal family, I did, and shook hands with Princess Alexandra. A real beauty she is and all. And wore my blue dress and had a blue bag to match and nylon stockings and all...' Then she gulped, put an arm round her son's neck, slightly tottering against him in the intoxication of memory, and hurried away — not a moment too soon as Mrs Roscommon-James, hearing their voices, had hurried up to investigate with a very suspicious look on her face. After that Glynis avoided Dev and he did not hear her say another word, but what she had said had given him more to think about than she could have believed.

But he preferred to make his discoveries and have his adventures alone and unaided and took to slipping out of the house before breakfast, climbing out of the window at the sound of Mrs Roscommon-James' approach, dodging Mrs Roscommon-James in the garden and spending the whole day out in the open. He was determined to seek, discover and win the England of his dreams and reading, the England he had quickly seen was the most poetic, the most innocent and enduring of Englands, in a secret campaign. At the end, he believed he did.

It was on his last afternoon in the village. Mrs Roscommon-James had gone to tea with a friend in Chandler's Ford. Mr Roscommon-James seemed to have gone underground like a mole shy of the sun, and Dev let himself out of the garden with some biscuits in his pocket, jubilant at the freedom and privacy he had won for himself in this free and private land. He took the lane down to the river. It took him past the churchyard where, amongst hillocks of grass and a riot of butter-centred daisies, the old cracked gravestones were bright with lichen. He passed cottages on fire with the most scandalous roses, where children with straw hair and clown faces sucked toffees under swinging washing lines and patches of tomatoes and plum trees, where men in shirtsleeves chopped wood and hoed, then down through fields of ripe, bending wheat and hay that showed aspects now of gold and now of lead to the ruffling breeze.

Tame and confined as the little country lane was, there were always glimpses to be had, from beneath a bird cherry tree, from over a paddock, not only of the rolling fields but of bits of the New Forest cradling in dips of the green downs, aquatically deep and still, hill-tops with blank white cliffs, of an expanse of lustrous sky in which clouds grazed lazily, of streams, and rivers crisscrossing in a cat's cradle of mercury, and these sudden visions, to be had at every turn of the lane made him feel buoyant and aflame with adventure, as though a gas balloon held him suspended a few feet over the earth, allowing him a bird's eye view of an idyllic land...

He climbed over a stile into a meadow of waist-high grasses of purple and loosestrife, of thistles and daisies, and at the bottom of it lay the river Test, as slow and placid as a wandering cow. Here he sat down, on the bank, and felt the sun gently knead his back. Sunlit weeds bent to the gentle current, trout and minnows darted in and out of the shelter of weeds — but calmly, unfrightenedly, all of life a musical dream to them. Across the river cows grazed somnolently. One of them looked up, noticed him and ambled up to the river's edge to stare across it at him. He sat still, scarcely breathing. The other cows noticed too and followed, and soon the entire herd was lined up along the bank, gazing at him with huge, wondering eyes, as children at a zoo will stare at a chimpanzee. For a worried moment he wondered if they would take it into their heads to cross the shallow river in order to get near him, perhaps taste him with their long, rough tongues, and prod him, exploringly, with their short horns. They looked intelligent enough to think of crossing by the footbridge, one by one. But no, they looked away at last and fell to grazing again. He breathed more easily and wondered if they would have treated every intruder to this deep scrutiny, or did they see in him, his dark skin and black eyes, something alien and exotic? For the first time in England, a thought of this order did not upset him as unjust or foolish — he saw it as fitting into the pattern of nature.

By keeping very still, he was rewarded with the sight of the little water moles playing in the river, swimming sleekly from one island of waterweeds to another, then diving into those little holes they build in the banks, safely hidden amongst the rushes. A moorhen sailed serenely by, not noticing him at all, followed by her chirruping brood. Trout flickered through an underwater chessboard of sunlight and shadow. The serenity, the plentitude of the scene so soothed, so lulled him that he was sure, if he lay back upon this bed of buttercups and rushes, he should fall fast asleep, stupefied with joy.

So he scrambled to his feet and walked along the river, crossing it by log footbridges, wading through banks of meadowsweet, bending low under the willows that washed their green hair in the stream perpetually till he came upon a grove of old and crooked pine trees. Here shadows brooded; coolness slept. Suddenly a large piece of the mud bank crashed loudly into the river. A brightbeaked moorhen flew shrieking away and he walked on, crossing and recrossing the river everywhere a log bridge invited him to do so, till he came to the sweet-scented, bee-filled field again and waded through it back to the stile, the lane, with the evening sun burning into his eyes, as ripe and russet as harvest itself. This, he thought, swaying from side to side as drunkenly as a bumblebee, this was the England her poets had celebrated so well that he, a foreigner, found every little wildflower, every mood and aspect of it eerily familiar. It was something he was visiting for the first time in his life, yet he had known it all along — in his reading, in his daydreams — and now he found his dreams had been an exact, a detailed, a brilliant and mirrorlike reflection of reality. English literature! English poetry! he wanted to shout and, instead raised his arms to the sky, clasped them in pagan worship, in schoolboy excitement.

Walking homewards, he found the gate of the churchyard swinging open and, taking this as another poetic invitation, he walked in and strolled amidst the gravestones, most of them so old and worn and covered with lichen that the engravings were no longer discernible. Grass and daisies grew in hummocks about them, cypresses dipped low over them. There was a profusion of violets, halfconcealed, waiting to be found. There was about this scene of death and decay a quietness and simplicity that implied, as softly as the evening light, that death and the end of time are not cruel, not hasty, not invincible, but merely the bringing to perfection of a pattern which is surely something to be striven for and accepted. It was a curiously Hindu atmosphere that spread this calm philosophy about the gravestones. Dev longed to say this out loud to someone, and thinking of Mrs. Roscoromon-James' or the Vicar's reaction to such blasphemy, he nearly laughed, then pushed open the door and entered the church.

The little church struck him at once as being far more beautiful and more moving than the great cathedrals of St. Paul's and Westminster Abbey. It had originally been Norman and then rebuilt in 1898, but the original stone arches and some of the wooden beams remained. He wondered if the stained glass did not also belong to a much earlier period. It had none of that livid and prosaic gaudiness that had made him look away in disappointment from the more famous stained glass of more famous chapels, but was delicate as an etching, exquisite, with the fine details and the tender expressions on the saintly faces of great Italian painting. Some of the windows had been repaned with plain glass, retaining only a few cracked panels of old stained glass faded to a lemon hue in which the lines had grown more fine and more distinct with the years.

He walked carefully so as not to make a sound or raise a mote of dust. The rounded pillars felt soft to his hand as do the stones in Hindu temples that have been touched by so many devout foreheads. The stone tiles were curved beneath his feet as are those of temples on which Hindu worshippers kneel and walk incessantly. The altar was decked with a few virginal calla lillies, as pure and simple in form as the curve of time. About it all was an air of piety and devotion — qualities that here assumed their natural simplicity and muteness. He had not sensed an iota of it in the great, busy, tourist-ridden cathedrals of London, those edifices to the might of the British empire with all its pomp and glory reflected, immemorialised in them, dazzling and impressive. Those had only to do with empire, temporal power and the drama and meanness of history, very little with Christianity and its essential austerity. These he found existmg here, in this old small and silent village church.

He was touched by it as by few things in this adventure, as a cynic, an unbeliever, an atheist will be washed off his feet by an unexpected wave of sentimentality, and he left the church on tiptoe, wishing he had a stick of incense to burn, a handful of jasmine or marigold to offer, Hindu fashion, to the grace of Christianity. But, probably, it was more fitting, he comforted himself, to enter silently and to leave alone silently.

As he shut the churchyard gate behind him, he saw that a farmer, leaning over a fence on fire with nasturtiums, had been watching him. He gave him a veiled look, on edge and defensive again. But the farmer only said, 'Had a nice walk then ?' and he, mumbling a 'Thank you,' an absurdly English 'Lovely evening, isn't it?' hurried away to the Roscommon-James' house next door. There he saw the car parked in the garage, and, seeing that his hostess was back from her tea party, slipped in through a window to his bedroom and sat there on the bed, smoking a cigarette with his eyes shut, going through every step of the paradisiacal walk in his mind, again and again, richly in detail, as though to imprint it all on his mind as one memorises a poem one knows one will want to recite to oneself later, again and again.

Part III

Departure

6

For the Sens, it had not been an unusual weekend. Most that they had spent with Sarah's parents in Hampshire were marred by tactlessness, by inane misunderstandings, by loud underlining of the basic disharmony of the situation. Normally Adit caught the train back to London with a singing sense of relief, a huge relief at having got it over with. Settling down to the evening papers, he would begin to gloss it over, to see it as having been silly, amusing, enjoyable, so that by the time he got back to London and started cooking his first solid meal in two days, he was able to laugh, sing and assure Sarah that it had all been wonderful. While she waited for him to get dinner ready, rapidly gulping down a glass or two of sherry before the television set, even Sarah began to feel her taut nerves uncoil and relax till she was no longer aware of them.

This weekend was different. It had been such a strain on both of them that Sarah's face was white and pinched as she waved goodbye to her receding mother from the window, and Adit sat back wordlessly, the evening papers folded on his knee. He said nothing to Sarah. He stared out of the window at the drops of rain that were now breaking upon the pane and the clouds that were hanging low over the fields like sodden smoke. He felt drained of the brightness of life, as though blood had ceased to flow inside him. He wondered, a little fearfully, if he had ever felt so depressed before. Normally, at the first hint of depression, he would settle down comfortably and arrange to have a coddled time of it, relishing

Sarah's concern, relishing his self-pity, relishing the drama of it all till there was nothing left to relish — and then it would be over. But now he felt depression pouring into him like lead, hot when it entered in the form of Mrs. Roscommon-James' sniffs and barks and Dev's angry sarcasm, then quickly cooled to a dull, solid mass inside him, weighing him down till he felt like a great lump of cold, grey metal. Sarah, glancing at him saw his face almost unrecognisably glum, even sullen as he sat staring at the rain, with black rings of lifelessness forming beneath his eyes. The weekend was over, yet he felt none of the usual relief, the forgiving pleasure. He only reviewed it and saw it as hateful, ugly, irredeemable.

Why had this happened? Mrs Roscommon-James had scolded him before, had shot maddening looks of pity at Sarah before. His arguments with Dev had been nothing new either, mere repetitions of things they had often said before, out of a sense of duty rather than antagonism. He could not tell himself. 'My mother-in-law hates and despises me. Dev makes fun of the life I lead and the ideals I profess. Therefore I am angry. I am hurt.' It was nothing so precise and definable. This was not the sole or even the main reason for his mood. This mood had begun to enter him, circulate within him and alter him during the drive out of London, through the Hampshire fields, had accompanied him through the dismal dinner and the night when Sarah had shut him out, with a bang and a snap, from her childhood of one-eared pandas and large jigsaw puzzles. The hysteria of the noisy tea party and the chase of the thrush had only temporarily obscured the true mood of the weekend. Adit had always been one to make the most of his moods, dramatise and enlarge them till they collapsed of their own weight — but moods of anxiety and abstract pain were new to him. Faced with one he was unable to deal with it — he merely stood still and felt his leaden feet sink in as though in quicksands.

Staring out at the dripping countryside and the dull evening, he felt again the sorrow and the sense of injustice that had made him briefly eloquent, even elegiac, on the drive out. Basically an urbanite, a lover of the steamy smells of the crowded bus and the warmth of an evening pub, he had not reacted with the ecstasy so strangely aroused in the more guarded Dev. The abundance and the beauty growing so green about him had filled him only with a curious anger and sorrow. It was as though some black magician had placed an evil pair of spectacles on his eyes which led him to see, not what was before him, but what the black magician wished him to see, distorted and terrifying.

As he had told his friends, in short sentences born of his panic at this strange and confusing state of his eyes, in a mild voice that hardly betrayed the tightness inside him, what he saw around him was not the sweet, sap-filled land of Hampshire at all, but the landscape of India, that vast moonscape of dust, rock and barren earth, broken only by a huddle of mud huts here, a dead tree there, a tree that raised its arms helplessly, dead before it had ever borne bud or flower, leaf or fruit. It was not the huge, sleek cows and picture-book pigs and turkeys that Adit saw in the country lanes and farmyards, but hordes of soundless Indian cattle, all ribcage and meditative eyes and spatterings of dung. The friendly hens, the fiery pheasant gave him no poetic thrill; he saw, instead, the vultures of India, those great, heavyboned birds with their reptilian necks rising out of rhinoceros shoulders and bloodcaked feathers, perched on thorn-bushes around the corpse of a buffalo that had collapsed of starvation, or a pariah dog run over in the street, or a pile of ashes in a riverbank crematorium.

When he had leaned over the bridge and gazed down at the river Test and laughed at the downy cygnets following their regal parent under the silver-leaved willows, the insane spectacles on his eyes had actually shown him the rivers of India — the shameful little Jumna, so unworthy of its mythical glory; the mud and slush of the Ganges with its temples and yogis, its jackals and alligators lining the banks; the murderous Mahanadi, each year going berserk like an elephant, trampling those who sought to pacify it in riverside temples with marigolds and oil lamps; the uncivilised, mosquitoridden Brahmaputra swirling through the jungles; the five silver fingers of Punjab's rivers raking the scorched earth...He saw them shrivelled, each summer, despairing gutters of mud stranded in vast beds of sand about which women with empty pots and cattle with lolling tongues stood in silence. He saw them as they were after the monsoon each year, breaking their banks, frenziedly swamping fields in which crops had stood hopefully, villages in which men and cattle quietly drowned together.

The long, lingering twilight of the English summer trembling over the garden had seemed to him like an invalid stricken with anaemia, had aroused in him a sudden clamour, like a child's tantrum, to see again an Indian sunset, its wild conflagaration, rose and orange, flamingo pink and lemon, scattering into a million sparks in the night sky.

When he lay in Sarah's bed that night, it was not the large, unhurried owl's cry that he heard, but the raving of peacocks and jackals that make the Indian night loud with reminders of the emptiness, the melancholy of everything.

Walking in that summer luxuriance of southern England, when all the hedges were wreathed with wild flowers, all cottages painted with roses, and church bells pealed the tunes of peace and plenty, rivers were full of trout and fields of grain, he had walked, seeing a landscape as different as a negative is from a photograph. He had had a dream that night, unconfessed to Sarah who was not interested in dreams, of taking photographs with a camera handed to him by an invisible hand, one of those that within seconds, produce the printed photograph. Ripping out one after the other, he was stunned to find no technicoloured print as promised to him by the silent voice, but negatives in ghostly black and white.

'Adit.'

'What is it?' he asked, turning to her slowly. 'Waterloo,' she said, and they were drawing up at the platform already and the blank lights of the station filled its halls with the brightness that hospital corridors and tube stations have. It seemed to dazzle and blind Adit, and Sarah had to find their luggage, their tickets, the exit, a taxi.

Normally they climbed with mounting relief the stairs of the Clapham house from the layer Dev had named Black to the one he had named Black-and-White, slamming the green door behind them as if to enclose themselves with the walls of warmth and familiarity and sighing as at the moment when a large, formal party is over and a smaller, gayer one begins. But Adit stood in the hall, blinking, not recognising his cat or his home, exactly like a stranger arrived at an hotel in a strange city.

'Adit!' Sarah cried, touching his elbow. 'Come on, put the rice on. Let's have an Indian meal tonight.'

'Yes,' said Adit. 'You cook it.' He went into the living room then and found himself a bottle of whiskey and a glass. Pouring out half a glass, he sat down and drank it in gulps, then waited to see what effect it would have on the cold, colourless metal that filled his limbs. It made the metal heavier. He could scarcely move his legs or raise his head. The room was cold but he could do nothing about it. He sat there drinking and listening to Sarah trying to be quiet in the kitchen.

There was no glass of sherry or time for relaxation for Sarah. She chopped and stirred, sprinkled and bustled, and, when dinner was ready, called him. He got up but first went to the record-player to put on a record, then came to the table. As they sat down, Bismillah Khan's *shehnai* began its long-drawn lament, the melancholy notes sweeping low on the floor in writhing coils of dark blue and purple. Sarah was careful not to clatter her fork on the plate. 'Shall I fetch the mango *chutney*?' she asked once.

'Not for me,' he snapped. 'Sweet mango *chutney* is for Anglo-Indian colonels and their memsahibs. Don't go offering it to an Indian.'

She raised her eyebrows and, another time, would have pointed out that he had finished the last bottle in three days, but then she saw how he ate, shovelling in his food angrily, without appetite and without satisfaction, concentrating intently on the uncoiling wails of the *shehnai* and she knew the time had not come to help him.

He went to bed. After heavily finishing the cleaning, she followed. Entering, she saw him lying with his arms stretched over his head, staring at the black ceiling with a look of disbelief that invalids have when their disease is still new, their pain still unaccustomed, their rage at misfortune just beginning to burn. She quickly picked up her nightclothes and went to change in the bathroom, returning to slip into bed very unwillingly. She lay stiffly, shivering slightly in her cotton nightgown, not knowing what words to say. Then Adit returned to her and, reaching out his arms, drew her to him and clung to her till he hurt her. But he would not say a word and she was not to know that he was seeing, even in the outspread hair about her shoulders, that Indian landscape. His embrace signified only that the first shock of the memory of its starkness and poverty was beginning to end and he was beginning to see its wild, wide grandeur, its supreme grandeur, its loneliness and black, glittering enchantment.

There was no opera in the bath next morning, no shouts of 'Hey Sally, send me to work on an egg!' Nor the next. Adit, instead of heaving himself out of his confused despair, sank consistently deeper into it. Sarah was at first alarmed by the silence of the house that had so rung and clanged with his noisiness. It was as though a holiday had come to an end. Then, shrugging, she went about her work and took on some of his chores as well, her lips tighter and thinner as she grew consistently more silent and more intensely reserved.

When Adit left the house for work, he stepped out with a look of astonishment on his face. He simply could not recognise this workaday, weary London as his once golden Mecca. He took to tramping it after office hours in a kind of morbid search. He gazed at Big Ben's face looming through the first autumnal mists, and at the chipped and dented surface of the sunlit Thames beneath Tower Bridge. He crawled up Threadneedle Street and sat sagging on the steps of the Albert Memorial. He visited all his favourite places and could recognise none of them. Then he went into all the pubs he had ever known, one by one, and in each was hunted out by the black sensation of not belonging. It was as though, in the one summer night that he had been away, London had been blitzed and he returned to find the grey ash of a nuclear war fallen from the skies already frosted with winter's breath, and the whole city shrouded with it. The footsteps on the pavement sounded different — there was no gay briskness, no determined bustle in them, but a furtive hurriedness, the sound of a shameful escape. Voices, laughter ringing out in the glittering white caves of the tube stations had a sinister ring to them, profane and conspiratorial, like the laughter and voices of enemies and schemers.

In the tube, one day, he was brought up short so suddenly that a pair of lovers behind him bumped into him violently. Without apologising, as he would once have so effusively, he stood staring, not at one of the posters he so delighted in but at a piece of *Nigger, go home* graffiti on the walls that had previously merely skidded off the surface of his eyeballs without actually penetrating. Now he screwed up his eyes and studied it as though it were a very pertinent signboard. Then he nodded to himself and walked on. The shuffle of his feet, the hunch of his shoulders and the sideways look of his eyes out of an enclosed, darkened face exactly resembled the looks and posture of those Indians whom Adit had so despised — the eternal immigrants who can never accept their new home and continue to walk the streets like strangers in enemy territory, frozen, listless, but dutifully trying to be busy, unobtrusive and, however superficially, to belong. Adit had always put down their diffidence and their failure to lack of preparation by education and a lack of the necessary instinct that enables one man through its possession, to be an international citizen and another, through lack of it, not to be one. But now his own education, his 'feel' for British history and poetry, fell away from him like a coat that has been secretly undermined by moths so that its sinews and tendons are gone and, upon being touched, crumbles quietly to dust upon the wearer's shoulders. Unclothed, Adit began to shiver in the cold and fear the approaching winter.

In the office, his colleagues found him so forgetful, so slipshod that they accused him of a descent into middle age. The lighthearted Girl Friday of the office who brewed his tea, asked him why he did not take a holiday.

'How can I?' he snapped. 'I'm saving up for my next visit home — do you know how much that costs?' he asked so savagely that she overturned the sugar bowl in surprise.

He snapped at Sarah as well when she tried to please him by getting mustard oil for his fish or an aubergine to fry. 'Fakes!' he shouted and she was helpless.

The truth was that when Sarah proudly laid the gleaming aubergine on the table before him, he saw — with that bewildering distortion of eyesight that seemed to have become a chronic affliction — a Bengali feast prepared by his mother. He saw it and smelt it with an intensity that made his eyes glaze and his nostrils quiver — that *hilsa* fish baked inside green banana leaves, that hill of rice flavoured with saffron and sprinkled with nuts and raisins, that clay pot full of *paish*[1] made with date palm jaggery cooked in the creamiest milk till it was thick and soft and bubbling... Then he became aware of the aubergine smiling a shining smile at him and 'Fake!' he snapped at it.

Similarly, when his Girl Friday, nonchalantly tossing her fringe out of her eyes, suggested a holiday on the Costa Brava, he was led to recall the thunder of an Indian railway station, the redshirted coolies hobbling under monstrous bedding-rolls and tiffin-carriers, the barrows steaming with hot fried snacks, the unbearable excitement of a small boy, released from school, going to Puri or to Darjeeling for a summer. Puri, where the ocean and the sky met in a landscape so elemental and primitive, unpeopled except for fishermen plunging into the waves in nutshell-frail boats, that Brighton and Blackpool seemed a mockery to Adit who had stood in the surf of Puri, listening to the wild roar of silence. Darjeeling, where a spume of snow was always flying off the peak of a towering Kanchenjunga and Tibetan women in striped aprons and warmly folded *bakkus* sold pieces of amber and turquoise on the streets. 'I'm saving for my next visit home!' he shouted with such fierceness as to spill sugar in crackling atoms of astonishment across his desk.

The ferocity of his growing nostalgia broke that stone dam that had silenced him for so long and he began to tell Sarah of this nostalgia that had become an illness, an ache. She listened intently gravely, hoping to find a way that would make her husband's

---

[10]Rice pudding.

background, not a black magic spell, a burdensome incongruity, but a portion, a large portion of their lives. It was very difficult because what he told her she found barely comprehensible. His torrential, often incoherent words constructed for her a vision of a deep veranda with round white pillars — 'Roman pillars?' She murmured, and he replied, 'Colonial, I should think' — and a tangle of flowering shrubs and creepers at its edge — 'All night-flowering? All white?' she asked in wonder — in which her mother-in-law, an almost speechless woman in a white sari bordered with vermilion— 'Always? But why?' — wandered, plucking offerings for the altar at which she spent most of her day — 'An altar? In a private house? In the *kitchen?*' asked Sarah. He talked of the buffaloes in the yard, of the pigeons that were kept on the rooftop, of the *Puja* season in Calcutta when prayers were conducted in the house every evening and visits were made from one private or community altar to the other, everyone dressed in the newest of clothes and fed on the richest of sweets, of the great-uncle who lived the life of a recluse, emerging only to crawl about the compound, from anthill to anthill, scattering flour drawn from a bag at his waist — 'Feeding *ants?*' cried Sarah. 'An act of piety,' Adit solemnly explained — of flying kites on the terraces, of the jars of aromatic pickles pickling in the sun from which the schoolboy Adit had stolen; of the evening sounds of his sisters learning to play the harmonium and the *veena*...No shadow intruded upon this multicoloured and headily perfumed world Adit created for his wife, no memory of tiles or dung-heaps, of beggars at the gate or servants kept at work till midnight, of a widowed aunt gone mad with rage at her seclusion, her boredom, and Sarah, seeing in a haze what he wished her to see, shook her head sorrowfully, thinking it would be impossible to fit such splendour into this dismal Clapham flat, this routine of catching buses into the city that had no attraction left for Adit.

She began to see now what heaved and whirled inside Adit during the long evenings when he sat silent and unoccupied. She wondered how he had kept this amount of yearning shut up and enclosed inside him for so long, releasing it now like a dam that releases its water when it is full to bursting. Adit himself could not have explained. All he knew was that it had happened on the weekend in the country. It was the beauty and contentment he had seen there that had proved too much for a mind, a stomach born to emptier, starker, less tamed and cultivated fare, and he could no longer take another insipid swallow of it. It was not the occasional slights and insults directed against him as a stranger, a non-belonger, that had finally proved too much for him, but the placidity, the munificence and the ease of England.

September was a month of anniversaries and celebrations, giving Adit ample opportunity to compare, with bitterness, the rarity, thinness and drabness of such events in England with the abandon and colour of festivals in India. He longed with pain to see the fireworks and oil-lamps of a Diwali night again, to join in a Holi romp of flying coloured water and powder and leaping to the music of drums. Instead, he trudged tiredly up three flights of stairs to Bella's and Samar's flat on Ebury Street to celebrate Bella's birthday.

He had spent many evenings in these rooms of theirs, cooked vast Bengali meals on their gas-ring, sung Tagore's songs sitting cross-legged on their rug. He had always enjoyed Bella's sprightliness and good humour which was like a marigold blooming in a city windowbox, and he secretly admired Samar whom he had heard spoken highly of as a doctor in a busy hospital, and who, he saw, had managed to create for himself that small, curtained, flannel-lined world that an exile must build about himself if he is to survive the northern clime. Although he knew Sarah had as little in common with Bella as she had with Jasbir's wife, Mala, he had always insisted she take an active part in this friendship which dated back to his own bachelor days and Sarah, not unwillingly, came with him, helped grind the spices for the curry and listened with, perhaps, a strained smile to their singing.

But this evening, the Ebury Street room, the tawdry attempt at an East-West decor, the eternal lamb curry and rice and the somewhat too glib jocularities of Bella and Samar, especially polished and displayed for the occasion, all combined to depress him hugely. As it was considered a 'party', Bella had already prepared the dinner and she was not a very good cook, so Samar and Adit ate glumly, then sat with an unaccustomed stiffness while Bella turned the pages of their photograph album for Sarah to see. Then she showed them the bathroom which she and Samar had recently re-tiled and prepared themselves.

'Why don't you show them the coffee table too?' Samar asked, standing in the doorway with his arms against the doorposts, while the others stood in the bathroom, noting the neatness with which the blue and the yellow tiles fitted together.

Bella looked as though she had suddenly come to the boil. 'I won't,' she snapped with a childish pout. 'I'm not going to take it out of the cupboard unless you promise to throw it away.'

'My wife!' Samar exclaimed with that anniversary coyness that made Adit curl his toes inside his shoes. 'I bring her a slab of marble for a coffee tabletop as a birthday gift — in addition to the bought and paid-for one, of course — and she asks me to throw it down the stairs.'

'Don't you like marble, Bella ?'

'I do — but not *stolen* marble,' hissed Bella, clicking her small teeth angrily together so that she looked like an angry vixen as she marched them back to the living room. 'I'm not going to have *stolen* goods in my house, I told Samar that, and I'm telling him again.'

'Come on, Bella, you're being a spoilsport,' Adit came to the support of his friend who had not expected quite such a vehement reaction from Bella, tactless at a party, and looked like a monkey who had been handed a cigarette stub instead of a peanut. 'I didn't know about this new talent of yours, Samar — tell us.'

'Well, I'd been seeing these pieces of marble every day on my way to the hospital, piled up in a small garden outside an old house that is being pulled down and rebuilt. They hadn't been touched by the workmen in weeks — I'm sure they were surplus. So the other night I drove down in Jasbir's car, picked up this little piece, put it in the car and drove back. No one saw me — I swear, Bella. I think she's scared of having the police up here.'

Bella was dancing on her small high heels with rage. 'What if anyone had seen you? What if you had been caught picking up someone else's marble? What would you have *done?* You can laugh about it to me, but what if anyone had *seen* you? What would you have said?'

'It was worth trying, Bella,' Samar protested.

'It wasn't, it wasn't! Just think, if you were caught and put in jail and written up about in the dailies. Why, that's what criminals do, and those crazy boys, and if they'd caught an *Indian* doing it, they would have gone on and on about immigrants in London, and how would you have *felt*, getting a bad name for your *people?*' Now that she had come to the crux of the matter, so long bottled up out of a wifely tact, she could barely restrain herself and her mouth and her chin quivered and her feet wobbled on those angry heels.

Samar and Adit, acutely embarrassed, lolled against their cushions and laughed.

This made Bella angrier and she appealed to Sarah. 'Sarah, what would *you* have said? If Adit had gone and brought you something he'd stolen, what would you have done?'

Sarah looked wildly at Adit for help, but he was laughing so loudly he held onto his ribs and his mouth was twisted as though he were at a dentist's.

Bella stamped her foot and shouted. 'It's all very well to laugh, but you're Indians, you're *foreigners,* you've got to be that careful, you do, and what's a joke to you would have looked like a dirty Asian's cheek to the bobbies, and how would you feel then? And what about how *I'd* feel then? Just think about that, too.'

Adit suddenly snapped his jaws together and sat up silenced. His amusement had been faked and now it was over. It had bored him. He simply could not take another minute of it — the falsehood, the fakery, the unnatural strain of it all. He simply wanted to take Sarah by the arm and get out, get away from Bella and her shrill rage at the complication of her once happily ordinary life, from Samar and his offended-monkey look. He wanted to get away from the album of wedding photographs, the empty brown ale bottles lying under the Indian brass table, the clutter of greeting cards and ivory elephants on the mantelpiece, the odours of greasy leavings in the tiny kitchen.

'Oh God,' he groaned, holding his head in his hands. 'Why does everything have to come to this — that we're Indians and you're English and we're living in your country and therefore we've all got to behave in a special way, different from normal people?'

'Well, that's the way it is, and it's best to look things in the eye and speak out, I always say,' Bella began, but more uncertainly — partly because she was alarmed at seeing Adit look so grim for the first time since she had known him, and partly because her natural good humour was beginning to overtake this unusual spurt of anger. 'Don't you think so, Sarah?' she asked.

Sarah got up with the languid movements of one utterly fatigued and began to pull on her gloves. She said nothing.

'Don't you get fed up too, Samar?' Adit asked his friend, also attempting a lighter tone, but unsuccessfully. 'Sometimes it stifles me — this business of always hanging together with people like ourselves, all wearing the label *Indian Immigrant,* never daring to try and make contact outside this circle. This business of burrowing about those grisly sidestreets, looking for Indian shops and Indian restaurants. All our jokes about Indians in England, all our talk about our own situation — never about anyone or anything else. It's so *stifling* — all the time, all the damned time — being aware of who one is and where one is. God, I am fed up!'

Tableau. Two third floor rooms on Ebury Street at night, smelling of the leftovers of an Indian meal. Two Indians, two Englishwomen, frozen in the stances of players on a stage who have not been told what to do next. Somewhere, in a locked closet, a slab of marble like a blank gravestone awaiting an engraving, a grave and a bunch of dead flowers.

To everyone's immense relief — since no one seemed to know what to do, exactly as if they had forgotten their lines in a confused and unfinished play they were being made to act — the prompter arrived in the large form of Jasbir who had been held up at the hospital by an emergency, and Mala dressed flamboyantly for the occasion in her best Kanchipuram sari.

'Hullo, hullo *ji,*' Jasbir roared shaking off his overcoat. 'Got any food left for me? Do I smell lamb curry and rice, Bella?'

Dev returned.

Sarah, looking up from the kitchen table where she was preparing the lamb curry for dinner, exclaimed, 'Oh, you look quite changed too!'

'Too ? Who else does ?' Dev asked, and walked into the drawing room where he saw exactly what Sarah meant: Adit sat collapsed in a chair, a drink in his hand, staring at a television set that he had not switched on, his eyes dead in his immobile head. 'What's the matter?' he cried. 'You look like an old, old man regretting his miserable past. What's the matter, *yar?*'

'It's not only the old who have regrets,' Adit retorted heavily, stung to alertness by Dev's very appearance.

'So what have you gone and done, *yar?* Have you murdered your landlady? Are you under sentence of death?'

Adit growled inside his throat, but said nothing. Dev, ebullient at being amongst friends again after a week's solitude began to sing.

'The north wind doth blow
And we shall have snow...'

making Adit snarl so dangerously that Dev was obliged to return to the kitchen for conversation. But Sarah was a notably poor conversationalist and Dev did not stay with the Sens much longer. A week later he got a job as salesman in Foyle's bookshop. When telling others about it, he was inclined to stress the word 'bookshop' and mumble, or even leave out, the word 'salesman.' A week after that he found himself a room in a kind of youth hostel in Battersea where, he said, he would stay till he could afford something better. In the meantime he was not unduly depressed by the window that would not open, the rarity hot baths or the din of youths, mostly African and Commonwealth scholarship students who were living their lives at the top of their voices in rooms separated from his by the thinnest of planks. He was working at last. He was earning money, a little, and one Sunday morning he went to Portobello Road and squandered a week's salary on a pair of glass salt-cellars, one of them badly chipped, for the pleasure of having them handed to him by a girl called Rose whose long hair was folded about her face like the wings of a white bird and whose somewhat protruding eyes studied him calmly and curiously, making him rock from side to side as he walked unsteadily away. Then he had to go to the Sens' for dinner for the rest of the week and try not to let Adit's dreariness and Sarah's silence obscure his rising sun.

A gold-edged invitation on thick paper arrived, inviting the Sens to Christine Langford's wedding. She was marrying a designer of men's clothes who arrived at his wedding in a disappointingly conservative morning coat and white carnation in his lapel. The church was all roses and carnations, the bride all organdy and lace, the breakfast all champagne. The Sens knew no one else at the party. Sarah's expression was not unlike that of a country waif come up to town to see the Christmas lights and Adit, watching her hawk-like, was torn between pity for her deprivation of a similar picturebook wedding, of fear that she might be filled with self-pity for the same reason, and a rage that it could possibly be so.

'So much for that bitch,' said Adit, taking her home. 'She's got what she deserves — a spottyfaced, ginger-haired clothes-hanger, as dumb as they come.'

'Oh Adit, you haven't even had two words with him.'

'Did one need to? Couldn't one see it all in his grin and Christine's smirk? But I suppose you thought it was all charming, touching, heart-wringing.'

'I did,' said Sarah simply. 'I've never been to a Hindu wedding so I don't know how to compare, but I do know that a Christian wedding is touching and charming and — heart-wringing.'

Adit groaned.

He began to hear music, Indian music. Struck with fear for his health, for his mental balance, he stood frozen on the pavement, his head sunk into the collar of his overcoat but his eyes glancing sideways and upwards, travelling the length of the street and the height of the walls for help. He shook his head and walked on a few steps, but he could still hear the exquisite tinkling of a sitar exploring a brooding mood, questioningly and tenderly. Its faint and so exquisitely foreign sounds pierced the damp, dull haze of a September evening, curled about Adit's ears and filtered into him sweetly.

Giving his head another shake, he darted sideways into a chemist's shop he had suddenly spied. Here he bought vitamins and combinations of vitamins in something of a frenzy, in a bid to recover his lost robustness, his formerly rock-solid mental and emotional balance. He had a dreadful vision of himself in the white shift and shuffling slippers of a lunatic's garb at an asylum, an outsider not only by virtue of his colour but by an imagination run amuck.

Hurrying out of the shop, away from the suspicious scrutiny of the salesman, he nearly bumped into a long-haired beatnik in a tattered black sweater who had run down a flight of stairs into the street, carrying a sitar in his arms. He apologised politely to Adit and Adit stood staring as he disappeared down the road.

He sent a party of lady schoolteachers from Birmingham to Venice for a holiday and forgot to make their return bookings which they were then unable to get for the required date. Indignant telegrams arrived at the office. The Manager pressed his lips together and advised Adit to 'go easy, boy, go easy.'

He spent half of a wet Sunday in the Indian miniatures section of the Victoria and Albert Museum, lingering over those minute, wispy figures robed in gold-embroidered gowns who sported on rose-bordered lawns beside fountains, on balconies, amidst peacocks and parrots, sipping wine, strumming lutes or fondling lovers, while others sat upright on horses, brandishing swords, riding through densely strewn battlefields. He strayed amongst them, distracted, the fantasy of the picture world mingling with that of his memory to whirl him about dizzily, till the Museum shut and enclosed itself in the clandestine secrecy of a Sunday night.

He stood in the middle of Oxford Street, watching the traffic that kept him trapped on an island. Bus, taxi, car swept by — bus, taxi, car, with a monotony, a predictability that made him burn with longing to see one bullock-cart wander into the fray, only to make an alteration in the single, swift tempo of the London traffic. A slowly meandering, creaking bullock-cart, he prayed, or a monkey *wallah* with his frocked and capped monkeys jingling the bells on their delicate ankles, or a marriage procession preceded by a brass band, decked in marigolds and tinsel — anything, he prayed, anything different in colour, tempo, sound, flavour; anything individual and eccentric, unruly and unplanned, anything Indian at all.

Entering a store, he felt he could not bear to see one more pale, expressionless British face. If one more were to approach him, he would hit it, hit it. He put his shaking hands inside his pockets and left furtively.

Once a year, on their wedding anniversary, the Sens splurged on a dinner at an expensive and, therefore, glamorous restaurant. There would be much discussion on the choice of locale, but this year there was none. Adit did not even mention the occasion till Sarah, standing before an open cupboard and wondering what to wear, declared, 'I can't choose a dress till you tell me where we are going.'

'There's only one place to go,' Adit said shortly. 'Veeraswamy's.'

This was the usual place for Indians in London to choose for any major celebration, but formerly Adit had roved happily amidst a more liberal choice of eating places. Now he did not even ask for Sarah's suggestion and, after deliberating a bit she silently took down a blue wool dress from its hanger, when Adit marched across to her cupboard and said belligerently. 'No, wear a sari tonight.'

'Oh Adit, not tonight. It's raining. I'll ruin the hem.'

'Why should you? Don't Indian women wear saris in the rain?' and he chose for her a sari that his sisters had once sent her, and refused to listen to her protests or recognise the embarrassment in her tone. He stood by, seeing to it that she draped it as correctly as possible. 'And the gold necklace,' he added, referring to a heavy chain of golden mangoes sent by his mother as a wedding present. It was the one his mother used to wear during the festive Puja season.

'But now I feel like a Christmas tree.' Sarah murmured bowing her head awkwardly while he fastened the clasp.

He snapped the clasp shut and flared up in anger. 'You feel like a Christmas tree! I suppose all Indian women look like Christmas trees to you or perhaps like clowns, because they wear saris and jewellery. You — you — English people and your xenophobia! You'll never accept anything but your own drab, dingy standards and your own dull, boring ways. Anything else looks clownish to you, laughable—'

'I didn't say that — any of that,' Sarah interrupted, her pallor altered to a flush. 'I never thought that. You imagine these things yourself and try and put them in my mouth.'

'Oh yes, it was I who said you look like a Christmas tree, wasn't it? It was I who laughed because for once you are dressed the way a woman should dress, with a bit of glamour and romance, instead of that bloody mackintosh you wear day in and day out...'

It could have gone on all evening and kept them indoors, wrangling, while the rain washed all brightness, all life out of the London sky, but they were halted, interrupted and turned onto another course by a ring of the door bell and Dev's entrance. He staggered a bit at seeing Sarah in her green and gold flamboyance, stammered awkwardly and tried to get away. But Sarah and Adit both grasped him by the arms fiercely, both insisted he stay with them and 'join the party.' A third man's neutral presence was exactly what they needed that night if there was to be a cease fire in which the annual celebration could be carried out, if not in reality, then at least in imitation.

It took Dev three whiskies at the bar before he could begin to play his role with the proper diplomatic elan of a UN officer, but by then he had forgotten the scene he had come upon in their flat, even forgotten the occasion they were here to honour, and begun to enjoy himself as he invariably did when given a new scene to explore, mock and vanquish. Adit kept up with him, peg for peg, and at the end of the third was looking at Sarah and the way the green silk about her shoulders made her hair more pale and fine, and the way the chain of gold mangoes — with which he had toyed as a child on his mother's hip — brought out the lustre of the white skin of her neck. She glanced up, saw him looking and smiling, and began to smile a little herself.

'Do you know what this place reminds me of?' Dev asked, gazing around in fascination.

'A maharaja's palace,' Sarah said promptly.

'Not at all. It has the atmosphere one finds in district clubs and gymkhanas in India — the ones that are very deep in the provinces and years behind the times, so that there is still something of the British Raj left about them. They still have those faded grey and yellow prints of fox hunts and polo games on their walls, and in the lounges you meet ancient relics of the Empire, turning the leaves of English papers like *Town and Country* and *Blackwoods*, while they drink tea and eat very thin bread and butter served by bearded old servants who've been trained by the British sahibs, and shuffle about on their bare feet, not discreetly, but very ostentatiously, all obeisance and respect.'

Adit smacked the golden tabletop and laughed. 'You see that kind of thing *here?*' he asked, flinging his hand at the people thronging the bar, waiting for a table to fall vacant in the vast, glittering hall.

'Well, of course, there *is* a difference. In those district clubs in India, it is only a ghost of the Raj that one sees lingering on, all dusty and cobwebbed and sad. Here you have the real thing — the very essence of the Raj, of the role of the *sahib log* — in its fullest bloom.'

Sarah, listening to a rather drunken Dev's flamboyant words, looked about her again and thought she saw what he meant. Through his eyes, she saw that essence, that living bloom in these halls — brilliant, exotic, gold-dusted, rose-tinted. Here were the tiger skins and the gold leaf elephants, the chandeliers and rainbow-coloured Jaipur furniture, the crimson carpets and the starched turbans of another age, another world — all a bit outsize, more brilliant than they had been in real life, in India, for here there was no clammy tropical heat, no insidious dust, no insecurity, no shadow of history to shake or darken or wilt them. Here was only that essence, that rose bloom, transported to a climate that touched more gently on human dreams; here it could flower and shed its perfume in the safety of a mirror-lined, carpet laid hallucination. Even the grace and good manners of the Indian servants were a little more theatrical than they would have been in India. Everyone seemed to be playing a part in a technicoloured film about the East — even I, thought Sarah, fingering the gold chain at her neck.

When they were called to a free table to dine, they found it loaded with large portions that were also survivals of another era. Dev raised his eyebrows at the little bowls full of outlandish condiments — pineapple chunks and sour gherkins with which no meal in India would have been served. He tasted the food and declared, '*Now* I know what this is. It is not Indian at all, Sarah, but it *is* authentically Anglo-Indian.'

'Really? But I love it,' she said.

'Of course. It is the kind of food English people in India used to love. Look at that old baldie by the window, shovelling in rice and *vindaloo* as though it were his last supper. He must be a retired colonel, coming here to revive memories of better days in Poona.'

'And those three Indian men there. They look like Madrasis, come on some kind of Commonwealth delegation, who've been fed by kind British hosts on Irish stew for the last ten days. They're eating enough to last them the next ten days.'

'And that Sikh buck in a purple turban — a student, do you think? Or an apprentice motor mechanic? He's showing his *au pair* girlfriend how he really keeps his fingers clean even if he eats with them.'

'And what about that young couple there with a baker's dozen of children? Where could they have picked them all up, and why?'

'They must be prospective VSOs or Oxfammers, practising charity the pleasant way before the going gets rough.'

'But who could those two old ladies in cotton frocks and cardigans be? They're blowing their noses and wiping their eyes, but they keep shovelling down those chillies all the same.'

'Perhaps they are English missionaries home on furlough from the wilds of Bihar. Oh yes, definitely — look at those white cotton stockings and court shoes. They're bound to have their *sola topees* tucked away somewhere.'

They laughed, they ate, they dipped their fingers in scented water and ordered mangoes and litchees and Bengali *rossogollas*. They stared unashamedly, played their guessing game in a kind of half-mocking reverie which might have been the distorted reflection of the kind of reverie enjoyed by the English in another land, another time. Infected by the overdone atmosphere, everyone at every table seemed to have relaxed and to be eating more slowly and talking more loudly than they would have elsewhere — so catching is the laze and leisure of the East. Adit was almost prostrate by the end of the evening by a combination of the rich food, the lazy pace and highly coloured emphasis of it all.

The next morning Adit got out of bed, seized the papers and read the news that India and Pakistan were at war. He was still standing barefoot with the papers in his hand when Sarah raced out of the kitchen, crying 'Oh Adit, I've already made your toast and you're still —' and then stopped short and gave a quick look at the headlines. A minute later Emma Moffit flew in, in her dressing gown and curlers, crying 'Oh Adit. I've come to say how shocked — how sorry — how—'

Then both women stopped and stared concernedly at Adit who was still staring at the same lines in the papers. He was not looking at them, he was looking at a memory he had, put far back in the darkest portion of his mind, never before revived or spoken of — a memory of Calcutta in 1947 when Muslims and Hindus who had learnt through the reign of the Moghuls, to regard each other as one people, now learnt at the end of the British reign to slaughter each other, burn each other's houses, rape each other's wives and toss the children aside like broken twigs. He remembered going up to the terrace at night with his father and seeing the sky livid with innumerable fires all over the city. He remembered the steady, surreptitious pacing of the men of the family who patrolled the compound by night. He remembered his mother placing his shoes by his bed at night, in case they had to rise and flee. He also remembered, he heard it again, a certain scream — a deserted alley, a sudden pandemonium at the end of it, footsteps running, and the scream. That scream. He clutched the papers and shook them, hearing again that scream, seeing the scene repeated. It was happening again — in India. Not riot, but war. War in India. What was going on?

'Aré baba,' he said, using a phrase from his childhood that Sarah had never heard him use before. He said it in an old man's voice, tremulous and baffled. *'Aré baba.'*

'Sit down, Adit, sit down,' Sarah urged and Emma bubbled 'Of course there isn't a *thing* to worry about. The Indian army — Oliver used to say — is the finest little army in the world. Don't you be alarmed, Adit, it will be over in a few days, I'm sure of it — Oliver always said — and then, it is in the desert, and the armaments will soon run out, so the papers say, and the Pakistanis, after all — oh, I read *such* an interesting book the other day...'

'Sit *down,'* Sarah urged.

But there was no time to sit down. Rousing himself from the confusion that for a few moments had made this news reported in the papers seem a nightmare repetition of what he himself had lived through as a child in Calcutta, he found he was no longer interested in sitting, in sulking and brooding. The time for that was over and action was now to begin. A furred sensation and a bitter tang in his mouth, he found himself moving, hurrying at last, with impatience and passion.

The days that followed were ruled by the black lines of print in the newspapers, by the crisp words of the BBC commentators. Maps of India and Pakistan were acquired and marked. Indian newspapers were sought and scrutinised. Time began to move at a new, busy speed, the hours marching from one news commentary to the other with military footsteps.

Indian troops crossed the ceasefire line in Tithwal. The Pakistan army blew up the Mirpur bridge. The Indian army captured the Haji Pir Pass. The Pakistan army bombed Amritsar. Pakistan — India — Pakistan — India — now they captured Dograi, on the Ichhogil Canal, now they lost it. Pakistan — India — Pakistan — India — now they advanced, now they retreated at Khem Karan. Indian aeroplanes were shot down, Pakistani Patton tanks were destroyed. There was fighting in Uri and Poonch, in Hudiara and Burki, in Philora and Chawinda, in Sargodha and in Sind. One newspaper reported a victory for Pakistan, the next paper reported a victory for India. One paper reported so many Pakistani soldiers killed, so many Patton tanks destroyed, another paper gave an altogether different set of figures. The facts seemed to vary with the policies of the papers. The news on the radio varied too, from one station to another.

The crowds that gathered in India House each day jostled each other in utter confusion.

'The bloody BBC!' one highly-wrought student screamed. 'Always partisan, always prejudiced. These British — they always sided with the Muslims — now it's out in the open, you can see it quite clearly.'

'Here's the *Hindustan Times,* just come !'

'Here, let me read it out.'

A roar went up. 'Ninety-seven Patton tanks destroyed!' they cried in exultation. 'Boo to America! Boo to Britain! Boo to the Big Powers.'

'Our *jawans*[2],' exulted another voice, 'God, what I'd give to be with them now, on the banks of the Ichhogil Canal, lobbing bombs right into Lahore!'

This was in the milling centre of the crowd. On the fringe stood the quieter ones, musing. 'In '47 they shot my father before my eyes. I saw my mother and sisters dragged away. I spent three months searching for them before I found them, in a refugee camp.' A man, leaning against the wall softly said to no one, 'I saw them kill my wife and son.' Beside him a small man said, 'I saw a train filled with the dead cross the border for us to bury them.'

'The *Times of India!*' went up an excited shout and the crowd jostled harder. Adit jostled too and Jasbir, Samar, all their friends. They lived in an excitement all the more intense for their being so far from the scene, not knowing the exact truth of the reports, allowing their imagination and their emotions the fullest play. They made plans. One was giving up his job and flying home to fight. Another was waiting for conscription orders to be passed. A third felt that at the moment the best he could do was collect funds here in England. They collected funds. They sent cheques and parcels. They waited feverishly for mail, for news.

Out in the streets, in buses and tubes, they ran into the placid figures of the British, their silence, their composure, and a madness stirred inside them, making them long to scream, 'Do you know what's happening? Do you know there's a war on? Do you know what Pakistan is doing to India? Don't you care?' Choking they stood in ferocious silence, but there were some occasions when the pressure proved too enormous, someone's temper went berserk, a voice shrieked accusations, and there was bewilderment and white frozen cold all around.

---

[2] Soldiers

One evening, just before the declaration of ceasefire, Adit telephoned Sarah at the school and asked her to meet him in the City.

Standing at the Head's desk, she clutched the phone agitatedly, saying, 'Yes, yes, all right,' and then returned to her room and sat there with her hands to her temples. She had a headache, it made her feel sick, she had no idea how she would drag herself after school to Victoria Street where he had asked her to meet him. She wanted only to lie down and close her eyes. But there was no going against Adit in any matter whatsoever these days. She could not tell what effect the smallest refusal or contradiction might have on him — he might start beating his chest and complaining of being misunderstood, he might start screaming accusations at her, he might shut himself up and weep... anything was possible in his highly-strung and dramatic condition. She dreaded such a reaction. Rather she would sacrifice anything, anything at all, in order to maintain, however superficially, a semblance of order and discipline in her house, in her relationship with him. His whole personality seemed to her to have cracked apart into an unbearable number of disjointed pieces, rattling together noisily and disharmoniously. If she allowed this chaos to reflect upon their marriage, she knew its fragments would not remain jangling together but would scatter, drift and crumble. So, she had clutched the mouthpiece of the Head's telephone and mumbled, 'Yes, yes, all right' and swallowed a few aspirins to still her headache. The nausea remained.

'How did it go?' she asked him, referring to an art exhibition to which all the Indian painters in London had contributed and at which the pictures had been auctioned off in aid of India's defence.

'Very well,' he said but so glumly that she saw he was no longer in his former mood of near hysteria, but had passed on to another phase. It was not a noisy one — there was some relief in that — but it was depressing.

She waited till he had found them an empty table in a tea shop. They lurched past full booths and tables to it, sat down and Sarah untied the scarf about her head. Then she asked him how much money they had made.

He drew down the corners of his mouth and made a disgusted motion with his hands. 'What does it matter?' he said. 'We're only fooling ourselves. By the time we've collected a few hundred pounds here, a few hundred pounds there, put them together and presented them to Shastri-*ji,* the war will be over. Look at the way things are going. The Anglo-American embargo on shipment of arms has been clamped down. Both armies are running out of arms. It'll all dwindle and finish soon and then drag on — the kind of skirmishes and sabotage that have always been going on.'

Sarah bent to study the menu in order to keep from saying that, that was surely the best that could happen at present.

'And here we are, organising little *art* exhibitions, for God's sake, little *jumble* sales, selling bottles of Indian *pickles* and pretending that will make India a great power and finish off Pakistan. I tell you, I'm not going to play auntie anymore. This is just a farce. Think what people at home are going through...'

Sarah sipped her tea, strong and bitter, and listened to him talk himself into his former manner of garrulous threats, complaints and prophesies. But there was now a hollowness in the centre of it, a tiredness born of days of too much intensity and excitement. Like the armaments of the Indian and Pakistani armies, his romantic involvement seemed to be dwindling.

When they came out on the street he was silent and gripped her by the arm as if for support. His weight on her made her totter and grit her teeth, she felt she would crumple. She bore it upto the bus stop before she broke away under pretext of having to open her handbag. She gazed down into it, wondering if she would faint before the bus arrived.

'What's the matter ? You're dropping all your papers,' he said sharply and did not bend to help her collect them.

On the bus they sat shoulder to shoulder, Sarah staring out of the window at the light that spliced and blurred the darkness, he gazing at the knots of his fingers bunched on his knees.

When they opened the door to their flat, he exploded. 'I can't stand it, Sarah. I tell you, I've had enough. It's all got to end now. There must be a change. A — a big change. I've got to do it. You — you understand? Now don't stop me, don't say anything, I've made up my mind—'

She looked at him in astonishment. She had never heard him stammer before. His very accent had changed. His vowels had become short and sharp, his consonants long and hissing, as they had been when he had first arrived from India. She saw his mouth quivering loosely as he stood by her, gripping his hands together stammering.

'Don't — don't just stare, dammit,' he shouted. 'Say it. Say what you want to say. Say I'm not sticking to my promise. Say I'm mad, I'm a fool. But I'm not — not going to listen. I've made up my mind, I tell you, I've got to — got to—'

'But what, Adit, what ?' she asked, frightened. 'What are you telling me? What promise?'

He flung himself into a kitchen chair and stared at her where she stood, clutching her cat.

'It's all over,' he blurted.

When he said that, an idea passed through her mind, a brilliant one that exploded in her mind like some fiery bloom in a desert, its fragments darting across brightly before they fell.

She let go the cat and hugged herself instead and began slowly pacing up and down, considering this idea. It had nothing to do with Adit, with the war in India, with his plans and decisions, his promises or desertions. It had only to do with her — her body, its coldness, fear and nausea. She held it with a kind of tenderness, protecting it from Adit's panicky assault. It was the assault that had suddenly made her aware of the secret inside her. Carefully, she folded her arms about her to guard it from whatever was coming to attack it.

'What do you mean ?' she asked at last. 'Adit?'

'It's over,' he said, 'over.'

'You mean — I ? Our marriage?'

Startled, he was knocked out of his paralysing concern with himself, and explained to her, 'No — England! England. I've done with England now. Sarah, I'm going back.'

'To India ?'

'To India — home.'

She held herself tightly, with frozen fingers, casting her eyes downwards, regarding her secret. Then he meant to leave, to abandon her and her secret?

But he said, 'Come, Sarah, come, we must go.'

In her relief she let go her hold on herself and sank down against the edge of the table, heavily, and dipped her head low so that her hair, escaping from its tortoiseshell clasp, swooped about her face and hid it.

He could not see if she was crying. He grasped her knee and shook it. 'You will come, Sarah? You see why I must go? I'm not being crazy. I'm not thinking of going off to fight for my country, nothing like that. The war will be over any minute, and I'm no soldier. It's nothing like that. But I must be in India. I don't know if Pakistan will ever attack India again, or if the Chinese will invade. I can't promise you anything. Only it's all so changed now, I can't live here any more. Our lives here — they've been so unreal, don't you feel it ? Little India in London. All our records and lamb curries and sing-songs, it's all so unreal. It has no reality at all, we just pretend all the time. I'm twentyseven now. I've got to go home and start living a real life. I don't know what real life there will mean. I can't tell you if it won't be war, Islam, Communism, famine, anarchy or what. Whatever it is it will be Indian, it will be my natural condition, my true circumstance. I must go and face all that now. It's been wonderful here. Sarah, you know I've loved England more than you, I've often felt myself half-English, but it was only a pretence, Sally. Now it has to be the real thing. I must go. You will come ?'

She was crying, he saw now, for convulsions shook her shoulders and, behind her hair, he saw her face as red and contorted as a child's.

He shook her knee again, impatient for her answer. 'You won't, Sarah?'

'Oh I will,' she cried, 'of course I will. I must. Adit, I think I am going to have a baby.'

He abruptly let go her knee, threw himself back in his chair and shut his eyes. She stopped crying and brushed the hair out of her face to see the advent of the notion of fatherhood on his face. But he kept his eyes so tightly shut, for so long, that she had to look away, turning cold, thinking — he does not want it, and beginning to feel the wave of anger lap at her.

But then he reached out for her hand and his eyes were open, on fire. 'He will be born in India, Sarah,' he said, 'My son will be born in India.'

Sarah, her hand clasped in his, felt a sudden, huge revulsion against the theatricality of the scene, of their words, the way emotions were dragging her this way and that, as though she were their victim. She turned away abruptly, blew her nose, then went to the stove and put the kettle on. 'Let's have a cup of tea,' she said.

7

'Yes, Miss Morris, thank you, Miss Morris,' Sarah said again and again, holding herself together with difficulty while the backs of her knees perspired and her face seemed to be melting into pieces of wet paper. She was freezing, she was perspiring. Only the repetition of the words 'Yes' and 'Thank you' and 'Certainly, Miss Morris' seemed to make her feet move, one follow the other down the matted passage to her office under the stairs. She half-crawled, half-swam towards it and then threw herself into her chair and laid her face against its green leatherback. It was cool and authoritative as a doctor's rubber-fingered touch. Revived, she straightened herself and groped in her bag for a pill which she swallowed down with the remains of the cold tea in her cup. 'Yes, Miss Morris, thank you, Miss Morris,' she whispered, nodding, and stared at the registers lying open on her desk trying to study them, to submit the confusion inside her to the severe red lines and neat rows of figures, to the discipline of thought they demanded. But the confusion remained even after she had stopped perspiring and shivering and mumbling 'Thank you' and 'Yes' and 'Certainly, Miss Morris.'

The fact was that too much demanded her attention at the same time, too many unwieldy shapes rose and heaved about her. Formerly the problem had been the emptiness of her life. She had jettisoned most things out of it when she had married — childhood, family, friends: all the normal ordinary things with which an ordinary person of no talent must fill and adorn his life. With an Anglo-Saxon composure and serenity, she had put them away from her, meaning to fill her life anew, with what her husband brought her. He seemed so rich to her, he seemed to have so much to give her so many relations and attachments, pictures and stories, legends, promises and warnings. More than willing to accept them, she had been worried to find that there were really not enough of them: they were too light in substance, too thin in texture, too pale in colour. That was why she herself lacked substance and skittered about Clapham Common like a pony on uncertain legs, startled by each gnat and mayfly. That was why each blue-rimmed cup in the kitchen, each letter slipped under the door assumed such vast proportions: she herself inflated them, making of them screens with which to surround and protect herself.

Now suddenly her life was being filled, willy-nilly, with more than she could manage. Everyone about her had decided, suddenly, to dump their surplus onto her. It was becoming an avalanche.

There was the baby. There was the voyage. The uprooting. And all at a time when she felt capable of doing no more than quietly sitting down and quietly cradling her child inside the fluids that rocked and heaved inside her body.

Sitting in her office, she had been trying to soothe this rocking-horse child, lull it to stillness, and to adjust to Adit's decision, still unaccustomed. She was trying to fit herself and her baby into the pattern Adit had now arbitrarily laid before her — when the Head called her in and, smiling like a mother cat watching her brood devour a mouse she had brought them, told Sarah that she, Miss Edwina Morris, was being transferred to a bigger, better, more expensive and up-to-date school in Kensington. She, Miss Edwina Morris, had been asked to take it on and reorganise it. And she had chosen Sarah, of all her staff in this decrepit, rain-and-ink smudged old Clapham school, to follow her, to accompany her to her new charge, and there head the office staff. What an opportunity, she miaowed, opening her claws, preparing to receive the grateful licks and bows of her most docile and therefore best rewarded kitten.

Sarah knew she disappointed gravely by not rising to the occasion, crying out her thanks by falling upon the Head's bony neck and mewing her thanks. All she did was bob her head, blow her nose and mutter, 'I'll think it over. You see, I must — I must think it over before I can let you know — but thank you, Miss Morris, thank you.'

Now she sat holding her head in her hands, waiting for the pill to exercise its steadying influence on her and trying to keep from splitting into three splinters — one pursuing Adit on his voyage to the East, one holding back to cradle and comfort the uneasy, unborn child, and the third tackling the exigencies of a career that had surprisingly revealed a future.

She was still in that huddled position when Miss Pimm flew in, screaming, 'Oh dear, Sarah, you haven't put the kettle on. Ooh dear, now I shan't have my tea before I'm to go back — and my migraine is killing me.'

Sarah had only been able to decide one thing — that it would not do to cope with these problems single-handed as she had done with all the others, that she would have to change, ask for help and accept it. 'Oh, Miss Pimm,' she sighed, 'do put it on yourself. I am sorry but I'm going to have a baby and it makes me so ill.'

Miss Pimm stopped, thunderstruck, the very hairpins falling from her hair pausing momentarily between her head and her shoulders before they slipped slowly to the floor. 'Ooh, ooh,' gasped Miss Pimm and she was still blinking her pink eyes when the other teachers flew in, demanding tea, and so they all had to be told. Sarah listened to them a while — they had so much to say — and then stopped listening, out of an immense weariness, feeling her restless body cut loose and drift away from the poky office room, its chalk boxes, its gas ring and circle of twittering, startled spinsters, and put out to sea.

She was only sufficiently aware of the old world and its old characters to hear Julia Baines say, a minute before obeying the ring of the bell, 'Now your'e not worrying about what the kid will look like are you, dear? You're not to worry, you know. I think those Indian kids are perfectly sweet — especially those tiny boys with the giant turbans, they're that cute.'

'I'm not worrying Julia,' she roused herself to say, 'and my husband doesn't wear a turban, nor will his son.' Then she had to get up and flee crying ,'Excuse me, Julia.'

She made herself walk across the Common every day, stoically ignoring the weather. It rained now as she walked home, her usual swift, nervous stride only slightly hampered by her growing weight, and she found a medicinal restorative in the chill drizzle, the soft sinking of her feet into dead leaves and rotting grasses, the odours and colours of a Common deserted except along the edges which were lamplit, glistening, populated. Often she said to herself: This is one of the last walks I shall have. Soon I shall leave it all. She felt a small contraction of unwillingness followed by a large, warm expansion of heart that the adventurers of old must have felt when they cut loose from the shore and set sail for what was then a fabulous land.

She felt it again — this tight, pinching contraction inside her chest followed by a throb and flowering of warmth — when she entered her flat and saw it already stripped of half its furnishing, open boxes lined against the wall, while her cat disconsolately nosed about the contents of one, then the other — all the disorder and promise of a house about to be abandoned.

There was so much to be done. But at least there was Emma Moffit to bring her a cup of tea and to urge her on with her breathlessly envious chatter. Listening to her abstractedly, she felt quite guilty that it was she who was going to have this great adventure and not Emma who so deserved it after a lifetime yearning and daydreaming.

Emma's chilblained fingers wrapped parcels for her, locked and unlocked boxes, sorted clothes and books, all the while panting and gasping with an excitement that outdid anyone else's.

'Dear Sarah, is there really only a month left before you will be gone and the flat will be empty beneath me? And there will be nothing, nothing at all to show me you have lived here...' she sighed clumsily stacking books.

'There'll be Bruce,' said Sarah scratching the creature's stiff, scarred ears, trying to make him relax on her lap. It had been been decided — after Sarah's mother had been approached and she had said no, there was her Peke's old age and ill temper to consider — that Bruce was to be left with Emma. Sarah had first asked Adit, indirectly and hesitantly, whether she might take Bruce with her and he had replied, directly and unhesitantly, that she might not.

'Ah, Bruce, Bruce, of course,' said Miss Moffit, patting him absently and then crossing to the bookshelf to draw out an armful of old magazines. 'Shall you be taking these, Sarah?' she asked and seated herself on the floor to sort them. 'I'll just look through and see if there's anything I might keep,' she said, shuffling through them, and went on, 'To think that at Christmas we shall be snowed in, in our little attic, Bruce and I, while you shall be in the sun under the coconut trees. Oh my, isn't it all strange? Shall you miss an English Christmas, do you think?'

'No. It has always been such a strain — going home to my parents, I mean, and all that.'

'Yes, yes. I know. And think, you shall dine on peacock and mangoes, perhaps. I shall think of you so. You lucky, lucky girl. All my life I've loved to go to India — Oliver did write me such beautiful letters from there, you know. I'm not sure even now if I'm not wrong in staying here when perhaps I *could* do more if I were there...'

'But Adit says you are doing absolutely indispensable work for the Defence Fund over here,' Sarah said quickly. She felt guilty about leaving Emma behind with that secret sense of relief, after Emma had suggested, at first timidly and later not so timidly, that she accompany them to India. She knew, of course, as well as Adit who had pointed it out to her, that Emma would only be a burden to them while they were struggling with all the problems of settling there. Also, he had said, Emma was one of those women who, as sure as sure can be, would go off her head in India. The Indian sun had that effect on giddy old spinsters with souls, he declared, and in no time they would find themselves searching for her in the *ashrams*[1]

---
[1] Hermitages

of Calcutta and the Himalayas, to save her from the clutches of fake yogis. No, he would not take the responsibility, he declared, and Sarah said gently, 'Perhaps next year you could follow us out — after we've found ourselves a house and Adit has a job and we can look after you and show you around ourselves.'

Emma did not reply. She stood up abruptly, letting the old magazines scatter across the rug, and stood with her back to Sarah, sadly taking out the many volumes of Kipling, Hickey's *Diaries*, Todd's *Antiquities of Rajasthan* — all the books of India Sarah had pains takingly accumulated.

When Sarah could no longer bear her sighing and snuffling and keeping her back so ostentatiously turned, she burst out, 'Oh, don't pack those books, Emma. Those are for you. I want you to have them.'

Emma swung around, clutching the books, and uttered all the expected squeals and gasps of surprise and pleasure, but at the same time a shadow seemed to creep forward and seize her, enclose her and wrap her so that she shrank and shrank and Sarah saw how thin and dried she had grown in these past weeks of hectic activity for India's defence fund, how old and dry she seemed, like a roll of yellowed newspaper, fading and shrinking into a roll of dead paper, a strip of dessicated bark. It struck her that it would only be appropriate to take Emma to India to die. Whereas she, Sarah, with her baby — she placed her hands about it and wondered if she was doing right in going to India herself, to give birth to a child in a land made for the old, the dying, the unattached, but hardly for infants, for the young, the growing. Old stories came to life against her will — the warnings of heat, sunstroke, disease, epidemics... And they would be strangers, she and the baby. Awed, she cried, half laughing, 'Emma, You ought to be the one to go. I — I don't believe I have the courage, really.'

Emma stopped fluttering and, brushing the snow storm hair off her face and giving her onyx chain a sharp rattle, said briskly, 'Nonsense, dear. You'll manage beautifully. Just think how nice it will be to have a baby in a country where you don't have to keep muffling it up in shawls and blankets and worrying about colds. Just think what fun it will be for the child to grow up amongst monkeys and parrots, like a little Mowgli...'

Thus the women spent their October afternoons, like two timid, careful girls on a see-saw, alternately sinking and rising, sinking and rising. When Adit came home he found them too exhausted by such exertions to react to his own wild enthusiasms and worries. He took to bringing home his friends with him, so that the flat was loud with their advice, suggestions, taunts and laughter, while bottles of Guinness and whiskey sprouted on the table like a seasonal eruption of mushrooms.

Jasbir, lying back with a glass of whiskey in his hand, grew eloquent with nostalgia freshly aroused by Adit's decision. He grew garrulous on the subject of Punjabi food and pickles as prepared by his mother, about the abandon and revelry of Punjabi festivals, about the warmth and wonder of the Indian nights and repeatedly interrupted his flow of reminiscence to remind Adit to send him a report on the state of hospitals in India and the prospects an anaesthetist would have there. On receiving that report, he declared he would decide whether or not to follow Adit. Of course if there was another Pakistani attack, he would not even wait for the report or for a job, but come immediately. 'I belong to the warrior class,' he boomed. 'I must fight.'

Samar, too asked Adit to 'report' on hospitals in India, on the prospects a doctor would have there — had they changed since he was last in India? He wondered. But he seemed more pessimistic, more unsure than Jasbir and related many stories of his experience of Indian hospitals, the lack of equipment, the poor cooperation, the ignorance and stubbornness of the patients... 'Write and tell me, is it still like that?' Then there was another thing, the one he did not speak of — his English wife who was terrified of snakes, spiders, centipedes, dacoits, dirt, cholera, the sun, could not live anywhere, really, but in her native London.

The wives had less time than their men to come and watch the Sens prepare for their departure, but when they came, they were much livelier and more practical. They seemed excited by this one decision, this one activity that had occurred in their stagnant circle, so given to long ruminations and reminiscence in which all ambition and decisiveness seemed to spend itself in the effort of talk. They were infected by the bustle and change in the Sens' household and joined in with a gaiety that made their husbands eye them with some apprehension.

Mala looked busily through Sarah's packed trunks and turned quite unexpectedly practical, making Sarah wonder if, in her proper setting, she was not quite an efficient and able person after all. 'But what have you done with all your woollens?' she cried. 'What if Adit finds a job in northern India? You'll need your woollens there, Sarah. And don't go buying so many clothes for the baby: they are so expensive here and in India you'll be able to get a tailor to come and sit on your veranda and sew you dozens of things for a few rupees.' She examined the kitchen. 'Don't throw away your gadgets and utensils, Sarah. Take them. You'll get a shock when you see what Indian kitchens are like, I warn you.'

'But she may have a cook,' Jasbir called from the drawing room. 'Adit will get her a cook, and an ayah for the baby.'

'Don't give her ideas,' Adit warned hastily. He was beginning to descend to the level of the earth now that dreams were no longer dreams but were being rapidly converted to the hard coin of reality. He no longer talked to Sarah of that romantic India in which all flowers were perfumed, all homes harmonious and everyday a festival. 'She's not going to live in a maharaja's palace, you know. She's going to live in a family of in-laws, a very big one, and learn their language and habits. Then, till I get a job and perhaps after that, for a while, she's got to help out. Don't you go imagining a life of luxury, Sarah,' he said so sternly, with such a worried look, that Sarah laughed and that annoyed him. He was finding it somewhat difficult to equate the dreams on which he had nourished himself as an exile with memories of the reality that had been refreshed now that he was forced to be realistic, and with his growing worries of the changes that had taken place at home since he left. Not the least of his worries — one he had not had to consider previously — was what his parents would think of their daughter-in law and what she would think of them. He became aware of the great gulf between her country home in Hampshire and his own over-filled city home in Calcutta — a gulf he had leapt over himself, but which she might not be able to tackle. Growing more observant, he saw how very Anglo-Saxon she was inspite of her Oriental gentleness and submissiveness. When he saw her at work in her kitchen — neat, organised and quick — he tried to picture her transferred to the sprawling noisiness, untidiness and unpunctuality of his mother's kitchen, and then his brow darkened by a shade or two.

Then there was the child. Adit was surprised sometimes, in secret, to find how little he thought of it. He was no worshipper of the pregnant female and was aroused to no especial tenderness by Sarah's 'condition.' When he remembered, he would get up and lift a heavy box or shift a piece of furniture for her but, more often than not, it did not occur to him that she might need help. He was more or less confident that when his son arrived — of course it would be a son, that he never doubted — he would be proud of it, it would be affectionate towards him and his parents would dote on it. But these pleasant aspects of fatherhood were mostly overshadowed by his worries about it — Sarah's confinement, the expense, the problems of raising a child with an English mother to be an Indian child... When he thought of the child at all, and he usually did only when he heard Sarah being sick in the bathroom, it was mainly these aspects that occupied him and it was no wonder then that Sarah, when she emerged from the bathroom, very pale and cold, found him somewhat lacking in sympathy.

The one who made up for his lack of concern and enthusiasm was, surprisingly, Dev. Dev, who was quite unmoved by Adit's decision to leave England and was highly cynical about the whole project, taunting Adit about being a wog who needed to return to the blacks to show them how much a white sahib he had become, and warning Sarah with malicious glee against the giant spiders, the lizards, the dirt and germs she would find lurking in her Indian home, this Dev proved curiously excited by Sarah's pregnancy, inexplicably anxious about her condition. He was constantly jumping up at her approach as though prepared to catch her if she were to faint. She was amused by this nervous, jumpy concern he showed, and laughed at the questions with which he piled her. How had she felt about the baby yesterday and how did she feel about it today? What was her opinion of natural childbirth? Did she find herself resenting the child or loving it without any reservation ever? What was her philosophy of child-rearing?

Sarah was no more loquacious on this subject than on any other but Dev would sit at her feet, persisting in his questions, enlarging upon her monosyllabic replies, gazing at her with an interest as though she were an egg that might at any moment crack apart and produce the magic infant. He would break off his questioning only to scold Adit for his lack of interest and his callousness.

'I think he's got a girl,' Adit said one evening when Dev had stormed out of the house in rage at Adit having allowed Sarah to hammer and close two packingcases of kitchenware. 'He's going soft,' Adit said.

'He was always soft,' Sarah said. 'He's always defending himself as if he's afraid everyone around him has knives.'

'Who?'

'You. Everybody. Things. England,' Sarah said absently, nursing a thumb she had hammered by accident. 'I couldn't fit this broom in — Mala says I should take it — but surely I can get a broom in India!'

But that evening, upset by the surprise sprung on her by Miss Morris, Sarah was not so energetic. She sat on a cushion, hugging her knees, till Adit came home. She told him about Miss Morris' offer.

He looked as though he would hurl something — his hat, his umbrella, his newspaper — at the wall. Then he flung himself on the divan and groaned 'I knew it — I knew it would happen. It had to, I ought to have been prepared.'

'Adit, stop groaning. What do you mean?' Emma interrupted, shocked by his behaviour which had exploded the tender mauve light of feminine brooding.

'She'll never come with me,' Adit shouted, pointing at Sarah. 'She's got cold feet. She's seen to it that I've burnt my boats and am ready to go, then she breaks it to me. Always, gently, always quietly. But I knew it all along. She hasn't the courage, she's backing out—'

'I think you are talking more foolishly than I have ever heard anyone speak in my whole life.' Emma snapped. It was the first attack she had ever made on Adit who had always been representative to her of her imagined Mecca, and Sarah gaped with disbelief. Emma continued, in a voice like glass, 'The most intelligent thing you ever did was to marry Sarah, and what courage she has—'

'Emma, Adit, all I said was that Miss Morris had offered me a job in another school. That was all,' Sarah cried hurrying to make up for her lapse and stop things from whirling about her till they made her sick. Calm, stillness, order — she had to have them. 'Why you should think, Adit, that I could want to accept, or consider accepting it, I just cannot tell — with our tickets bought, our things packed, all preparation made. You know I want to leave.'

'Yes, I had better leave myself,' Emma said making both Adit and Sarah panic at the implications of her words, but she only gathered her books together and said, wanly, 'I must go up and get my supper now. Excuse me.'

They begged her, feelingly, to stay.

When she had read the letter with the Hants postmark, Sarah tossed it on the table with the casualness with which she treated all such letters. Adit, upon reading it, could not understand how she could react so coolly to the stream of outrage, ill will and dire warning in it. It shook him so that, in no time, he found himself unsure again, and beginning to look at their adventure with Mrs Roscommon-James' cold eyes.

'Sarah, do you think she could possibly be right? There's a lot of common sense in it, you know. English women never could stand the climate, and she says you are already in poor health and it would ruin you. You should at least ask your doctor what he thinks, Sally—'

'Nonsense,' she snapped, flipping over the eggs in the pan with her eyes drawn into grey slits.

'And the child. It is quite natural for her to worry about her grandchild, Sarah, you must admit that,' he went on worriedly. 'I never thought about all that she says, it just didn't occur to me, but I suppose it might be awful for the child not to know which country it belongs to and be torn between the two—'

'Bunk,' said Sarah, more loudly, and fat flew from the pan.

'Now, Sarah, don't be so harsh with your mother. I always have told you, you're not nearly grateful or considerate enough to them, Sally, and it's very, very wrong.'

'Don't call me Sally!' she cried, turning on him, and he quailed at the anger and coldness of her face. 'Don't you treat me the way she always does — as though I'm not an individual with my own life to lead, but just — just some appendage to them, with nothing but duties and responsibilities instead — instead of rights. If I were you, I'd be ashamed to listen to that nonsense for one moment.'

'Sally!'

'Don't — Sally — me,' she breathed fiercely at him, then returned to the making of a scorched and punishing breakfast, and he was awed into an ashamed silence by her determination.

'But at least we must go and see them,' he said, quite timidly, after obediently eating up the burnt eggs.

'Yes,' she agreed, carelessly. 'I suppose so. We could go and see them after we've done with London, and then she could drive us to Southampton to catch the boat. I have to pick up some things I left with them. And my father — I must say good bye to him. I might not ever see them again,' she added reflectively, after a bit, sitting down to a cup of tea and a cigarette, but without a trace, Adit noted, of sadness.

He packed his briefcase, rolled up the *Times* and left the house. shaking his head over the lack of emotion, of humanity — 'just weakness, sentimentality,' Sarah would have corrected him — in English relationships.

Drawing a swath through the moisture on the window pane with her crabbed hand, the old Sikh matriarch peeped at Sarah who stood struggling on the steps with her umbrella and mackintosh, then tapped on the glass and beckoned, smiling gaptoothedly and conspiratorially.

Sarah had never been in the Sikhs' flat before. Now its heat, its swaddling odours, its monotone of din, its curious bareness that somehow combined with an appearance of lavish untidiness, all struck her together as the old lady drew her in and down onto a bed that served as a divan, covered, with many layers of blankets and banked with white bolsters. A daughter-in-law, the clever one who had picked up a smattering of English from television, was called in to translate, but Sarah found herself, as in a dream, actually understanding the old lady's forceful, rhythmic Punjabi far better than she understood the young woman's chipped and metallic, broken English. She sat there, holding her wet mackintosh and dripping umbrella, wondering if India was going to be an extension of this small but overpowering scene, loud with the unknown but strangely comprehensible sounds she was listening to now, wafted over, not with the fabled perfumes of tuberoses and jasmine, but with very different odours with which this room was thick. The Christmas tinsel tacked onto the pink nylon of the young woman's sari, the tinkling of gold and glass bangles on the busy wrists of the girls going in and out, the paper-cut brightness of their clothes and slippers, their embroidery and the metal tumblers of tea were all flickers of light and colour beckoning from the other side of the ocean she was soon to cross.

The theme of the old lady's speech was that now Sarah was going away to India, she would be leaving her British citizenship behind and, if she wished to be happy there, she would have to turn herself into an Indian wife, an Indian daughter-in-law and, quite soon, cackled the old lady, an Indian mother.

'When I hear of our boys coming here and marrying English girls, I always feel pain here inside me. I feel pain for the girl and also for the boy because I know how hard their life will be and that the

English girl can never belong to us. But when I look at you, when I see you going out in the morning and coming home, always so quiet with your head bent, not looking at anyone, then I think you are one of our own. You will have no trouble when you go to India. You will see it is your own country. Always I had this thought in my mind when I looked at you — there, Ratna is laughing at me, but listen, I will tell you my thought — it is that you were an Indian girl in a past incarnation. I don't think you were a Punjabi girl, or a Sikh, but perhaps you were born a Bengali or a South Indian, and that is why, in this birth you found a husband who would take you back to India. Ratna, don't cackle like that in my ear, it is not so foolish. She is so much like an Indian girl — how else can you explain it?'

Sarah, suddenly spoke up, looking into the old woman's face with its hawk-like nose and wide-spaced eyes and cat's cradle of wrinkles. 'I think you may be right,' she said. 'I think when I go to India, I will not find it so strange after all. I am sure I shall feel quite at home very soon.'

The two women laughed in delight at her words, and then began to ply her with practical advice — how to be always silent in her father-in-law's presence and never contradict her mother-in-law, how to prepare for the birth of a beautiful baby by eating almonds every morning as soon as she rose from bed, how to be sure to learn her husband's language and speak only that to her child, how to avoid food cooked in oil and prepare it only in pure *ghee*...

And Sarah would take a parcel back to India or their relations there? And message? And would she visit their cousins, their uncle who lived in Calcutta, and tell them about England? Would she, could she...

Sarah accepted a tumbler of spiced tea, refused the sweets handed to her on a tray and nodded, nodded, nodded.

'I wonder,' said Mrs Miller. drawing her lips together as though she were crumpling up a rubber band, 'I wonder how you will like being in India.'

'I am looking forward to finding out,' said Sarah stiltedly, as a poor actress might speak her lines. But what else was there to say to Mrs Miller? Suddenly she wondered why Mrs Miller always poured out only half-cups of tea and she set down her cup in protest.

'But a mistake,' said Mrs Miller, raising one bony finger and wagging it. 'I warn you, a mistake to go like this, bag and baggage, without first having made a — a reconnaissance.'

'And the political situation,' rumbled old Mr Miller stirring and stirring his half cup of tea. 'It does seem rather unstable at the moment doesn't it ?'

'You mean, Pakistan?' Adit asked. 'No, no, that is all over. All finished with. India is so well prepared now, we can take on anyone — Pakistan, China, anyone.'

'But if they were to attack again, you might have to fight, too, you know, Mr Sen,' Mrs Miller reminded him tartly.

'Of course' Adit said loudly. 'My country, I must fight for my country.'

'But there won't be another attack,' Sarah said.

Mrs Miller jerked up her grey eyebrows at her. 'You sound very sure, my dear. I suppose you must persuade yourself of such things otherwise it would seem too dangerous, too risky.'

'What — to return to India? To Adit's home? How could that be dangerous or risky?' Sarah asked, sharply for her, and Adit hastened to put an end to the quarrel which even he scented.

'You can't imagine *how* excited the old people are about seeing Sarah,' he said, beaming. 'They will love her. And for her it will be so interesting.'

'Hmmm,' hummed Mrs Miller, stretching out the rubber band of her lips. 'Of course it is a very good thing that you are going back at last, Mr Sen,' she said, and he smiled, then stopped smiling and looked to Sarah for help. She rose.

'But you haven't finished your tea, Mrs Sen,' the old lady objected.

In the centre of the scrubbed kitchen table the caramel cat lay. curled like a glowing lamp. At its edge stood a blue-rimmed cup of tea. Looking over its top at the wash of thin light on the windowpane, Sarah felt an assurance and certainty melt inside her, at first breaking apart into little isles of comfort in a yellow sea of sadness, then sinking and disintegrating till all that was left was this lemon sharpness of fear inside her.

The flat was almost bare now. All that was to be sold was sold, all that was to be given away was given away, what was to be packed was already in the fresh smelling packingcases and crates along the walls. So little was left, so little of what had been till now familiar and comforting and that little looked helpless and exposed in the cold, stark November rooms.

Sarah felt herself as nothing more than a chipped cup that was not worth the trouble af packing up or giving away but was best left here, like the remains of a picnic, a holiday on a lonely bank or a deserted beach. She listened to the waves receding down this beach on which she had been left, listened to footsteps sinking down the road. At this moment her curiosity and her courage shrank inside her into a single drop of rain, a flake of ice, and she could hardly believe that Adit would be able to lift her and to transport her to a land where she would regain warmth and personality. If she was to come to life there again, she was sure it would be as a new, a different personality. Perhaps this would make it all easier for her, for Adit, for everyone. But that afternoon when she sat alone — Emma was upstairs, conducting a committee meeting — she felt all the pangs af saying goodbye to her past twentyfour years.

It was her English self that was receding and fading and dying, she knew, it was her English self to which she must say goodbye. That was what hurt — not saying goodbye to England, because England would remain as it was, only at a greater distance from her, but always within the scope af a return visit. England, she whispered, but the word aroused no special longing or possessiveness in her. English, she whispered, and then her instinctive reaction was to clutch at something and held on to what was slipping through her fingers already.

There was a flurry of brisk hand-clapping and shoe-stamping upstairs, loud enough to make Bruce twitch his tail in annoyance at being disturbed, loud enough to rouse Sarah and change the line of her thought and make her get up and go to the window. She looked out at Laurel Lane, deserted now in the afternoon, all softened with the tawny moss of a November afternoon's sunshine. The tiles and chimneypots, the potted chrysanthemums and the bright spokes of pram and bicycle wheels, all were golden and fuzzed with the saffron light. No car disturbed this best-loved territory of Sarah's, not even a cat chose to step across it and claim it from her. Only the breeze ruffled it, making a pair of striped pyjamas flap on a washing line, giving it the breath of reality instead of the static chill of a realistically painted picture.

Then there was a chiming, tinkling sound, the purr of a motor and Mr Yogi's icecream van came rolling down the road like a naughty child left over from a summer's day, refusing to admit to the end of warmth, stealing back to the scene of the party with a sly gaiety. And from all the houses and gates up and down Laurel Lane tumbled the children who were more than ready to agree that sunshine on such a late day surely meant a return of summer and party time. Out they slipped with pennies clinking inside patch pockets and rolled fists, rushing towards the van with those soft, bird-like voices that English children maintain even at the height of excitement and pleasure.

Sarah stood watching them buy their multicoloured ices then dissolving into little groups and pairs that wandered about, licking with hesitant tongues the frozen ices that were not quite so enjoyable on a November day as Mr Yogi's sweetly tinkling bells had led them to expect. It occurred to her that her own child would not know the pleasure, however doubtful in such a climate, of running down Laurel Lane to buy an ice from a picture-covered van with its Pied Piper music. She began rapidly to draw up a mental list of the things her child would not know and enjoy and tried to stop herself by attending to another list, the list of things the child *would* know and enjoy, but inspite of the substantial length of this list, she could not help biting her lips and casting another look at the pleasures it would have to forego.

It was Adit's birthday. He did not suggest dinner at Veeraswamy's. He did not invite his friends to a lavish Indian meal. He took Sarah to a small inn as English as he could find, and there they silently chewed their roast mutton and brussels sprouts, in a setting of brown dinginess, staring at the rim of grime in the cap of the tomato ketchup bottle, the fat and gristle clinging to the pieces of mutton, the windowpanes so smeared with dirt and moisture as to allow only the dimmest filtration of light, the dumpy doughlike waitress cleaning her fingernails in the corner, impatiently waiting for them to finish.

It made him reach out and squeeze Sarah's hand under the table. 'If we don't like it, we'll come back,' he said, through a constriction in his throat. 'We can always come back, can't we?' he pleaded.

Sarah, who had grown hugely depressed by the drabness of the inn and the melancholy of the occasion, was so astonished she let drop a splash of gravy on the grey tablecloth. 'Do you think you might want to ?' she asked, unable to believe she would ever miss Englishness such as this.

'Oh yes,' he said feelingly. 'Often.'

'How perfectly sweet!' said Christine when Sarah confessed that Adit's decision had been made during the war with Pakistan. 'Now if my Simon were to find himself in such a spot, he'd funk, he would, my Simon. When there was such a flap about Cuba and Russia and darling Kennedy was ever so brave, Simon wanted to flee to Greenland. Greenland! I told him, "My dear, we might as well flee to India." And here you are, actually *fleeing*. Did I ever tell you,' she went on, 'about my uncle who was Governor or something of Delhi or somewhere? He used to talk of those poor, poor widows who had to burn themselves when their husbands died.'

'I'm not thinking of being a widow yet, you know,' Sarah said.

'Of course you're not to, darling. You're a mother — about to be one, I mean,' Christine cried, eyeing Sarah with upraised eyebrows. Then she drew at her cigarette thoughtfully, tapped her heel and hummed till she could no longer hold her tongue and burst out 'Have you thought about the child, darling? I mean about — what it will be?'

'You mean, boy or girl? I don't mind either,' Sarah paused, then added 'Or do you mean who it will look like, Adit or me? I hope it will look like Adit, brown as brown, with black hair and black, black eyes.'

'Well, in that case, darling,' said Christine, ceasing to tap and hum, 'I suppose it *will* be better to have the child in India.'

The room was nearly empty. Only a bare divan stood there, and the television set that had not yet been fetched away. So they sat on the divan and watched, on the rain-shredded screen, an old Satyajit Ray film. The sounds of a sitar throbbing passionately, with a stormy despair, swept about the room in dark clouds. On the screen a mother crouched, weeping. There was a mud hut, mouldering in the forest. The thatch hung askew, a single window gaped like an ache. A man stood alone with an umbrella. A breeze rushed across a field. A child's eyes widened and welled. A train came wailing up and drew wailing away...

Silent, frozen on the divan, Sarah and Adit held hands like a pair of children, feeling Bengal, feeling India sweep into their room like a flooded river, drowning all that had been English in it, all that had been theirs, friendly and private and comfortable, drowning it all and replacing it with the emptiness and sorrow, the despair and rage, the flat grey melancholy and the black glamour of India. They themselves were tossed about by the flood like flotsam and then became a part of it, the black flood.

8

Waterloo Station, early in the morning, had the flatness, the indistinctness of an old film. The Union Jack colours of London had not yet woken up, were still furled, asleep, and all was in film shades of grey, black and white. Even the tea in the cups was grey, its steam white. Women in white mackintoshes, men in grey overcoats. The sudden, distinct clanking of iron chains; then silence, then a great spume of smoke rising to the ceiling of the wind-blown station, and silence. As in an old film, the dialogue was blurred, almost inaudible, merely an accompaniment to the scene.

'Early snow —'

'Christmas under palm trees —'

'Come back. Perhaps—'

'Don't forget—'

'A message to my old man—'

'Write—'

'No—'

'Write—'

'You—'

'We—'

Words snatched away and sunk into the haze of departure, the fog of preconceived absence.

Adit alone felt himself clad in robes of rash and startling colours — the robes, purple and peacock, pinned and striped with gold and amethyst, the garments of the ambassador he had been. Surrounded by his friends, his court, he felt very much the retiring ambassador bidding farewell to his faithful staff. (Only Emma had stayed away: she had flu.) And now he was going to carry the message of England to the East — not the old message of the colonist, the tradesman or the missionary, but the new message of the free convert, the international citizen, a message of progress and good cheer, advance and good will. The umbrella in his hand was nothing less than a sealed scroll, a document of vital importance to this country and his own, to be carried with care and pride over the seas. He felt regal with importance, with pride, and drew himself to his full height as though he heard the drum, the trumpet and the fife, as though he saw the Union Jack being lowered in sadness at his departure and saw the Indian tricolour rising upon the opposite horizon.

'Yes, I shall write,' he was assuring them 'I shall give the message — I shall deliver the parcel — I shall send you a parcel, a message, depend on me—'

Sarah, beside him, wrapped in the customary drabness of her old mackintosh, her face green tinged with morning sickness and the prospect of travel in this condition, felt herself, on the other hand, fading, fading — like a creature in *Alice in Wonderland*, in a dream world that bordered on nightmare. Her body, with its rules and wants, kept slipping out of her hold, acting strangely and irresponsibly, shrinking and threatening to disappear. Even the smile she felt lingering behind in the English fog was a strained smile, slipping — like her mind — from a brightly tinted dream into a shadowy, opaque nightmare, and back again. When the train blew steam, blew whistles, rang bells and roared, she clutched at Adit's arm and momentarily her face lit up with the thrill of a journey and the prospect of a new world. But the train remained stationary, their friends shifted restlessly from one foot to the other and blew on frozen fingers, and she felt herself once more in the grip of apprehension, ignorance and doubt.

'I wish we were coming to Southampton to see you off, *yar*,' Jasbir said, clasping Adit's shoulder. 'I'd like to make sure you actually leave. I can't believe it otherwise — you, the most *pukka* sahib of all, going back to India and leaving all the *kala*[1] sahibs here.'

'It's fate,' Adit said cheerfully. 'I leave everything to fate again, like the good Hindu I am fast becoming.'

'No one will believe that at home,' Mala smiled. She looked unaccustomedly wistful in the folds of her sari and the great collar of her coat. 'You will be made to travel up to Hardwar and take a dip in the Ganga to cleanse yourself before they accept you again.'

'Nonsense. Stop frightening my wife,' Adit shouted. 'Those days are over, Sarah, don't you worry. You'll find everyone as advanced and progressive as we are here.'

'Not too much, I hope. I'm looking forward to all the servants and the leisure, remember,' she smiled a bit.

'Sarah, what will you call the baby?' Bella suddenly wanted to know. 'Let's choose a name. Come on, everybody, think.'

They thought. They made suggestions, ideas coming on with an urgency created by the warning whistles of the train, the hurrying of porters, the knowledge that only a few moments were left. The Indian names they intoned in staccato were like an incantation in that smoky morning air. Standing in a semi-circle about the two travellers, they chanted these names as if they were casting a spell that would lift and waft the pair to a foreign land by their charm, their magic, their power.

'Bharat — Brahma — Chandralekha—'

'Durjaya — Dushyanta — Nayantara—'

'Lakshaman — Lavana — Madhavi—'

'Nishith — Nandini — Ambapali—'

'Rothin — Arjun — Mrinalini—'

'Sita — Draupadi — Shakuntala—'

---

[1] Black

'Uma —Rahul — Vasanta—'

'Trisura — Tani— Sagarika—'

'Vir — Vijay — Siddharta —'

The chant droned itself out in spirals that wound closer and closer about the encircled pair till it finally caught them, lifted them and swept them up the steps into the railway carriage. Then the circle of sorcerers on the platform fell silent, stepped back, breaking the magic ring, the spell and left the pair free to go at last. The train lurched, a whistle shrilled. Smoke spumed. The fog parted to allow it a passage. The train burrowed into its grey tunnel.

Adit leaned out — one arm swinging its purple sleeve, its gold chain, its furled flag. He shouted in a voice that expanded and exploded with feeling. He gazed at the dark knot on the platform, waving. The last he saw of it was Bella's bright head in its midst, like the rounded flame of an Indian oil lamp, symbol of the warmth that awaited him.

Sarah leaned out — one arm waving, briefly, slowly, in doubt or unwillingness, she herself could not say. She called out a subdued goodbye to the little dark knot on the platform, waving. The last she saw of it was Bella's bright head in its midst, like a saucy marigold in a city window box, last symbol of London's cockney staunchness that she was losing now, had lost already.

Dev stood silent, watching, for the most complex feelings of all tumbled and tossed inside him, clamouring for attention, for resolution. If plans and prophesies had any strength in them at all, it would have been he steaming out on the train to catch the boat back to India. This was what he had planned and, for some time, sincerely believed. It was Adit who had found himself a pleasant groove to fit into, with his English wife and the education that had, he so repeatedly told them, brought him up to love and understand England. Why then was it Adit who was leaving while he stayed on? What had made them exchange the garments of visitor and exile?

There had been time enough in which to think of replies, sort them out and suitably dress them in conviction. But, somehow, both he and Adit had avoided the ultimate question, and they parted in ignorance of the answer. Somewhere, at some point that summer, England's green and gold fingers had let go of Adit and clutched at Dev instead. England had let Adit drop and fall away as if she had done with him or realised that he had done with her, and caught and enmeshed his friend Dev. It was as though this were an arbitrary act of England's, an abstract law to which Adit and Dev had quite unwittingly succumbed. Adit had found it simpler to say it was Pakistan's attack on India that had decided him on his return. The truth was that his disenchantment with England had begun sometime before he read the news in the papers, but this he stowed away in his subconscious, and it was the myth he lived by and acted on.

But why was Dev not returning to fight for his country? Or, less theatrically, to carry back an academic degree, search for a job in a school or college there and educate the illiterate masses? A far more difficult question to answer than the one regarding Adit. Something had happened — he remembered it clearly enough — when he sat on the banks of the trout stream in Hampshire, watching the water moles slide in and out of the rushes, feeling the soft sun knead his back, listening to the cows munch mouths full of grass. At that moment England had ceased to be an aggressor who tried to enmesh, subjugate and victimise him with the weapons of Empire, something to be taunted and mocked and fought. It had inexplicably become something quite small and soft, something he could hold in his cupped hands like a bird, something he could hold and tame and even love. It was a sensation completely unlike that aroused by the thunderous splendour of India which spurns pursuers, escapes capture and insults and defeats enemies and lovers alike. For the first time Dev felt the rapture of a victor, a rapture that accompanied him back to London, so that he no longer saw it with the eye of a member of a once-conquered race, or of an apprehensive and shortsighted visitor, but of someone before whom vistas of love, success and joy had opened.

Walking out of Waterloo Station, he walked out of the diffidence and uncertainty of his old existence in London and into the groove already cut and warmed for him by Adit. Adit had bequeathed him a job in his office not exactly his own job but one created by a reshuffle of staff brought on by his resignation, so it was Dev who now sat beneath the posters of Spain's sunflower sun and Jamaica's sloping palms, drinking tea brewed by the fringed and freckled Girl Friday, breathing the exquisite relief of the unemployed at last employed. Sarah had persuaded him, after weeks of hunting a bedsitter in Kensington and Bayswater, to take on their own flat in Clapham and it was for the Clapham bus he waited now, enjoying the thought of spending a Sunday in its privacy, moving his bookcase from one wall to the other, hanging up pictures first on one nail, then the other, wrecking the kitchen while cooking an egg to go with his rice and indulging in the unsuccessful, shortlived but childishly happy business of setting up house.

The bus drove up, he swung himself on. While buying his ticket he felt certain — and then not so certain — that he saw a glint of scorn in the conductor's eye, the abrupt way in which he handed him his ticket and then kept him waiting for his change. He wondered if the old lady beside whom he sat down did not clutch her handbag and lean away from him as though she suspected a smell. But, he told himself, it didn't matter. The London fog lapped the windows and through it the early morning lights of the city glowed in a way that made him feel he was riding into the heart of a painting by Turner. As they rumbled over the bridge, he had a definite sensation of the bright water flowing beneath him. Thinking momentarily of Sarah and Adit on their journey to India, he murmured, as a kind of parting salute to them and also as a prayer for himself:

> 'Make my bed and light the light,
>   I'll arrive late tonight.
> Blackbird, bye-bye.'

□□□